FRIGHT ON
STAGE RIGHT

By G. B. Ralph

FRIGHT ON
STAGE RIGHT
A Milverton Mystery

G. B. RALPH

ISBN 978-1-99-118294-4 (Paperback POD)
ISBN 978-1-99-118298-2 (Ebook EPUB)

A catalogue record for this book is available from the National Library of New Zealand.

G. B. Ralph
www.gbralph.com

For my LGBTQ+ readers,
you'll always be welcome in Milverton.

Chapter 1

It was all for show. Nobody would be getting slaughtered tonight.

That's what Addison had to remind himself after he arrived at Milverton Town Hall and looked up to find it transformed. Wrought iron lanterns flanked the doors, with lights flickering as if they could go out at any moment. The 'Milverton' carved into the stone above the doors remained clear, but the 'Town Hall' had been obscured by a seemingly blood-spattered banner with thick, red brush strokes spelling out 'Slaughterhouse'.

The doors themselves had been flung wide open and haunting choral music poured out, overlaid with occasional high-pitched whistling and distant screams.

Addison's skin prickled, goosebumps lifting the hairs on his forearms as he ascended the steps. He had to shake his head clear – he was being silly and he knew it. The last thing he wanted was to embarrass himself in front of Jake, so best to start practising now before his date arrived.

Showtime was scheduled for eight o'clock – a little over half an hour away – and about when the sun dropped below the horizon at this time of year. Even so, it had already taken the last of its warmth along with it.

Addison stepped inside.

Just as the Milverton Town Hall facade had been made over for the evening, so had the interior – almost unrecognisable compared to the last time Addison had seen it. Of course, the bones of the space remained, the ceiling for example, at least double height by Addison's inexpert estimation, perhaps even triple height. And hanging from that ceiling was an immense rail, running from one side of the hall to the other, holding up a deep red curtain which dropped all the way to brush the polished timber floorboards – not that Addison could see all that much of the floor through the swirling, low-lying layer of fog.

The curtain divided the vast space about a third of the way along, leaving this side to function as a foyer and bar area and the far side presumably for the seating and the stage. Projected onto its rippled surface were a succession of scenes in silhouette. In the brief time Addison watched, he witnessed what appeared to be a witch's cottage, a dark forest, a dread lord's tower, a crumbling cemetery, a haunted house, a dank cave, and a Victorian mental asylum.

Shifting from the slideshow, his gaze caught on the great threads and tattered shrouds of cobwebs criss-crossing overhead, with the occasional spider or bat dangling beneath – quite the shift from the joyful bunting of the Spring Craft Fair that he'd once helped string up.

In summary, the wildly inconsistent interior decor told no cohesive narrative, nor did it fit with the slaughterhouse theme. However, they were here for the 'Spooky Showcase' which suggested what? A variety show? A talent competition? Nothing with any coherent storyline, anyway. All Addison knew was that drag performers would be taking the stage, and if they were shooting for a general spooky vibe, then Addison supposed they had succeeded. And that was OK.

Much of his job in marketing, at least the creative side of it, involved storytelling. The story tended to involve taking potential customers on a journey to discover how wonderful and necessary a product or service was, how much they needed it in their life. So when he saw something that was just a bunch of vaguely themed *stuff* put together, his fingers itched to put it right.

On the other hand, Addison was conscious that he needed to suppress his big-city snobbish tendencies, because really, it was all good spooky fun. Not that anyone else was there to enjoy it, apparently – the place was practically empty.

Where was everyone?

With no apparent box office or other source of information, Addison cut through the fog on his way to the makeshift bar – they were bound to know what was, or was not, going on. If he happened to pick up a drink in the process, so be it.

The bartender was nowhere to be seen. At least there was someone else at the bar waiting – a woman with her dazzling black handbag perched on the counter, she was perhaps half a head shorter than himself, with long, straight, jet-black hair, clad all in black. The form-fitting, floor-length dress flared out at the bottom and was layered with black lace, occasional jewels, and something else that caused her to subtly sparkle all over. The long sleeves extended well beyond her wrists and across the backs of her hands to loop around her middle fingers. Each finger featured a chunky, Gothic-style ring and ended in a nail painted a dark red and sharpened to a point. They were slowly drumming the surface of the bar, from pinkie to index finger, and again, and again.

To see off any potential awkwardness, Addison made small talk by greeting her and asking how long she'd been waiting.

The drumming of the fingers abruptly halted and the woman turned her attention to him. Her powdered face with bright red painted lips and dark eye shadow completed the look and gave Addison his first proper fright of the night. Though it wasn't the makeup that startled him, but the person wearing it.

'Oh, Addison, you're here,' she said, her warm, genuine smile in contrast to her fierce and rather iconic outfit. He'd been prepared for idle chit-chat with a stranger sharing his drinkless predicament, not greeting the septuagenarian troublemaker Mabel Zhou.

'Quite the Halloween transformation.' Addison smiled, giving her costume another once-over. 'Morticia, I take it?'

'Well done. You are correct, young man. Here I am.' Mabel flourished her talons and drew her red lips into a severe line. 'Morticia Addams, a pleasure to meet you,' she said, slowly raising an arm, strips of black lace draped from the sleeve following her movement.

Addison took the proffered hand in his and dutifully kissed it. 'The pleasure is all mine.'

Mabel beamed, immediately breaking character, before batting his hand away. 'You are very good, humouring me like this.'

'Of course. The least I could do after you've gone to all this effort. I didn't even recognise you,' Addison said. 'It was the height that first threw me off, I think.'

'Oh yes, aren't they good?' Mabel rested her arm on the bar and put one leg out to show off her black platform heels. 'They add a good few inches, at least. The things you can see from all the way up here! I picked them up from Jojo's Co Clo. Johanna put me on to them.'

'Yoyo's cocoa? Coke low? Cloak oh?'

'Johanna's Costume Closet,' Mabel said by way of explanation.

'Ah, right.'

'A real institution, that place. Must've been there oh, ten, twenty years plus. She put me on to this wig too.'

'Yes, that too. Quite the change from your usual do.'

'It is, isn't it? I had hair just like this once upon a time.' Mabel ran her fingers through the flowing faux hair. 'Perhaps not quite this long, but not far off.'

'Well, you can still pull it off, that's for sure.'

'You are too kind,' Mabel said, patting Addison's hand. 'But I think it's more likely that I will be *literally* pulling it off before the night is through.'

'What? Why?'

'It is very hot under here, and itchy too,' Mabel said, gently scratching behind her ear with one of her sharpened fingernails as if to underscore her point. But then she whipped her hand away and shook out the wig, a faint grimace of discomfort on her face. Her attention shifted to her nails, which she splayed out in front of Addison. 'These fingernails though, aren't they a wonder?'

'I take it you haven't filed down your real nails then?'

'No, no. I'm not that committed to the costume. Sophia showed me – she's good to her old nana. Helped me glue them on, much to her mother's horror.' Mabel tittered, apparently delighted by the situation. 'They feel so strange and I can't help tapping them.' She did just that, staring at her own fingers for a moment as she did so before once again pulling her hand back and shaking her head.

She turned to Addison. 'And who are you supposed to be, my dear? Actually, what's this?' Mabel said, plucking some ginger fur off Addison's shoulder and holding it up for inspection.

'Ah, I thought I'd caught it all.' He lifted his elbow to make sure there wasn't any more evidence of Keith's shedding.

'Anyway,' Mabel said, shaking the cat hair off her fingers as she tilted her head in question. 'Who are you?'

'I'm, you know, just me.'

He may not have put together a costume or anything, but he had at least put *some* thought into his clothes, with the subtlest of nods to the spooky season. A pair of black high-tops on his feet, slim black jeans, and a loose-fitting, deep purple velour T-shirt. It had such a luxurious texture – what Addison imagined a royal robe might feel like, though probably a fair bit less expensive – and with the rich, regal colour, it gave off low-key King of the Night vibes.

Mabel tapped a finger on her chin, thoughtful. 'Goth royalty? Perhaps on a lazy Sunday hanging about the house?'

Addison scoffed, feeling a little called out. 'I didn't realise it was a proper dress-up thing.'

'Addison, Addison, Addison...' Mabel said, clearly unimpressed. 'It's Halloween. Of course it's a dress-up thing. Not only that, tonight is a *drag* variety show so there's no room for subtlety. More is more.'

'Yeah, for the performers. Not us, surely?'

'Pish posh. Live a little.'

'I am living plenty, thank you,' Addison said. 'Besides, it's only Halloween Eve.'

Mabel waved the comment away. 'You are clutching, my dear. But don't worry yourself. I'm sure plenty of others will be dressed just as' – Mabel paused, pursing her lips as she considered her next word – 'just as *underwhelmingly*.'

Addison ignored the jab, instead focusing on the aforementioned but as-yet-nonexistent 'others'. He was about to ask where they were when Mabel raised a taloned hand, running it through the air over Addison's shoulder. 'I do love this fabric though...' She trailed off, looking uncertain, something Addison recognised from previous times he'd worn the top back in Wellington.

He laughed. 'You may touch it, if you like.'

'No, no,' Mabel said, her hand dropping immediately to her side as she let out an uncomfortable laugh of her own. 'No. I can't be making grabby hands at handsome young men – I already have enough of a reputation without adding *that* into the mix.'

Addison rolled his eyes. 'Don't be silly,' he said, pulling the hem out towards her expectantly.

Mabel waited for a beat, tsked, and then reached out to run the fabric between her thumb and fingers. 'Oh... it is lovely, isn't it? Almost like a mink coat – not that you see those anymore these days. Yes, very nice. Why haven't I seen you in this before?' Then, before he could respond, she continued. 'No, I suppose it's a bit too much for a weekday morning while working remotely.'

Addison blew a raspberry. '"Too much" now, is it? I thought it was "underwhelming"?' He raised an eyebrow, confident in his minor triumph. 'You can only pick one.'

Mabel slowly raised her hands in surrender, a sly smile

taking over her face. 'I take it back.'

Addison strongly suspected his little victory was to be short-lived. 'But…' he said, recognising he might as well get it over with.

'But nothing. I'm just coming to realise you put rather more thought into this outfit than I first suspected.'

And what exactly did she mean by that? Addison raised an eyebrow, communicating the thought without him having to open his mouth.

'With fabric as enticing as this, I'm sure Sergeant Jake Murphy won't be able to keep his hands off you.'

Blood immediately rushed to Addison's face, as often happened at any mention of his fledgling relationship with the sergeant, let alone the man's hands. He would have been lying if he said the thought hadn't crossed his mind, or that it hadn't factored into his decision-making. He couldn't deny, so he knew he had to deflect.

Addison cleared his throat. 'To answer your earlier question, you haven't seen me in this top before because I only just brought it back with me today. And regarding Jake and his hands, unless he's scuttling around under the fog somewhere in costume as a *disembodied* hand—'

'Dressed as Thing, you mean?' Mabel clapped her hands together, delighted at the notion. 'Wouldn't that be something? The beginnings of an Addams Family reunion!'

'Alas, it doesn't appear Jake is here yet, in costume or otherwise. Nor is anyone else for that matter.' Addison turned his attention from the bar, gesturing to the practically empty foyer area. 'Where is everyone?'

Not that he would admit it to Mabel, but wondering after other members of the audience was very much secondary to wondering – or more accurately worrying

14

about – where his date was. Jake had seemed receptive when Addison presented the tickets, and had given all indications that he was looking forward to tonight's show. He said he needed to finish up some things and would meet Addison at the show. So, where was he?

Chapter 2

It was then that Addison caught sight of a case of wine floating through the air. A shock of bright purple curls followed closely behind the box as it bustled along, heading directly for him. The case came to an abrupt halt opposite Addison and dropped onto the temporary bar with a thud and a clatter to reveal the woman beneath the violently violet hairdo. She was dressed all in black, though it was plain, matte black, with not a rhinestone, sparkle, or wisp of lace in sight.

It was Deirdre Dodds, who Addison realised he should've been able to identify from the unique hair alone. The driving force behind the Spring Craft Fair had now apparently returned to haunt Milverton Town Hall for the night. She adjusted her blocky, emerald green specs with one hand, the other hand now firmly set on her hip, as she turned her gaze on her prospective customers.

'Mabel. Addison.' Deirdre said their names less in greeting and more in grudging acknowledgement of their presence. 'That there's the last box. You know, I could've done with you, Addison, about ten minutes ago.'

'Oh, uh, sorry?'

'You're sorry?'

'Sorry I wasn't here to help out.'

'You're not sorry,' Deirdre said, and she was right – he was not sorry. He'd had no idea he might've been of use until approximately ten seconds ago, let alone ten minutes. It was just something you said, wasn't it?

Regardless, with his date's imminent arrival, he didn't want to be working up a sweat – not just yet, anyhow.

'You're right, I'm not sorry. But to make up for it, you can put me down for box hauling, stall setup, and other such manual labour at your next craft fair,' Addison said with what he hoped was a winning smile.

It was not an entirely selfless offer. He had enough enemies without collecting more unnecessarily or accidentally, and deep, deep down, Addison suspected Deirdre might be a future ally. So he hoped it was worth cultivating a positive relationship. Also, more imminently, Deirdre appeared to be the one serving the drinks tonight. Always important to have the bartender on side.

His smile earnt him a shadow of one in return from Deirde, followed by a solitary nod. 'I'll hold you to that.' She sighed as if nothing would ever get done if it weren't for her, shaking her head before slapping the bar top. 'Anyway, everyone had better drink up tonight because I'm not lugging all these boxes back to the van.'

'Now I'm sure *that* is something Mabel and I can help you with.'

'All right,' Deirdre said as she pulled out bottles of wine and lined them up on the bar. 'What am I getting you, then?'

'What are our options?' Addison said.

Deirdre took in a deep breath, slowly letting it out again as she scanned the bottles already on the bar and those still in the boxes at her feet. 'I have a lovely merlot and a dangerously drinkable pinot gris from over the hill in Hawke's Bay. A couple of local beers from just downriver in Palmerston North – Brew Union's Lager and their Swamp Juice, which is a hazy IPA. Then further downriver to Foxton, if you're looking for soft drinks, we have the full Foxton Fizz range.'

'It's all very local, isn't it?' Mabel was clearly impressed.

'Of course,' Deirdre said, as if she wouldn't have it any other way. 'And upriver, I guess, or upstream at least, we have Turitea's Finest, served on the rocks.'

'Oh, that sounds nice,' Mabel said.

'It's all about the marketing. Isn't that right, Addison?'

'Right... but I don't—'

'Turitea's Finest is tap water,' Deirdre said, 'with ice.'

Mabel hooted. 'Overselling it a bit, don't you think?'

'It is complimentary,' Deirdre said, remaining deadpan. 'I cannot be accused of overselling if it's free.'

Mabel conceded that was true.

'Named for the Turitea Stream?' Addison said.

'Yes, or the Turitea Dam which is used for the town's water supply.'

'You can keep your rebranded tap water, Deirdre,' Mabel said. 'I'll have a pinot gris.'

'Same for me, please.'

Deirdre poured their wines, took their payment, and then immediately forgot they were there, returning at once to unloading boxes.

Wines in hand, Addison and Mabel drifted away from the bar.

'Let's hope tonight's performers can muster more joyful exuberance, more vim and vigour than our Deirdre,' Mabel said.

'At least she wasn't shy with her pours.' Addison raised his glass in appreciation.

'Yes, cheers to that.' Mabel smiled, clinking her glass against Addison's.

They both sipped, their lips simultaneously curling a little in response.

'Room temperature white wine,' Mabel said.

Addison nodded. 'I knew it was too good to be true.'

***

In the minutes since Addison's arrival, a handful of people had trickled through the doors, but still far too few to warrant hiring out Milverton Town Hall.

'At this rate,' Addison said, 'we could've had this show in the front room back at the house.'

'Keep your hair on. Curtain-up isn't scheduled for another twenty minutes. And knowing this lot, it'll be another ten or so after that before things get underway. Plenty of time. Look, there's Linda and Jon heading for the bar. And that's Johanna – the one with the costume shop I mentioned before. That has to be Brodie there by the curtain – dressed all in black, as usual. And there are the Wagners just coming through the door now.'

Between the low lighting, the wisping fog, and the different directions they were facing, Addison struggled to get more than a vague impression of the newcomers Mabel had indicated. Not that he recognised the names anyway, for the most part. What he did recognise was Mabel's attempt to pump up what was looking increasingly like it was going to be a poorly attended event, and he said as much.

'You mustn't take this the wrong way, dear,' Mabel said, patting his arm. 'But for someone so switched-on, you can sometimes – hmm, how can I say this? – you can sometimes struggle to process the evidence before your eyes.'

Addison felt his back going up, but recognised the truth in his friend's words, and knew the intention wasn't mocking. He slowly said, 'What do you mean, in this particular instance?'

'There were no queues on the footpath with everyone waiting to get in, were there?'

'No, because there were no bag checks.'

'Right. And we'll be lucky if someone even checks our tickets – which is another common potential pinch point at the theatre.'

'What's to stop someone sneaking in for a free show?'

'Other than the shame? Everyone in town knowing you're a cheapskate who thinks they can get away with ripping off the already struggling arts sector?'

'Well yes, other than that.'

'It's assigned seating, so if you sneak in and grab a seat, it'll be obvious you're not meant to be there when the person who paid for that seat turns up.'

Addison laughed. 'True enough.'

'What else? Well, we're working on a different scale, aren't we? Milverton Town Hall is a lovely venue, and impressive for the size of our town, but our seats are just through there,' Mabel said, gesturing to the edge of the curtain dividing the space. 'It's no grand old opera house with thousands of seats and multiple tiers. We don't have to navigate a labyrinth of corridors in order to find the right door for our seats.'

'All potentially very time consuming.'

'And without any of that—'

'Most people are going to stroll on in as the curtains are going up.'

Mabel shrugged and smiled. 'You're not in the city anymore, Addison.'

'This is a whole other world.' Addison laughed, shaking his head.

'Milverton is a big change after the capital, that's for sure. You're still getting used to life here, but once you have, you'll wonder how you ever managed before the move. Fewer people, less frantic, less drama.'

'That's not entirely true though, is it?'

Mabel pursed her lips. 'You have had a particularly rocky few weeks, I'll give you that much.'

'"Rocky" indeed,' Addison said. 'Let's hope we don't have any more pitfalls to navigate anytime soon.'

'I'll drink to that,' Mabel said, raising her glass.

They sipped their drinks.

'Oof, that's going straight to my head,' Addison said after a brief wave of dizziness. He shook his head to clear it.

'Have you eaten, dear?'

Addison was about to protest, to say he didn't appreciate being mothered. That was, until he realised he had not, in fact, eaten.

He hadn't had a spare second to grab anything for dinner, what with getting back to Harper House then getting ready to come out. Rushing around Wellington and wrapping things up at his old job, he hadn't had time for lunch either. 'Oh, this morning, down in Wellington, the barista gave me a bit of biscotti with my coffee.' Was that really all he'd eaten all day? 'I had a banana at some stage too – on the train down, I think.'

'It's no wonder you're not at peak mental performance this evening. Just a couple of wind-up monkeys banging away on their cymbals up there.' Mabel hooked her arm around Addison's and led him over to a dark corner of the hall.

'Where—' He lurched at the sight of a skeleton lurking there in top hat and tails. Apparently Addison was neither perceptive nor particularly observant tonight. He quickly recovered himself, reassuring the fight-or-flight part of his brain that he wasn't about to be attacked by a Halloween decoration.

'Meet Sir Harold the Skeleton. He is put to work regularly throughout the year – quite dashing in a Santa suit, if a little ridiculous. The spooky season though, this is his time to shine. He really comes into his own and the kids love him.'

It was then Addison noticed the silver tray Sir Harold held before him. Rows and rows of miniature mince pies, potato top pies, sausage rolls, and club sandwiches cut into small triangles. Perched amongst the pastries was a note inviting him to 'Help yourself'.

'I think I love him too, right about now,' Addison said as he considered the offerings. 'I hate to question it, but what's with the complimentary savouries?'

'I suspect it's a requirement of their liquor licence. They're serving alcohol so they need to have some food too.'

Addison nodded along to the explanation. His first instinct was to question why they weren't *selling* the food. Instead, he accepted they tended to do things differently in Milverton. And so he did as the note instructed and discreetly inhaled a miniature mince pie, immediately

22

feeling it take the edge off.

Imminent starvation averted, Addison returned his attention to the rest of the hall – it was starting to fill up. 'It's good to see a few more people coming in,' he said, recognising some faces he'd seen before around town, but nobody he'd met, and still no Jake.

'Don't worry,' Mabel said. 'He'll be here soon enough.'

'Am I really that transparent?'

'Practically a spectre. I can see right through you.' Mabel rolled her eyes. 'Anyway, I've barely seen you all week, what's been happening?'

'Now who's being transparent?'

'Are you going to let me distract you or not?'

How was she right, yet again?

'I took my granddaughter to the Diwali festivities in Palmerston North,' Mabel said, apparently deciding Addison would be getting distracted whether he liked it or not. 'Quite magical with all the lights and music and dancing. And the food, my goodness – I couldn't stop myself, had to try everything. Sophia and I had a wonderful evening. You'll have to join us next year.'

'Yeah, that'd be great.'

'At least you're not missing out on Halloween this weekend. And then there's Guy Fawkes next weekend. It's all going on!'

'Does Milverton do a bonfire and fireworks and all that for Guy Fawkes?'

'Of course,' Mabel said, taking the final bite from her small triangle of sandwich. 'What did you get up to this week? Did you get your bike sorted out?'

'Yep, good as new.'

'And you, Addison?'

'Me?'

'Are you as good as new too?'

'I'll get there.' Addison sighed and slowly smiled. 'And what about you? How goes the car hunt?'

Mabel looked as if she were about to press, but then decided otherwise. 'The car hunt has gone very well, in fact, thank you. I knew it the moment I saw it, and I took it home right then and there. Just what I'd been looking for.'

'Small, red, hybrid?'

'Exactly that. I'm very up to date.'

'Watch out, Milverton.'

Mabel looked up at Addison from beneath her brow. 'You had better watch yourself, dear. Remind me: who is it, out of the two of us, who is legally allowed to drive? Hmm?'

'Touché, Mabel, touché.' Addison raised his hands, a smile on his lips. 'I take it back, and I apologise.'

'Apology accepted. And yes, I will.'

'You'll what?'

'Teach you how to drive in it.'

'Ah…' Considering the last time he'd been in her passenger seat they'd ended up in someone's front garden, he thought it might take him a minute to come around to the idea. 'That is very generous, Mabel. But I don't even have my learner licence yet, so I'm not allowed on the road, even with someone supervising from the passenger seat.'

'Well, chop chop.'

'I was studying my road code on the train journey back this evening, actually. I'm booked in to take the theory test next week, and all going well, they'll issue me my learner licence.'

'That is excellent news. And I'm sure our sergeant will be very happy to help you study for that,' Mabel said with a wink. 'You couldn't have a more qualified tutor.'

Addison sipped his wine in lieu of responding, but Mabel wasn't having it.

'Why are you looking so shady?'

Reluctant, Addison lowered his drink. 'I haven't told him.'

'Why not? Wasn't he the one who gave you the road code? I'm sure he'd be pleased to hear you're taking it seriously.'

'I'm sure he would be too, but, well…'

Mabel snorted. 'You're worried you're going to fail.'

'I will tell him the moment I've passed, but not before, in case it takes me a couple of attempts.'

'Oh, Addison,' Mabel said, hand on his forearm. 'You'll be fine. You really ought to trust yourself, and the sergeant too.'

'Yeah, yeah…' Addison did trust Jake, and he'd had more than a few occasions recently to learn just how deep that trust was becoming. That didn't mean he hadn't kept plenty from Jake in the past, usually in his capacity as Sergeant Murphy, and almost always when it involved Addison doing something he probably shouldn't – that is, getting himself involved in police business. In this instance, getting his driver's licence was doing something right, and it was absolutely his own business, so the situations were not comparable. Jake didn't need to know everything he was doing, even if he was quite invested in it. It didn't sit completely right with Addison, but it was a minor thing, and would hopefully be resolved shortly anyway. 'All in good time.'

Mabel raised an eyebrow. 'No time like the present.'

Addison raised one of his own. 'Better late than never.'

'Time waits for no one.'

'One day at a time.'

'The early bird catches the worm.'

Addison chewed his lip. 'All good things must come to an end?'

'Good try, but not quite,' Mabel said with a laugh.

'I'm fresh out of time-related cliches.' Addison laughed along with his friend. 'But I did finish up my old job in Wellington today, returned my laptop and everything.'

Mabel gasped. 'Ready to start your new one for the mayor? When?'

'On Monday.'

'No rest for the wicked!'

'Mabel, you're better than that.'

'What?'

'I think one flurry of cliches per day is more than enough for anyone.'

'Oh, you. Spoilsport,' Mabel said with a wink before raising her glass. 'To you, Addison, and your new role right here, in Milverton, where you belong.'

'Yes, yes, OK.' Addison raised his glass.

Mabel had a wicked grin on. 'Out with the old, in with the new,' she said, clinking Addison's glass before he could pull it away. She shrugged. 'I couldn't help myself.'

Addison was busy mentally jotting down how he might exact his revenge when someone appeared at his shoulder.

Chapter 3

'Out with the old, is it?' Percival Foster had a cheeky smile on his weathered and wrinkled face, and a twinkle in his eye. A man more than twice Addison's age, though he proudly refused to act it. 'Well, that's me gone, then.'

'Not a chance, dear,' Mabel said. 'They won't be getting rid of us anytime soon. How are you?'

'I'm happy to hear it. And I'm very well, thank you.' Percy air-kissed Mabel on each cheek, careful not to make contact and smudge her Morticia makeup. 'It's good to see you.'

'We were talking about how Addison is currently between jobs.'

'Oh that is a shame. But don't worry, young Master Harper, a clever lad like you will find something in no time.'

Addison laughed as he clarified that he was only 'between jobs' for the weekend.

'Well, that's all right then. I take back my commiserations and instead offer congratulations.' Percy put out a rough hand to shake Addison's before pulling him in for a quick hug.

'Thanks,' Addison said, a little surprised to find his arms

27

suddenly pinned to his sides.

When Percy pulled back, there was a glassiness in his eyes that wasn't there before. 'Good to see you again,' he said, patting Addison's arm before he cleared his throat and turned to Mabel. 'He reminds me of the old boy.'

'I can see that.' Mabel's face softened in response, which didn't quite fit with the whole Morticia Addams thing, but it was the thought that counted.

Percy turned to Addison. 'How are you doing after the bicycle incident?'

'Oh yeah, still a bit of healing to go, but nothing to worry about.'

'That is good to hear. And how's the bicycle? Back in top shape?' Percy said, offering a small smile. 'Or do you need to borrow my three-wheeler?'

'No, no. My replacement wheel came in this week, and I've already taken it for a test ride. Not on the road, just along the riverside pathway.'

'Good, yes, that's good.' Percy nodded. 'The best for recovery – physically and mentally.'

Mabel murmured her agreement. 'Get right back on that horse, so to speak.'

Addison recognised the truth in their words, but responded with only a tight-lipped smile and a nod. He was doing all right, but he wasn't in a hurry to relive the incident. 'Speaking of recovery,' he said instead, 'how are your goats doing? Brutus and Beatrice, was it?'

Percy laughed, looking pleased. 'Well remembered. And yes, they're back to full mischief.'

'I wonder where they learnt that from?' Mabel's smile challenged Percy to disagree.

He didn't, instead conceding the point with a shrug of

the shoulder. 'Takes one to know one.'

Addison let out an unexpected laugh, delighted to find someone holding their own against his friend.

Mabel flicked a dirty look in his direction before returning her attention to Percy. 'Now, I wasn't expecting to see you tonight, at least not until after the show?'

'No, I shouldn't really be out here. I have an important job backstage tonight,' Percy said in full stage whisper which he backed up with a wink. 'Just popped out to see if Lynne had brought in the goods, and so she has. She's a good egg, that one.' He made a show of glancing back over each shoulder before reaching out to nab a sausage roll. 'And I see Sir Harold is on duty tonight as keeper of the snacks.'

It was only then, as Percy reached out, that Addison registered what he was wearing and what that meant. Of course, not noticing was the whole point of stage blacks – black shirt, black trousers, black belt, black socks, and black shoes with black laces – allowing the crew to fade into the darkness and not draw the audience's attention from the main action on the stage.

'How's it all going behind the scenes tonight?' Addison said.

Percy's eyes flashed wide as he finished chewing his first bite. 'Well, yes. Busy, busy. Everyone's coming and going. It's chaos is what it is, but that's par for the course. It's all got a bit tense back there too, to say the least. That's the other reason I'm out here. And I'm not needed for anything at the minute, not specifically, so I took the chance to take a breather, have a little break… and a snack.'

'That is very fair,' Mabel said. 'But while you're here, you might as well make yourself useful.'

29

'I might as well, might I?' Percy said, eyebrow raised as he took another bite of his sausage roll. 'And how do you suggest I do that?'

'A little peek behind the curtains—'

'You don't want to go back there just now – shatters the illusion if you see them beforehand. You know, faces all done up but shapewear, silicone, and padding still on full display,' Percy said, gesturing to the air in front of his chest and hips as he did so. 'You want the music building, the big cloud of smoke, the spotlight swinging into focus on stage as each performer makes their dramatic appearance.'

'No, no,' Mabel said. 'I meant – what's the word? – *metaphorically*. A metaphorical peek behind the curtains.'

Percy tsked and rolled his eyes. 'You want all the juicy goss? The drama, the scandal, the scoop, the tea?'

Mabel smiled and ever-so-slightly lifted a shoulder. 'Think of it as a little pre-show entertainment for me and Addison. Dazzle us.'

'Well, Mabel Zhou, when you put it like that, who am I to resist?'

'That's my Percy.'

'Give me a sip of that first. Just a little taste – have to keep my wits about me.' He accepted a sip of Mabel's wine and immediately drew his chin back into his neck, wincing. 'It's warm.'

Mabel rolled her eyes as if she hadn't reacted just as badly only minutes earlier. 'You'll survive.'

'Nice and fruity though.'

'Takes one to know one,' Mabel said with a smirk, echoing the man's earlier comment.

'Indeed.' Percy laughed. 'Anyway, one mustn't gossip on a dry throat.'

Mabel said nothing, her face loud with expectation.

'A few of the drama llamas are saying the production is cursed.'

'Cursed?' Mabel's attempt at horror was lost under the weight of her anticipation.

'Which is nonsense, of course. It's taking the whole "spooky season" thing a step too far. Such comments are not helpful and only serve to unsettle our more sensitive souls. They're jumping at shadows, squawking any time a floorboard creaks.' Percy let out a breath, shaking his head.

'Why do they think it's *cursed*?'

If Addison wasn't mistaken, and he didn't think he was, Mabel was more excited for backstage drama than the show itself. Not that Addison was above such things either – he just quietly sipped his room-temperature pinot gris and listened.

Percy glanced between the two of them, tutted, and rolled his eyes. 'Quite the pair of gossipmongers, aren't you?'

'I think you will find, Percival Foster, it is called "taking an interest in our community".' Mabel's indignation was delivered with such a straight face that a casual observer might have believed it.

Taking Mabel's lead, Addison added, equally indignant, 'We only deal in the most organic, locally sourced, free-range gossip.'

Percy shook his head, chuckling as he did so. 'Yes, I'm sure your intentions are entirely pure.'

'If you don't want to tell us, that's, you know, that's fine too…' Addison knew Percy was well aware of what he was doing when he dropped the conversational crumb of the supposedly cursed production. Addison also knew that

31

Percy wouldn't have done such a thing if he wasn't dying to tell them all about it.

'Oh, fine, you twisted my arm.'

Mabel drew her lips into a line to stop herself from smiling.

Percy held out a thumb. 'The first setback, you two are already very familiar with.'

Addison didn't know what he meant by that but he had his suspicions. 'Penshaw Hall?'

'Precisely. Penshaw Hall was booked in to host tonight's show, but with centre stage a crater and the boards splintered into kindling, we had to scrabble for another venue only weeks out. Not the end of the world, and we were able to secure the town hall. A few favours had to be called in, but we managed it.'

'The show must go on.'

'That's right. But then we had Theo, one of the stagehands, helping build the sets. A sweet lad, but not the sharpest. The implement he was using, on the other hand – which he was wildly underqualified to use – that was certainly sharp. He almost lost a finger, and well, the screams wouldn't have been out of place in tonight's show. Poor boy got quite the fright, and was in a bit of pain, but he's had himself all stitched, splinted, and bandaged up now.'

'That's no good,' Addison said. 'But "cursed"? A last-minute venue change and a small, if serious, backstage injury is hardly enough to be trotting out the C word.'

'Oh, don't you worry, there's more,' Percy said with a wince. 'Just last weekend, during rehearsals, the driving force behind tonight's show, Patrick Laurence AKA Lady Perry Less – producer, hostess, and headline act – broke a leg.'

'What?' Addison and Mabel said together.

'As in… theatre "broke a leg"?' Addison added.

'Someone wished him good luck?' Mabel's eyes went wide and she grabbed Percy's arm. 'Or should I say someone wished *her* good luck?'

'Well, yes. It can all get a bit loosey-goosey with drag, can't it?' Percy said with a chuckle. 'I asked Patrick about this – I think it's always best to ask. He said that when he's in everyday, non-performance boy mode, he uses "he" and goes by Patrick, his given name. But when all dolled up in drag – in character as Lady Perry Less, putting on an act – for the purposes of the evening, she uses "she" and only answers to the name of her drag persona, not Patrick.'

'Yes, that's all very straightforward. It was rude of me to assume,' Mabel said, briefly scolding herself. 'But OK, so, this leg-breaking business?'

Percy nodded. 'Patrick slipped on stage while the performers were doing a run-through, quite literally broke a leg. He's casted and booted and everything. He's been able to continue organising tonight, even with the unexpected encumbrance. But he certainly won't be putting on any heels or pulling off the opening number's choreography. So, our beloved Lady Perry Less won't be making an appearance. This show is Patrick's baby, and he can still do everything for the production, just not perform on stage.'

'But the show's still on, without its leading lady?'

'Of course, as you said before, the show must go on. It's like what they do on that TV quiz show, you know? *Who Wants to Be a Millionaire?*'

'I do enjoy *Who Wants to Be a Millionaire?*' Mabel said. '*The Chase* is very good too. Anne is my favourite, "The

Governess". I would like to give her a run for the money.'

'"Phone a friend"?' Addison said, trying to bring the conversation back. 'That lifeline where they can call someone to help answer a question?'

'That's the one.' Percy snapped his fingers. 'Yes, Patrick called in a queen from Auckland to take over hosting the evening. We're lucky she was available, and willing to fly down for the night.'

'Who is it?' Mabel said.

Percy tapped the side of his nose. 'I don't want to give away all the secrets, but she's certainly made a splash recently, and you'll recognise her name.'

'Fine,' Mabel said with a faux huff. 'I'll be finding out shortly anyway, I guess.'

'That all sounds positive?' Addison said. 'So, things are back on track?'

Percy winced. 'We thought so, but we should've known better. Our new hostess flew in this morning, but one of her checked-in bags, unfortunately, did not.'

'I do hate it when that happens,' Mabel said. 'I've learnt my lesson on that front – always pack my medication, breath mints, and a spare pair of knickers in my handbag now.'

Percy's face said everything without him having to say a word before he quickly continued his tale. 'Poor Theo Robinson with his bandaged finger picked her up and bore the brunt of it. It's only a short drive from the airport in Palmerston North to here, but Theo was a bundle of tattered nerves and unshed tears by the time they arrived.'

'What was in the lost bag?'

'Her wigs.'

It was Addison's turn to wince. 'And I've learnt *my*

lesson on that front – never get between a queen and her *girls*.'

'She certainly needs something for that bald head of hers. We've been on the phone with customer services all day,' Percy said. 'Good news is they've located the bag—'

'That's great.'

'Bad news is it's in Dunedin.'

'Oh,' Addison said, 'only the far end of the country, then?'

'Yeah, they have no idea how it ended up there. And there was no chance they'd get it back here by tonight, so our hostess has had to… improvise. Let's just say she's not impressed.'

'I'll bet,' Addison said. 'Oh well, I'm sure she'll smash the performance and no one will be the wiser.'

'Here's hoping.'

'I dare not ask,' Addison said, 'but is that all?'

'All the issues? That I know of. Patrick is being a trouper, making the best of it, as is Brodie.'

'Is Brodie performing tonight too?' Mabel said. 'Not really his style, is it? I thought he tended to go for something more… what's the word?'

'Pretentious?' Percy suggested.

'Well, not the word I would use, but yes. Thoughtful, experimental, lofty?'

'No, you're right, not his style. He's just a bit out of sorts. Unfortunately, his new production wasn't picked up in the latest round of funding, but he's still part of our little arts community and keen to stay involved.'

'Funding cuts all around,' Addison said. 'It's such a shame. So terrible, and so short-sighted.'

'I don't know what they think anyone is supposed to do

35

of an evening without our creators – no books, no theatre, no TV, no movies.' Mabel looked thoughtful for a moment. 'I guess we might end up with another baby boom...'

'Yes, I'm sure folk would find ways to fill the time,' Percy said with a chuckle.

'But more divorces too, I expect, unfortunately,' Mabel said. 'Can you imagine, couples having to spend all that time in each other's company? Having to actually *speak* to each other?'

'Now that you mention it, that's adding to the – uh – the *discomfort* backstage. Kieran, our sound and lighting technician, is having to work alongside his ex. It's not the end of the world, and these things are bound to happen when you're moving in such small circles.' Percy shrugged. 'It's all very civilised, if a little strained. They're making the best of it but, well...'

'Everyone will be glad to be through it?' Addison said.

'Exactly. And of course there's your usual conflicting personalities, long-held grudges, divas who refuse to share a dressing room. But that's showbiz, baby.'

Addison took another sip of his wine, feeling it warm his throat as it went down. 'Sounds like we'll be lucky if we get through this evening unscathed.'

Chapter 4

'We really ought to stop lurking in the corner,' Mabel said after Percy had decided he'd probably shirked his duties long enough and headed off backstage again.

'Morticia should be haunting all of the town hall.'

'Yes, I didn't put all this on for nobody to see.'

'And we don't want to be accused of hogging Sir Harold.' Addison nodded his thanks to their skeletal waiter. 'Actually, just one last savoury – that should keep me going.' He'd been eyeing up the sausage rolls since Percy had tried one. Sausage meat wrapped in flaky puff pastry, served warm. So simple yet so delicious. Fancy folk often turn their noses up at the humble sausage roll, but at any given party up or down the country, that's the first tray to be demolished, without question – the smoked salmon blinis, bacon-wrapped figs, and tzatziki shrimp cucumber bites never stood a chance. Addison, however, had no such hangups about sampling delicious savouries.

He popped the entire thing in his mouth, turning away from Harold in time to see his date, Sergeant Jake Murphy, stepping through the front doors.

He looked very handsome.

Addison's eyes devoured him whole in the space of a breath. Dark trousers and a dark, forest green shirt open a little at the neck. Chest and shoulders he couldn't stop admiring, even after seeing the man so often in recent weeks. His warm, light brown skin, with dark hair cut short and tidy, facial hair trimmed. And eyes already locked on Addison's across the space.

Addison's breath caught, the slight intake of air lifting a flake of puff pastry from the sausage roll which landed feather-light at the back of his throat.

He coughed involuntarily. Hacking and wheezing, vision swimming as his eyes flooded with tears. It took way too long for his body to realise it was not, in fact, choking. He swallowed the mouthful of sausage roll and growled to clear the tickling sensation from his throat, wiping his eyes clear with the backs of his hands, only to be faced with the man who'd set off this whole sorry saga.

Jake's features wavered between concern and amusement, which was the best Addison could've realistically hoped for. Coughing one's lungs up hardly said 'come hither'. It would not have been at all unreasonable for Jake to turn right back around and head off again rather than associate himself with a liability like Addison. But considering he'd still come over, Jake had every right to at least wear a look of pained embarrassment. He did none of those things.

A small smile played on Jake's lips as it became clear Addison had regained control of his functions. 'This reminds me of the first time we met.'

'Uh uh. No, thank you. We don't need to hear about what you two got up to the first time you met,' Constable Manaia Edwards said as she emerged from behind her boss.

Constable Sean McGiffert quickly followed. 'Hi, Addison,' he said, a wide grin already plastered across his face. 'Our sergeant here was just *gagging* to see you too.'

'Who raised you, McGiffert? Have some class.' Edwards went to clip him around the ear but her colleague dodged the blow. 'Can't you see Mrs Zhou is here?'

'So formal,' Mabel said with a tsk. 'Mabel is just fine – how many times must I say it?'

'Sorry, Mabel. Just trying to recover some *manners*.' Edwards punctuated her words with a jab to McGiffert's chest, which he wasn't quick enough to dodge this time.

Undeterred, Sean smiled and shrugged. 'I think it's romantic. And I think it's for all our benefits that our sergeant is getting—'

'All right!' Edwards abruptly cut off her colleague. 'I need a drink. Anyone else?'

Addison held up his wine and said he was fine, thanks. Mabel did likewise.

'Murphy?' Sean said.

'Yeah, sure.' Jake glanced towards the makeshift bar for inspiration, but only saw lines of bottles and piles of boxes. 'Grab me something.'

Sean held out a hand, all puppy dog eyes.

Jake sighed and handed over a card.

'Thanks, boss. You are the best.'

'And *you* are about to be written up if you don't watch out.'

Sean's wide smile took a momentary dip before returning to full wattage as he looked to Addison and Mabel. 'He's a right joker, isn't he?'

'McGiffert.'

'Yep, yes. Off we go.'

Jake sighed. 'Hey, sorry I'm late, by the way – had to sort out something with my place.'

'Is everything OK?'

'Oh yeah. At least, I'm sure it will be,' Jake said with a smile. 'Nothing to worry about tonight, anyway.'

Addison wanted to ask – oh, how he wanted to ask – but Jake clearly didn't want to get into it. And Jake didn't seem worried about whatever it was, so Addison told himself that he wouldn't be either. 'Ah, I didn't know Sean and Manaia were coming out tonight,' he said instead. 'I would've asked, but didn't think it'd be their thing?'

'McGiffert heard we were coming, decided he had to come too, and then guilted Edwards into joining him. I'm sure a night at the theatre was not how she'd intended to spend her evening off.'

Addison shrugged. 'It's always good to take a break, have a laugh. Hopefully she'll still enjoy herself.'

'I'm sure she will,' Jake said, looking properly for the first time at the top two members of Milverton's unofficial sleuthing squad. 'Excellent job on the costume, Mabel.'

'"Costume?"' Mabel gasped, planting a taloned hand on her chest. 'Is that what I get for putting in a little effort to look nice? Out for a night at the theatre, not wanting to look like I've just rolled out of bed?'

Addison noticed Jake taking a moment to reassess Mabel's attire and confirm that yes, he was not mistaken, despite her protestations. 'And with a performance like that, you really should be up on the stage, not down here with us.'

'Oh, I don't know about that, but thank you for saying so.'

'Afraid you'd steal the show?'

'Yes, a very real danger.' Mabel looked grave. 'Wouldn't want to damage any delicate egos. But...'

'One day, perhaps.'

Mabel rested a hand on Addison's forearm, then Jake's, before saying in a melodramatic stage whisper, 'I'll be sure to get you boys front-row seats for opening night.'

'I want to come too,' Sean said, bustling back with what appeared to be a pint of lager in each hand. Not that he could have any idea what they'd been talking about, but he clearly didn't want to miss out, whatever it was.

'Of course, dear.'

He beamed, pleased to be included. 'Here you are, boss,' Sean said, handing one of the drinks over.

Manaia appeared a moment later, hazy IPA in hand, having edged her way around the gathering crowd. Despite the thickening fog, Addison spotted a few more familiar faces, nodding his head and raising his glass across the room in acknowledgement of Emily Smith, property manager and real estate agent; Sandra Campbell, environmental scientist at the regional council; her partner Ariana Harris, librarian and aficionado of oversized scarves; and Mrs Harriet Ferguson, Her Worship the Mayor of Milverton.

'And to think,' Mabel said, following Addison's gaze, 'you were worried we were going to be the only ones here. It's opening night!'

'Isn't this the only night?'

'All the more reason not to miss it,' Mabel said as the lights in the foyer area flickered. Faces throughout the space turned upwards in response to the change, and the overlapping conversations all paused mid-sentence.

Into that sudden, unexpected silence, a bell tolled. The

note rang out slow and resonant, reverberating around the space and through Addison's bones. The sound echoed, still fading when the next heavy strike followed.

A death knell summoning people to their seats.

Chapter 5

'You know, I'd be happy sitting somewhere in the middle.'

The middle was the safest place to be – out of sight and, more importantly, out of reach. When it came to comedians and drag queens, to sit in the front row or an aisle seat was to take your life into your own hands.

Addison remained on his feet, the stage and heavy crimson curtain immediately at his back as he looked along the front row.

'Lucky for you,' Mabel said, 'that's where we're sitting.'

'No, I mean the middle as in the centre, halfway back—'

'Nonsense,' Mabel said, patting the seat beside her. 'It's assigned seating, so you don't have a choice. The mayor is always given a handful of comp tickets by the Milverton Community Theatre so she can attend with a few guests. And she's always given prime seats. It is an *honour*.' Mabel emphasised this last word with a pointed look.

'I can't believe she gave you a ticket too.'

Mabel shrugged. 'It's always worth asking, dear. What's the worst that could happen? She says no? Now, stop quibbling and sit down. It would be an insult to the mayor, to the performers, and to the production team if you shunned their generosity by leaving an empty seat in the front row.'

Addison was still pussyfooting about when Jake took the seat next to Mabel, then looked up at Addison, an amused yet encouraging smile on his lips. He lifted an arm, resting it across the vacant seat to his other side. With an invitation like that, how could Addison refuse?

Apprehensive and not too happy about it, but emboldened by Jake's presence, Addison took the seat. Front and centre – Addison's worst nightmare.

Best not to think about it.

For lack of anything better to do, he went to throw a shady look at his supposed friend and caught her presenting something in her dazzling black handbag to Jake.

He briefly squeezed Addison's shoulder before withdrawing his arm to reach inside Mabel's handbag. He pulled out something diamond-shaped, about the size of his thumb, with a crumbly topping.

'What's that?' Addison said before he could help himself, his curiosity getting the better of him.

'Mabel smuggled some Diwali treats in,' Jake said, clearly amused. He popped the treat in his mouth, chewed, and nodded. 'It's nice.'

'They were giving food away out there. I don't think she needs to be so cloak-and-dagger about it.'

Mabel closed her handbag, pulled it back towards herself and gave him a stern look. 'Do you want one or not?'

'I do, yes, please.'

Mabel smugly presented her open bag to Addison over Jake's lap. 'Go on then. I'm embarrassed to say I can't remember what they're called. But they're pistachio.'

The moment he pulled one of the diamond-shaped treats

from the bag, she turned to Jake. 'See that, Sergeant? Accessory to my "cloak-and-dagger" crime. And in front of an officer of the law? How brazen! Lock him up.'

'I think we can let him off without any jail time, don't you?'

'Oh, I don't know…'

'I can assure you that the police will be keeping a close eye on him.' Jake smiled, glancing at Addison before returning his attention to Mabel. 'Actually, this case is of such critical importance that I will see to it personally.'

'Oh my goodness.' Mabel cackled, putting her smuggled treats away. 'That certainly backfired.'

Any satisfaction Addison derived from seeing Mabel's joke turned against her was immediately overwhelmed by the blood flooding his cheeks at the thought of what form Jake's personal attention might take.

As appealing as the various options his brain presented were, he could act on none of them in that moment. Instead, for want of anything better to do, he popped the unnamed diamond-shaped treat into his mouth.

Dense, with a soft marzipan-like texture and the occasional crunch. Rich, nutty, creamy, sweet, and was that cardamom?

Addison chewed, satisfactorily distracted and mollified. At least until he felt someone settling themself into the seat on his other side.

The newcomer wore a sparkly black top, three strings of pearls layered in concentric circles around her neck, and a simple, single pearl in each ear. Her clutch – continuing the pearl theme, this time on the clasp – rested in her lap. She glanced once at the stage immediately before her, then to her side.

'Good evening, Mr Harper,' she said, and in such a way that it was clear she was not yet convinced of its goodness, as if the evening was still working out its probationary period.

Or perhaps that was just where Addison's mind went. She was his boss, after all – as of Monday, anyway.

'Hi, Mayor Ferguson.'

'Very brave of you to sit up front.'

Addison was about to clarify that he had no choice in the matter, which she would know, and that he was there rather against his will – passed off as an amusing quip, of course – but then she nodded, as if in approval, and Addison decided he was happy to let her believe in his bravery.

He'd already been a little on edge about being on the front line, and having the mayor at his side was not helping.

She just sat there, facing forwards, apparently content to wait for things to get underway.

Addison was not content. He'd have preferred to continue talking to Jake and Mabel, but he couldn't bring himself to turn his back on the mayor. Nor could he sit there in silence, not when her presence seemed to grow by the second.

He might as well get a head start on his work, show willing and all that. Addison had been hired with the broad brief to 'market Milverton', part of the mayor's campaign to rebuild the town's reputation after the recent spate of deaths and associated bad press – off-putting to visitors, to say the least.

'I was chatting to Percy Foster earlier,' he said, the first vaguely relevant topic to come to mind. 'Sounds like there's been a bit of drama in the lead-up to tonight's show.'

Mayor Ferguson raised an eyebrow. 'Drama in the

dramatic arts? I'm shocked.'

'Well, yeah, I suppose,' Addison said, feeling a little silly but unconvinced it should be a foregone conclusion.

'I expect it's not too different from local politics – we all have our ideas about what's best for the community,' the mayor said before gesturing to the curtain before them. 'Just like all creatives have ideas about what's best for the production. Put that much ego and ambition in one room and something's bound to give.'

Addison conceded that she made a good point. 'But let's hope they've settled all that. It'll be good to get through one event without incident.'

'I'm sure they'll throw themselves into it and make Milverton proud.'

The moment the words were out of her mouth, the house lights abruptly cut off, plunging the space into darkness, broken a moment later by a bright flash of light and an ear-splitting scream.

Chapter 6

Gasps and screams burst from alarmed audience members, immediately followed by a smattering of self-conscious chuckles.

Everyone joined in the applause – with additional hooting, hollering, cheering, and whistling – as the heavy main curtain was raised. A low fog churned and swirled, spilling forth around the flickering jack-o'-lanterns piled at the stage front. A spotlight burst on against the dark backdrop, creating the illusion of a large, full moon.

Sparkly, twinkly, magical notes shimmered through the air, creating an almost hypnotic melody which was quickly drowned out by a wicked cackle that seemed to come at them from all sides, all at once.

The audience's attention was drawn back to the moon as it was partially obscured from the top. A cluster of bristles slowly descended, soon resolving into a broom, and then a figure mounted on it, silhouetted against the lunar glow.

The cackling ceased and a witchy, mischievous voice took its place, speaking of putting a spell on everyone, announcing her return, and describing how she was ready to exact her revenge.

Her steady descent stopped, leaving only her head and shoulders in silhouette as she mouthed the words of the song, her vibrant red, heart-shaped bouffant bobbing to the beat. On her powdered white face, the shade and shape of her lipstick matched the wig, giving the impression of an exaggerated pursing of the lips, her buck teeth in evidence even with her mouth closed.

Addison smiled, immediately recognising the tune and the costume from one of his favourite childhood films. His mum had recorded *Hocus Pocus* off the TV, even going so far as to pause the recording during ad breaks.

The witch stepped forwards, revealing shiny red patent leather boots with heels of at least six inches, drawing attention away from the harness attachments being swiftly hoisted into the fly space and the black-clad stagehands darting back into the wings.

Her stride was regal, matching the embroidered, lush green velvet dress with sleeves that reached all the way to the floor. Not that it was all that far, in truth. Even with the height afforded by the dangerously high heels and the alarmingly voluminous wig, Addison would've been surprised if she had to duck through your average doorway. The scale of her other assets more than made up for any perceived lack of height, though. Her chest had been exaggerated to comic proportions, her waist cinched disproportionately small, and her booty padded back out again.

She was soon lip-syncing a gibberish incantation, broomstick in hand. And then, at the final beat of the song, she plummeted into a death drop, falling back onto the stage with one knee bent and foot tucked underneath, the other thrust straight out, arms splayed to the sides.

The audience gasped and cheered, applauding as the performer got back to her feet. After patting herself down for a few moments, she jerked her head towards them and froze, as if caught in headlights. She held her broomstick upright with the bristles resting on the stage, and without moving any other muscles, slowly tilted the handle towards her sneering lips. 'Another glorious audience. You sicken me!' she said, her smoky, amplified voice pitched low with disdain. She loosened her posture, making a show of glancing around the hall. 'It's a full moon tonight, as you can see' – she gestured to the spotlight on the backdrop – 'and that's why all you crazy mortals are out, is it not?'

This drew more cheers from the audience, including Addison, his childhood self – and his adult self, if he was being honest – delighted to have the wicked Winifred Sanderson putting a spell on him.

'For the poor, uncultured wretches amongst you who didn't recognise that musical classic, that was the voice of Bette Midler singing "I Put a Spell on You" from the classic 1993 film *Hocus Pocus*. And the queen before you, your hostess tonight – you may recognise me from the televised drag extravaganza *Heel of Fortune*? Or perhaps from that spicy dream you were having last night? It is, of course, me – the one and only, Cilla Slay!'

The audience applauded, with a few pockets of extra-enthusiastic responses around the hall – some in the know, others just happy to go along with it. However, based on Cilla's subsequent frown and slight pause, this was apparently not the universal adoration she'd been anticipating.

'Yes, yes, admittedly, I didn't take the crown home after my appearance on the latest season. You may say that

50

coming runner-up is just a generous way of saying I was the first loser, the chief chump. Always the bridesmaid, never the bride. But what do those judges know? Certainly not what I am capable of,' she said before channelling her inner Winifred with her most maniacal cackle yet, sleeved arms slowly rising in a display of magical power. Abruptly she dropped her arms, and the character with them. 'How many televised talent shows have you seen where the winner burns bright for all of five minutes? But then it's the runner-up who goes on to have a sparkling career in the biz?' Lips pursed, she fanned out her nails before her, as if for inspection – a show of complete nonchalance and self-confidence.

'Anyway,' she said, flashing a wicked smile at her audience. 'How are we, Masterton?'

The collective cringe as everyone sunk into their seats was silent but so very loud at the same time. Nervous chuckles had started up when one brave soul a couple of rows behind Addison cleared his throat and said, loudly and clearly, 'It's Milverton.'

Cilla froze, eyes wide. 'Oh, that *is* embarrassing.' She barked a laugh. 'Milverton. Yes, of course – how could I forget? You won that Terrific Town Award, or something, recently?'

Addison's cringe deepened. He felt himself involuntarily shaking his head and suspected there were more than a few in the audience doing the same. Not that Cilla would be able to see through the glare of the stage lights. Though the lack of expected cheering was probably all she needed to know she'd erred once again.

'No? Well no, I suppose not. I wouldn't have given it to you, either.' The camp, witchy cackle that followed might have been intended to bring them into the joke with her, but after the quick succession of unsuccessful light-hearted insults, her formerly warm audience had rapidly cooled. The laugh now felt like it had a mocking edge to it.

'Swiftly moving on,' she said, each word punctuated with a clap, as if to draw a line under the flurry of faux pas. 'You may be wondering what has dragged me from civilisation to slum it with you in small-town New Zealand?'

OK, no. Nope, nuh-uh.

Cilla Slay had climbed right back onboard that fail train. Supposedly a professional performer, how did she not see how spectacularly badly her attempts at humour were landing?

The mayor's knuckles were white, Addison couldn't help noticing from the corner of his eye, clasping at her clutch as if she were wringing its neck.

'What dragged me all the way down to' – Cilla screwed up her mouth – 'this *place*?' The final word itself was neutral, but the delivery was not, using a tone generally reserved for speaking about faulty septic systems.

Addison may have only been a relatively recent arrival in Milverton, but the disparaging comments about the town smarted nonetheless. He had chosen to move there, after all. He tended to give everyone the benefit of the doubt, but Cilla Slay was swiftly burning through any of that remaining doubt.

'Especially when they weren't able to stump up for my usual fee. Well, I am very graciously doing it at a discount, as a favour to a dear friend.' Each sentence was accompanied with a strut across the stage, each full stop punctuated with a power pose and pivot before returning the way she'd come. 'We may have started out together, but where I have gone on to bigger and better things, my sweet sister has kept it small, local.'

Addison sighed. Such cattiness was sitting about as well as his lukewarm white wine.

'But then she went and had a little whoopsie, slipped over during rehearsal. Awww.' She drew out the sound with mocking melodrama, ending it with a pout. 'She really did take "break a leg" a little too literally. Now she can't even make it on stage for her own "big" show and has to run things from backstage. So, what did my girl do? She thought, "Hmm, who could possibly fill my low-rent, man-sized shoes tonight?" Well, anyone, probably – hah! – but she shot for the best.' Cilla slowly and demurely placed a hand on her chest, pausing to bat her eyelashes. 'And she's lucky I was feeling generous.'

'Now, I hope you know who I'm talking about here. I hope you recognise the name, because if not here in... *Milverton*, then where? I am of course talking about your very own Lady Perry Less.'

This announcement was met with applause, the first with any genuine enthusiasm since their hostess had first spoken into her broomstick-microphone.

From Addison's vantage point front and centre, he spotted a smiling face peeking out from behind the curtains on stage right. The man's face was only there a moment before it ducked back out of sight to be replaced by a pair of crutches, a moon boot, and then the rest of his black-clad self. He only came one swinging step onto the stage, enough to be seen by all, before he stopped and gave a little wave. This had to be Lady Perry Less out of drag, because his appearance set the crowd off.

Clearly adored by a loyal local fanbase, he blew the crowd a kiss and – with the mood sufficiently buoyed – swung himself back offstage.

Addison caught Cilla straining to maintain a smile, the squint giving her away even through all the makeup. With the applause only now coming to a close, their hostess snapped her fingers towards the opposite side of the stage, waving her fingers at her throat.

'Mama's thirsty,' she said by way of explanation as a stagehand dashed on with a glittering chalice, handing it over to Cilla. They'd barely made it halfway offstage again before Cilla had knocked it back and smacked her lips. 'Hang on,' she said, waving the chalice. 'Where do you think you're going? Take this away.'

She held the chalice between thumb and forefinger as if its emptiness disgusted her.

'Why was I cursed with such inept stage kittens?' she said to the audience in her amplified stage whisper before addressing the cupbearer. 'I'm going to need a few more of those if I'm to survive this night. So keep 'em coming, will you?'

With the stage to herself once more, Cilla Slay shook her head and let out a theatrical sigh before turning sharply back to the audience as if she'd forgotten they were there. 'Now, where was I?'

She stalked from one side of the stage to the other.

'Ah yes,' she said with a snap of the fingers. 'I am not at my best, called in at the last minute. Take this hideous wig for example – you can't have not noticed. Nasty. Such poor quality. I've never looked so *cheap*.' Cilla shook her head and held up a hand. 'No, I won't get into all that or I might never stop. Let's just say my girls – lovingly crafted, exceptionally expensive – are lost. Johanna did her best, I'm sure, but she didn't have much to work with in that tacky little shop of hers.'

She cackled again, as if to bring everyone in on the joke. And again, nobody joined in.

Not to be deterred, she patted the air to either side of the offending wig. 'That's OK though. This is good enough for you lot.'

The obliviousness was *breathtaking*. How could someone whose art was fuelled by live audience feedback be so incapable of reading the energy of the room?

If she didn't check her outsized attitude and ego, far from slaying the audience with her performance, Cilla Slay was in danger of being slayed herself.

Chapter 7

'All right, you wretches. It is time for your Spooky Showcase!'

Her reception thus far had been as cold as a day-old corpse, but this received a genuine cheer. If others were feeling anything like Addison, the enthusiasm was just as much about getting the hostess off the stage as it was about getting the night's performers on it.

'A talent show unlike any other. And I use the word "talent" here loosely, of course.' She flashed her eyes wide for emphasis. 'And now, some mathematics – so pay attention! We will have five contestants – four drag queens and one drag king – competing in three rounds. The contestants will be judged after each round, and the two found most unworthy will be' – she screeched, drawing her fingers in a line across her throat – 'they will be sent to the fiery depths for their sins.'

Cilla Slay slowly lifted a hand and the spotlight moon turned blood red, accompanied by the wailing of a dissonant choir overlaid with manic, demonic laughter. She dropped the raised hand and the moon returned to its usual pale yellow and the tortured sounds cut off in an instant.

'The first round is a drag staple – you know it, you love it – it is, of course, the lip-sync. Round two will be familiar for anyone who loves a beauty pageant. Will our surviving performers be modelling swimwear? Fortunately, no. There would not be nearly enough fabric involved to cover up all our secrets, and the risk of a wardrobe malfunction is just *too great*. No, round two will give our contestants the chance to show off their "special" talents.'

This last comment was accompanied by a salacious wink.

'Now, the sharper students amongst you will realise that leaves us with only one contestant for the final round. They will have the pleasure, the honour, the privilege of joining me, Cilla Slay, for the big finale. Supporting me in… singing an original song!'

Addison groaned internally.

At least, he thought he had. When Mabel leant forward and caught his eye a moment later, dark amusement written all over her face, he realised the groan had in fact been quite audible.

Wincing, Addison returned his attention to the stage only to find the gaze of their hostess boring holes into him. It appeared she too had caught the private thought he'd tactlessly and unintentionally shared aloud.

Addison was well on his way to imploding with cringe when Jake rested a hand on his knee, pinning him to the present and reassuring his brain, with its penchant for hyperbole, that he was not about to literally die of embarrassment. He gave Jake a grateful smile and tuned back in to what was being said.

'—you hags, that's enough notices,' Cilla Slay said, her attention back to the audience as a whole. 'Are you ready for round one?'

The audience dutifully applauded.

'That was – how do I say this nicely? – quite pathetic. Our contestants will be performing for their lives, their very souls! I said, *are you ready for a show*?'

This produced significantly more enthusiastic applause.

'We'll work on that,' she said with a sigh that suggested there really was little hope. 'Now, make sure you're paying attention during the performances, because afterwards I'm going to ask you to help me decide our winners and our *losers*. You shall pass judgement, as it were.'

Again, the moon turned red and the wails of hell flooded the hall before cutting off once more.

'Our first queen has come to us' – Cilla shook out a roll of parchment she'd pulled from one of her sleeves – 'all the way from Woodville, just on the other side of the gorge. Wowee. A town that surely can't be any more, um, *regional* than this place, but who knows what goes on around these parts?'

Addison checked back in with the mayor's knuckles, now as white as the pearls she wore.

'Without further ado – your first killer performance, please give it up for... Little Red Riding Wood!'

Cilla Slay and her broom departed stage left and a red-hooded figure ventured on from stage right to great cheers.

What came next was what everyone was here for: dazzling drag performances by the queens – and the king – from all around the region and beyond.

First up was Little Red Riding Wood's sultry and almost vicious interpretation of Duran Duran's 'Hungry Like the Wolf'. The 'Little' in her name was rather misleading, considering how much time she clearly spent at the gym, almost bursting out of her red, hooded cloak.

Pineapple Pizzazz from Palmerston North sashayed out to 'Sweet Dreams (Are Made of This)' by Eurythmics wearing what appeared to be some kind of pyjama-dress combo, topping off their outfit with an oversized pineapple nightcap.

Miss Candy Less from Milverton – the drag daughter of Lady Perry Less herself – went full glam-rock, storming the stage as Dr Frank-N-Furter for a wildly camp and chaotic rendition of 'The Time Warp' from *The Rocky Horror Picture Show*.

Richard Coxington III, the gentleman drag king from Levin, did a full, unabridged rendition of Meat Loaf's 'Bat Out of Hell.' At almost ten minutes long, the audience were subjected to more air guitaring than anybody could ever want, and they clapped more from relief than anything else when it mercifully came to an end.

And finally Dame Tuck Shop from Whanganui strutted out with her trolley cart serving looks and imaginary school lunches in equal measure, all while lip-synching to Dolly Parton's '9 to 5'.

Sure, some of the performances were a bit off-theme, the makeup was a little rough, and the sewing clearly not the work of a seamstress at the top of her game, but the choreography was creative and it was obvious the performers were having a great time. They were enthusiastic amateurs and their energy was infectious.

In between performances, Cilla Slay came out again in her role as hostess, nominally to thank and congratulate the preceding performer before introducing the next. But considering she'd also indulged in a couple of costume changes, Addison suspected the appearances were to ensure nobody forgot about her, and to re-centre the show back on herself at every opportunity. One particularly notable appearance was as Sigourney Weaver's Ellen Ripley from one of the *Alien* movie sequels, based on the attire, grubbiness, and especially the baldness, with the titular alien as a drooling sock puppet on her hand trying to take bites out of her.

Even with the repeated reminders, her shady presence didn't diminish the mood, which was uplifted further with each performance.

Dame Tuck Shop, the fifth and final contestant, finished her lip-sync performance with a flourish before tottering off the stage, pushing her trolley cart ahead of her on a wave of appreciative applause.

Cilla Slay re-emerged in yet another new costume – this one head-to-toe black but with a slash of red lipstick, shiny red heeled boots, and a single red rose clasped in her hand along with her microphone.

Another macabre and instantly recognisable character.

'Oh, Milverton,' she said breathily as the crowd quietened. From somewhere in her costume she produced secateurs which she used to lop off the head of the rose. 'Isn't it just so dark, so dire, so devoid of life? What a *dream*.'

Cilla was channelling another queen of the night from the nineties. This time it was, without doubt, Anjelica Huston's take on Morticia Addams.

She looked fantastic – there was no denying it. But after her earlier rant, Addison couldn't help scrutinising the wig. It wasn't quite as long, straight, or glossy as one might have expected – not like Mabel's. His friend had clearly scored the best wig for the role at Johanna's Costume Closet, leaving Cilla lumped with the second-best alternative on her last-minute visit. Addison felt an uncharitable flash of delight at that. He leant in ever so slightly, catching Mabel's eye, and she beamed back, clearly having had the very same wicked little thought.

'And that was, of course, Dame Tuck Shop. I'm a little peckish after that number, I must say. But do you know what I like to tuck into the most, what fills me up unlike anything else?' She raised an eyebrow as the moon shifted to blood red and the tortured soundtrack enveloped them once more before she said, '*Revenge.*'

Chapter 8

'Let's bring back my potential victims, shall we?' Cilla Slay waved them onto the stage, the eclectic mix of performers emerging from stage right to wild applause, lining up before the audience with a variety of winks, curtseys, air kisses, and 'call me' hand gestures.

Cilla stalked along the front of the stage, her back to the audience, giving each in the lineup her shadiest once-over as the cheers settled down.

'All right,' she said, turning to face the audience. 'How this works is I will hold my hand over each contestant, and if you want them gone, sent to the fiery depths, then you will yell, "DIE!" Easy enough, yes?'

The response from the crowd was a general rumble of uncertainty. Addison could appreciate the sentiment – it was counterintuitive to make some noise for someone you did *not* want to win. That aside, it was also rather mean-spirited.

'I know you lot, feigning innocence,' Cilla continued. 'Pretending to be so nicey-pie, wouldn't hurt a fly? What rot. You're all *killers*. I give you permission, here and now, on this spookiest of holidays, to let out your inner darkness.

We only have three places in the next round. They can't all go through. Two must die.'

The performers lined up across the stage wore expressions of exaggerated horror.

'Let's practise with this pumpkin.' Their hostess stalked over to the nearest pile, bent at the waist, selected the smallest of the sinisterly grinning jack-o'-lanterns, and then snapped back upright. An equally wicked smile now on her face, she held the carved orange pumpkin to the side in the palm of one hand, slowly moving the other to hover over it as she counted down. 'Three... two... one...'

A few uncertain calls, barely above regular conversational volume. Only the performers had responded with any real gusto.

Cilla whipped her hovering hand back and stomped a heeled boot. 'We have been through this, folks. Once more, with feeling,' she said before counting down again. 'Toru... rua... tahi...'

Perhaps fearful of what their tyrannical hostess might do if they didn't comply, the audience erupted with an unrestrained 'DIE!'

'Much better.' She dropped the pumpkin from on high, resulting in a moist explosion upon impact with the stage. Segments of pumpkin shell and pulp that hadn't been fully scooped out shot in all directions, including towards those sitting in the centre of the front row – namely Mabel, Jake, Addison, and Mayor Harriet Ferguson.

The alarm of the rest of the audience drowned out Addison's reaction – for which he was very grateful and relieved, as he feared it had been rather loud – and was once again followed up with a round of self-conscious chuckles.

It was the fright of the thing, with Addison getting off

relatively unscathed, only wearing a couple of pulpy pumpkin seeds, easily flicked off.

The mayor, however, copped the worst of it, being splattered with more than a few stringy orange clumps. This was swiftly dealt with by some furious swiping. The pulp residue may no longer have shown up against her sparkly black top, but she was fuming.

'And now, it is time,' Cilla said, drawing everyone's attention back to herself while clearly delighting in the chaos she'd caused. 'We have before us five on death row, two of whom are about to be dispatched to the fiery depths. The power is in *your* hands.'

Well primed, the audience voted by shouting their deathly demands as Cilla Slay stalked along behind the death row inmates, stopping to hover her hand over each in turn. She returned to a few performers for second assessments, eyes squinting as she judged the relative volume of each infernal vote.

She nodded, apparently satisfied, and returned to her favoured position at centre stage. 'You are all so wonderfully dreadful, voting with such gusto. I knew you could get there. I thank you for your contribution and invite you to give yourselves a round of applause.'

Again, the audience did as they were directed, clapping until their hostess waved them into silence. 'That's enough, don't get carried away. You are just sitting there, after all.'

Addison overheard Mabel mumbling from her seat on the other side of Jake, something about making up her mind already.

'Now, could the following contestants please step forward: your local baby queen, Miss Candy Less of Milverton—'

A few cheers and gasps rippled through the crowd – who had different ideas about what being called forward meant – quickly followed by shushing.

'—the ferocious flirt of the forest, Little Red Riding Wood of Woodville…'

Cilla let her sentence trail off, but nodded when her audience remained silent in anticipation.

'And Dame Tuck Shop, Whanganui's most matronly of dinner ladies.'

This time, their hostess paused, keeping her rapt audience in suspense as she slowly lifted her head to look down her nose at them. 'You have been judged worthy. You are safe, and you live to compete another round,' she said, her voice sweet yet ominous before turning wicked once more. 'Now, get out of my sight.' She shooed the top three off stage as they dropped into impromptu curtseys and blew kisses throughout their departure, to great applause.

'And that leaves two to meet their fate: Pineapple Pizzazz of Palmerston North and Richard Coxington III of Levin. Both dreadful performances – and I mean "dreadful" in the spookiest, most macabre way – but tonight you were not quite as dreadful as the other three, I'm afraid.'

Cilla Slay stepped aside, gesturing to the space she'd just vacated as the ever-present fog began to thicken, churning with malice and obscuring the view of the stage.

'Would you losers please take my place there at centre stage? Yes, both of you. See that big red X? Yes, right there, X marks the spot, as they say— No, don't stand *on* it, unless you want to be sent to the underworld for real? I didn't think so. Just behind it will do. Now, I suggest you take comfort in each other in the face of your imminent demise.'

The performers, each gracious in their defeat, did as

instructed by melodramatically holding onto each other as if for dear life, though they were barely visible now through the thickening fog.

'And now, my awful, terrible, despicable audience… What do we say? One more time, with feeling. Three… two… one…'

'DIE!'

A loud bang cracked as the moon flashed red and wails of the dead burst forth. From Addison's vantage point right at the front, he could see the faintest movement through the swirling mists as one figure appeared to descend through the stage, then a second, followed by a distinct *clunk*.

Cilla Slay swept through the fog, strutting past where the contestants had been only moments earlier. She cackled with glee, waving down at the stage floor. 'Bye now. Ta-ta. Au revoir. Haere rā. Auf Wiedersehen. Good riddance.' She dusted off her hands and returned her attention to the crowd. 'Oh, I do enjoy taking out the *trash*. And that is the end of the first round, folks. It's now time for a little interval. Mama's dying of thirst up here. I'll see you all again very shortly.'

The audience had started shuffling and their hostess was halfway off the stage before she abruptly turned back. 'Oh. Yes, yes, keep your panties on,' Cilla said, addressing someone offstage before returning her attention to the murmuring crowd. 'One thing before you dash. The sharper ones amongst you may have noticed that we are here at the Milverton Town Hall. Yes? I believe this evening's original venue, Penshaw Hall, is currently out of commission, much like your original hostess. I have been *reminded* to mention that proceeds from tonight's show will go towards funding the Penshaw Hall stage repairs. So please drink up, buy lots of popcorn, ice creams, merch, all that. And remember, the more you drink, the funnier and the prettier I get.'

Chapter 9

Either the audience had taken instruction from their hostess or they were all just desperate for a drink. Addison suspected the latter was the case, considering that was true for himself.

A large crowd had swarmed the bar, though they were being served surprisingly efficiently. Deirdre had pre-poured rows of red and white wine ready to go, pouring only the beers and fizzy drinks to order. She'd also roped in another two helpers, taking payments being their sole responsibility.

A slick operation. A major step up from the temporary volunteer-run bars Addison had endured at other community theatre events – they'd clearly meant well, but had no system and no direction and the lines had snaked through the foyer, blowing out the interval and holding up the second act.

Addison caught snippets of conversations around him and the general consensus was not surprising, with all proud to have such wonderful, talented local performers but, equally and oppositely, appalled by the evening's hostess.

'I hate to speak ill of the injured, but wow, couldn't our Lady Ferry Less have found someone – anyone! – else to host?'

'It's as if Cilla got more obnoxious with every appearance.'

'If it were up to me, I'd be sending her through that trapdoor next.'

This last was met with dark chuckles of agreement from many in the vicinity.

'I am enjoying the performances though.'

'Yes, absolutely. Worth it for that. Otherwise I might have snuck out to "use the loo" —'

'Never to return.'

Snorts of amusement and quiet laughs suggested more than a few people had had similar thoughts.

When Addison had asked what they wanted from the bar, Mabel had suggested 'something with alcohol, anything' and Jake had nodded, echoing the sentiment. Addison kept it simple and safe with three glasses of red – having learnt his lesson with the very much unchilled white wine of earlier.

With generously poured glasses of wine arranged between the fingers of both hands, Addison turned from the bar. He hadn't even taken a step when his elbow was jostled, sending a glug of red wine overboard and onto the front of someone at his side.

The splash was immediately followed by a string of curses from the unfortunate victim, who held his shoulders back, hands splayed, as if to get away from the spillage. He looked down, pulling at the various layers of his drapey black clothes.

'I'm *so* sorry,' Addison said, horrified. And then he

recognised the man as someone Mabel had pointed out earlier. 'Brodie, was it?'

'Yes,' Brodie said with a hiss and a huffed-out breath. 'This evening, already a stain on my soul, is now a stain on my clothes too, it seems.'

Addison repeated his apologies, before adding, 'Please let me know your details and I'll pay to have it—'

'No, don't bother.' Brodie scoffed and waved a dismissive hand. 'This top is ruined. Just get out of my way, will you? You have what you came for. If I didn't already need wine before, I certainly do now.'

'I'm so—'

'Just go,' Brodie said, stepping around Addison and up to the bar.

Addison considered insisting but reckoned that would only make the situation worse. Instead he took a breath and shook his head in an attempt to put the incident from his mind before navigating through the crowd on his way back to Jake and Mabel.

Careful to keep his elbows close, Addison passed Johanna in a heated conversation with Mayor Ferguson. He didn't catch the details, but the costume shop owner was clearly fuming about Cilla's disparaging wig-related commentary, and the mayor was doing an admirable job of nodding along, lending a receptive ear, and keeping her own thoughts to herself.

Mabel, however, had no such qualms about doling out more than a few choice words and phrases. She was in full flight when Addison returned with their drinks. 'Classic Napoleon complex,' she said. 'Trussed herself up in costume and given herself permission to be a total diva, maximum melodrama.'

'You wear it better, anyway,' Addison said, handing out their drinks.

'Thank you for getting these – yes, red, good idea. And what's that? What do I wear better?'

'The melodrama.'

'Oh, you!' Mabel smiled, batting his arm. 'The cheek.'

'Morticia Addams, I mean, of course. You're the number one Morticia tonight.'

'I don't know about that. But well, yes, I think you might be right. Did you see—'

'The second-rate wig? I did.'

Mabel tittered in dark delight. 'Don't you let Johanna hear you say that, but I clearly got in there first.' She ran a hand through her long, glossy black hair.

'Second-best on that TV show and now second-best in selecting her wig.'

'Always the bridesmaid, never the bride.'

'You know,' Addison said with a sigh, 'getting runner-up doesn't mean she can take it all out on us.'

'Yeah.' Jake shrugged. 'Whatever she's trying to do, she's missing the mark on sharp, witchy wit.'

'Overshot it, hasn't she?' Mabel said. 'By a significant margin.'

'She's landed somewhere that's not so much "witchy" as it is' – Addison considered for a moment – 'as it is a very similar sounding word that starts with B.'

'*Language.*' Mabel batted his arm, though any attempted reproval was negated by the twitch of her lips. 'But yes, a witch with a B. Even so, let's hope the second act goes off without a *hitch*.'

'Be a shame if she ended up in a *ditch*.'

It was Mabel's turn to roll her eyes, and Jake only shook

his head.

'Oh, come on,' Addison said. 'Just because *you* couldn't think of another one.'

'Sure thing, dear. Let's get back in there.' Mabel nodded back towards the gap between the dividing curtain and the edge of the hall, already seeing a trickle of people returning to their seats. 'Wouldn't want to miss any of the drama.'

Chapter 10

The lights dimmed as a few spooky, jazzy notes sounded and the heavy red curtains drew up to reveal an entirely new set.

On the audience's right – that is, stage left – was what appeared to be a stone sarcophagus, set on a diagonal.

Across the back, large constructed set pieces transformed the space into a dank dungeon or crypt, with wrought iron lanterns – much like those at the entrance to the town hall – flickering their feeble firelight and set against an oppressive stone wall.

Onto the stage stepped their hostess.

Addison caught glimpses of the same red heeled boots, giving her that extra height. Otherwise, she'd been completely transformed once again.

Glamorous in a floor-length, form-fitting dress of shiny, silver metallic fabric, with long sleeves, and oversized lapels framing a plunging neckline. The neck itself, practically braced in silver with jewellery, encircling and extending its entire length. The wig was one of long, wavy blonde hair. And the lips, pursed just so.

She was giving Addison serious Meryl Streep vibes… not

as frosty as her Miranda in *The Devil Wears Prada*, not as steely as her Thatcher in *The Iron Lady*, and certainly not as sunny as whatever character she played in *Mamma Mia!*, but he couldn't put his finger on it. He'd kick himself when he figured it out.

With a vial of swirling pink-purple liquid in hand, she posed this way and that. When the applause died down, she said, 'Do you think this outfit… becomes me?'

That was it. He'd been so close. The fading actress from *Death Becomes Her*, originally played by Meryl Streep. Another comedy horror from the nineties – who knew the decade had been stacked with so many?

'You did a serviceable job on the voting for our first round. It's no secret that I did not have high hopes for you lot, but you came through with the goods – eventually. And now, round two, where our remaining queens will perform for you their *special* talents.' She treated her audience to an exaggerated wink. 'They each only need to pull off one such talent, so let's hope they can manage that much.'

Cilla Slay stalked her way over to the sarcophagus.

'You may have noticed this grim addition to my stage? Yes,' she said, drawing out the hiss. 'For this next round, I will be forming an "expert" judging panel. Don't worry' – she held up a hand to halt the nonexistent protest – 'your voices will still be heard, but it is my judges who will have the final say. Shall we meet our first judge?'

Once the cheers in the affirmative had settled, Cilla continued. 'As you've already seen tonight, Lady Perry Less hasn't bothered to tuck it all away or otherwise put herself together – one broken limb and it all falls apart. So, in boring old boy mode, please drag yourself back out here, Patrick Laurence.'

He came in on crutches, leaning them against the sarcophagus as he dropped into a seat behind it. He acknowledged the raucous applause with a smile and brief wave.

'Now, for our second panellist, I believe your mayor has bribed the production team into giving her a position on my judging panel. Yes?'

Cilla turned to Patrick who was shaking his head.

'No?'

Patrick picked up a microphone from the sarcophagus. 'Yes to the position on the judging panel. No to the bribe.'

'Oh, of course – wink, wink, nudge, nudge. We'll discuss my cut later,' Cilla said before dropping her gaze to the front row. 'All right, your majesty? Up you come. Trot, trot.'

Mayor Ferguson's grip may have been white-knuckled before, but was now practically vice-like. Addison feared her clutch might be about to sustain mortal damage. She stood, her posture rigid, and joined Patrick on stage.

'And now we need one more,' Cilla said slowly, appearing to consider where she might find such a candidate before turning to the audience. 'Do I have any volunteers?'

Addison had absolutely no desire to volunteer, but an itch suddenly appeared on his nose, demanding to be scratched. And the back of his neck, just at the hairline. He kept his hands right where they were, not moving a muscle as Cilla Slay stalked from one side of the stage to the other. Addison didn't look down into his lap, because that'd be obvious. Instead he focused on a flickering lantern at the back of the stage, determined to avoid eye contact without appearing to be trying to do so. Did he have something in his eye?

'I need someone with a sharp mind—'

Out of the corner of his eye, Addison saw Mabel leaning forwards, trying to get his attention.

'—and a sharp eye.'

Mabel's eyes widened insistently and Addison was sure she was about to reach across to nudge him. He shook his head in what he hoped was a subtle yet clear response.

'I need someone who can make a quick assessment on the spot.'

Cilla Slay stopped right in front of Addison, and waited, not saying a word.

It had been seconds, multiple agonising seconds, when Addison couldn't take it any longer. He slowly, reluctantly shifted his attention to the looming drag queen, a wicked smile on her lips. But her eyes weren't on him, they were to his side.

'What about you, handsome man,' she said, her eyes practically eating Jake up. 'What do you do?'

Ever stoic, Jake simply said, 'I'm a cop.'

Cilla gasped, her hand flying up dramatically to flutter around her jaw, not daring to touch her face lest she spoil her makeup. 'You're a top? Goodness, it's not *that* kind of show, sir, but do come and see me later. I have my own dressing room and—'

'I'm a police officer.'

'Oh…' Cilla drew out the sound as if she didn't already know what he'd said. 'A *cop*, you say? Well, you'd be perfect for the job, but that just won't do. No, we can't have you working after hours. You stay there, in the front row where I can see you. Relax, conserve your strength – I'll be needing your services later.' She winked, leaving no doubt about her implication.

Addison didn't think himself the jealous type – at least, he liked to think he wasn't. But that didn't mean he couldn't be annoyed. He was literally *right there*. Soliciting his man before his very eyes? Brazen, tacky, and not even that funny.

And it was all for nought anyway. Jake wouldn't fall for such nonsense – he had better taste than that. Addison was thinking of himself, of course, reasoning that it wasn't arrogant to have some self-respect, recognise your own self-worth. Cilla Slay didn't stand a chance.

'Yoo hoo,' she said, snapping her fingers until Addison made eye contact. 'Yes, you. Welcome back, space cadet. What about you?'

'What—'

'You're the one who was groaning earlier' – she glanced at Jake and winked – 'and not in the way I intend to be later. You were not looking forward to hearing an original song, if I remember correctly?'

She had remembered correctly. And his confidence from moments earlier had shifted to discomfort at being called out.

'I'll take that as a yes. And what do you do?'

'I'm a marketing consultant.'

'Ah, yes, that sounds about right. Nobody here has a clue what that means and neither do I. But we do already know you're the judgy type, and with a job like yours, I expect you'll be well rested, so I think it's time we put you to work. Up you get, sweet cheeks.'

Addison didn't know where to start.

Should he defend his job and his work ethic? No, that'd just sound whiny, like he couldn't take a joke.

Explain what it was he did? No, that wouldn't play well, and even worse for a live performer doing crowd work, it'd be *boring*.

Should he object to the disparaging endearment? Who even called someone 'sweet cheeks'? No, he wasn't about to get into all that.

And as much as he might want to slap that smarmy smirk from Cilla Slay's face, assaulting someone – no matter how satisfying – was not an option. Even if a police officer, and a hall of other witnesses besides, weren't right there.

Finally, Addison considered quietly demurring but suspected that would only encourage their hostess.

Short of throwing a tantrum and storming off, he wasn't getting out of this.

Addison patted Jake's knee as if to draw strength from him, pulled on his best attempt at a smile, and got up without outward fuss. He stepped up on stage and took his seat next to the mayor, who looked about as pleased as he was to be there.

Chapter 11

The first thing Addison noticed about being on stage was the heat pouring from the lights. He didn't understand how the performers' makeup hadn't melted off their faces. The other thing about the lights was that they were bright, practically blinding. Addison could barely make out the audience from his newly elevated position, though there was no hiding the two eliminated contestants – with their big, bright costumes – who had joined the back of the audience to enjoy the second round.

The first contestant to return to the stage was Dame Tuck Shop, who entered once again pushing her trolley. However, she had switched out her matronly dinner lady costume for a sleek flight attendant's outfit. She showed off her business class service skills for the judging panel, first offering small hot towels with a set of tongs, presented with a great flourish for the audience's benefit. While they refreshed their hands, she served a selection of cheeses and crackers, with the cheese-to-cracker ratio heavily weighted towards the cheese, which Addison appreciated very much. And then she poured three glasses of bubbles, filling the flutes right to the brim, leaving the bottle in front of the mayor with the comment that she might need it.

The skit was part running commentary, part stand-up comedy routine, and entirely tongue in cheek. Loudly deferential, with much over-the-top complimenting of the judges' positive attributes, and many reminders that they were a *full-service* airline, that it would be her great *pleasure* to offer them her *personal touch*, all they need do was ask.

The audience was amused, laughing along at all the right points and ending with enthusiastic applause.

Addison happily sipped and munched away as Dame Tuck Shop finished her number and he considered the stack of large cards before him, numbered one to ten. From his perspective, the business class service deserved full marks, so he proudly held up the card bearing the number 10.

He finished his in-flight snacks as Dame Tuck Shop made her departure. He concentrated on the chewing and swallowing more than the average adult might, as he was known to forget such basic things, and the last thing he wanted right then was a choking fit on stage.

Still, he couldn't help noticing that, too distracted from waving her farewells, the dame accidentally rammed her trolley into the faux stone wall lining the back of the stage. He knew it was only a set piece, likely made of plywood, but it didn't budge at all – an impressively solid construction.

Her waving hand flew to her mouth in an exaggerated 'Oops!' before she quickly tottered off stage.

Addison took a moment to check his front for any crumbs, and when he looked back up, he found the next act had already taken the stage. It was Miss Candy Less looking like nothing so much as a gothic candy cane. Her form-fitting bodysuit sported bold red and white stripes, with bursts of black lace at the ankles, wrists, and neck.

She performed a choreographed dance and gymnastics routine to Lady Gaga's 'Abracadabra' – aerial cartwheels, backflips, handstand pirouettes, death drops, the lot, and all the more impressive for being done in heels.

As the song's end neared, Addison saw the mayor preparing her 10 card – the only correct score for a fan favourite in front of the home crowd. He did likewise, as did Patrick Laurence. The final note dropped and Miss Candy Less froze in a dramatic pose, the judges hoisting their cards to the roaring approval of the audience.

Candy took her time basking in the adulation, smiling and throwing out plenty of air kisses to a delighted crowd.

Addison was starting to relax into his unwanted role. Nobody paid the judges any real attention behind their sarcophagus, with all eyes on the performance until the moment they presented their scorecards. And provided they didn't throw up any particularly miserly scores, they ought to be safe.

The final contestant – Little Red Riding Wood – came out in a sparkly black dress under a black cape with a silky red satin lining, with a pair of long white gloves pushing what appeared to be an oversized wooden trunk.

From Addison's newly elevated position, he could see she was aiming for the large red X taped to the stage which Cilla had mentioned earlier. He could also see that it was centred on a square marked out by very narrow but distinct gaps in the floorboards.

The trapdoor.

The gateway to the underworld where the first round's unsuccessful contestants had been so dramatically banished.

Little Red Riding Wood positioned the trunk covering

81

the front and the side edges of the trapdoor, leaving only the back half of the trapdoor extending beyond the back of the trunk.

The latest contestant made a show of dusting herself down, wiping her brow, and touching up her wig just so. She then went through the motions of proving to the audience that there was nothing inside the trunk before bringing a microphone to her lips.

'Now, my darlings,' she said, drawing out the word as if everyone in attendance was her most special someone. 'Who would like to get into my box?'

A flurry of hands shot straight up into the air and after much deliberation by Little Red, Addison was pleased to see his friend in the front row selected as the magician's assistant.

A delighted Mabel bustled up onto the stage and was introduced to the audience before being hoisted into the box. Then, once she was safely inside, the lid was closed over her.

Little Red clapped her gloved hands together as if in delight, but Addison could see from his new vantage point that the gesture was to mask the sound of the trapdoor dropping open, revealing a ladder leading down to the space below stage.

What followed was much magical, mystical woo-woo from Little Red, with lots of hand waving and skipping about, all with a touch of theatricality and humour. Meanwhile, in full view of the judges but out of sight of the audience, Mabel picked her way down the ladder. She ducked out of the way as the trapdoor returned to its closed position, once more *clunking* into place, as if it had been there all along.

'And now for the magic word,' Little Red said with an air of impending triumph. 'You may recall it from the very talented and alarmingly flexible Miss Candy Less who just spent three minutes and forty-three seconds hurling herself around the stage to it. Do you know the magic word I'm talking about? Yes? OK, here we go: uno... dos... tres... abracadabra!'

With the final syllable, Little Red Riding Wood gripped the trunk's latch and flung the lid off, each of the sides falling back onto the stage with a *thunk* to reveal absolutely nothing. It was as if Mabel Zhou had magically vanished.

A simple trick. And Addison suspected more than a few Milverton residents knew about the trapdoor – especially after the previous round – but the talent was in the drama and spectacle of the execution. A captivating performance that earnt a well-deserved round of applause.

Little Red Riding Wood let the applause roll on for a few moments, flip-flopping between suggesting they were too much, really, and that they should keep going, please. She offered ostentatious bows throughout, and when the applause was finally petering out, she said, 'Thank you for coming out tonight, Milverton. If you've enjoyed my performance, I've been Little Red Riding Wood. If you haven't, I've been the Big Bad Wolf.' She started to walk off stage, to laughter, cheers, and a cacophony of calls which included 'Yes', 'Hey', 'Oi', and 'What', before settling on a chant – 'Bring her back! Bring her back!' – that soon had everyone joining in.

Fully off stage now and out of sight of the audience, Little Red stood alongside Miss Candy Less and Dame Tuck Shop, all waiting in the wings.

Little Red let the chant run a few more times before she

ducked her head back from behind the side curtain. 'Did you want me to bring her back?'

The crowd cheered their loudest yet, with the judging panel joining in too.

'Oh, all right then,' Little Red said, returning to her collapsed trunk at centre stage. 'Now, we smashed my box wide open a little earlier, so let me just put it back together or my lovely assistant – Morticia Addams herself – will have nowhere to reappear.' She made a show of bending over and lifting each of the sides back to vertical and snapping them into place before finally latching the lid closed again.

'OK, that's all set,' she said, levering herself back upright and wiping her brow from all the manual labour. 'So, we already know the magic word to make someone disappear? But what about making them reappear?'

'Abracadabra!'

'Kapow!'

'Ta-da!'

'Huzzah!'

'Voilà!'

'Please!'

'You're all wrong, I'm afraid,' Little Red said. 'But my favourite was the "please" – whoever said that, your mother would be so proud. No, you'll kick yourself when you hear it, especially anyone who was a Pokémon fan as a child. Or an adult, of course, no judgement here—'

'Alakazam.'

It wasn't until Little Red turned to face the judging panel behind the sarcophagus, locking onto Addison, that he realised he'd said it out loud – his second slip-up that evening.

He could already feel the blood crawling up his neck, but

instead of slipping into the familiar sensation of embarrassment, he took a deep breath and nodded once. Why shouldn't he know the answer? He was going to own it.

Addison may not have been able to remember where he'd left his keys, what he'd had for breakfast, or so often what he'd gone upstairs for, but you bet he could still rattle off the home phone number of his best friend from primary school as well as the names and key statistics of all 151 of the original Pokémon.

'That's correct,' Little Red said. 'It's like you read my mind. *Alakazam*. Now, just to be sure my box is ready for action again…' She tucked her microphone under one arm, clapped her gloved hands together, and the trapdoor dropped open just as it had done the first time. When no movement could be seen through the now-open trapdoor, Little Red directed her voice rather pointedly to the box and said, 'I sure hope my assistant is ready to return.'

Mabel took the hint, immediately working her way back up the ladder.

'All right, one last time, everybody. You know the magic word. Un… deux… trois…'

'Alakazam!'

Little Red flung back the lid of her box and Mabel popped her head out the top to great fanfare, much applause, and once again full marks from the judges.

Not even Mabel's slightly undignified hoisting from the box by the muscle-bound Little Red Riding Wood could diminish the joyous moment. The magician and her lovely assistant were taking their bows when Cilla Slay reappeared, clearly having had enough of others basking in the audience's adulation.

Chapter 12

Cilla Slay's latest costume sported overlapping green leaves plastered above her heavily made-up eyes, forming a pair of exaggerated eyebrows. Then there was the vibrant red hair wrapped into two horn-like cones atop her head, with the rest hanging down to her waist. She wore a neon green jumpsuit, alarming in both how bright and how form-fitting it was. Long strings of ivy were draped around her neck and over her shoulders, trailing across the stage behind her as she strutted, still in the shiny red heeled boots.

Addison immediately recognised Uma Thurman's villainess Poison Ivy from another nineties classic, *Batman & Robin*. Though that film had lodged itself firmly in his psyche for an entirely different reason. That being, of course, Robin's suit. The sculpted arms and chest and stomach and *ahem*, all that – formative in Addison's adolescence. His overactive imagination had shifted to picturing Jake in such a costume for next Halloween when he tuned back in to find Cilla Slay shooing Little Red Riding Wood and her box from the stage.

Mabel had taken that as her cue to leave and was already halfway across the stage when Cilla started clicking her fingers from her position near the large red X.

'Oh no, excuse me? Yes, you. Morticia the Short, where do you think you're going? Back here, to me.'

Mabel hesitated, clearly weighing up whether to respond with what was on her mind before deciding against it. She returned to centre stage, picking her way through Cilla's trailing vines – a trip hazard if ever there was one – and taking up position just to stage right of her.

'You did such a serviceable job in getting into and out of a box – yes, closer, right at my side, there,' Cilla Slay said, sighing as she rested a forearm and some of her weight on Mabel's shoulder. 'It's not easy being a leafy seductress, I hope you know? This lush lady garden doesn't tend herself. And all done in these heels, which are killing me, by the way. So, Mini Morticia, you have now been promoted to *my* assistant, and your sole task will be to stand there and help hold me upright, OK? Wonderful.'

Mabel gritted her teeth and widened her stance a touch, but otherwise didn't respond. Cilla Slay's Napoleon complex was on full display, picking on Mabel in an attempt to boost her own ego and stature. Though the outcome was less casually imperious and rather more comical because Cilla was still barely any taller than Mabel.

'Now, I think we can all agree that my judges were not up to the task, were they?' Cilla shot a poisonous look over her shoulder at the three sitting behind the sarcophagus before returning her attention to the crowd. 'People pleasers, the lot of them. Full marks for every performance?' She blew a raspberry. 'Please. Those were sixes or sevens out of ten, at best. No, it surprises me as much as you, but it looks like I'm going to have to rely on my audience again.'

Cilla Slay pursed her lips, glancing from the audience

before her to Mabel at her side, then back again, the low-lying fog churning and swirling as if in anticipation.

'Actually, before I call back tonight's performers, we're going to practise our voting. To make sure you haven't forgotten. We won't be banishing Little Morticia to the fiery depths, just back to her seat, OK? Yes? Are we ready?'

The audience responded with a combination of cheers, affirmations, and death wishes. The response may have been rather discordant but nonetheless showed they were ready.

Addison thought he was ready too, but he could not have been more wrong.

Still leaning on Mabel's shoulder, Cilla Slay raised her free hand to hover over Mabel's head and started counting down. This triggered so many things to happen and in such rapid succession that Addison could only watch in mounting horror, utterly powerless to stop any of it.

Together, the audience shouted 'DIE!' as the stage lights flashed red and the screaming of tortured souls tore from the speakers.

This was as expected for the macabre voting regime. What followed a moment later, however, was not.

With a bang, the trapdoor at centre stage flung open and Cilla Slay abruptly jerked to the side.

Her left foot, the one planted nearest the large red X, disappeared. The other, by Mabel, remained right where it was.

Hurtling sidewards, Cilla plunged through the trapdoor.

She was overturned completely, too swiftly for her to lift her arms or even scream.

The vines of her costume came alive as her head dropped from sight, followed immediately by her shoulders, chest, waist, and hips. A heartbeat later came a crack and a dull thump.

Her upended body slumped against the edge of the opening, only her trailing foot remaining aloft, sticking up through the open trapdoor.

And the shiny red, patent leather boot with six-inch heel that had stormed the stage all evening was now deathly still.

Chapter 13

Jostled by the weight suddenly lifted from her shoulder and the vines of Cilla's costume whipping past her ankles, Mabel lost her wig yet somehow kept her footing. Her eyes locked on the open trapdoor as she took first one step back, then another, before freezing in place.

The stunned audience looked on in silence, eyes flicking between the stage and their seat neighbours, unsure quite how to react.

What had they just witnessed?

Any chance it had been a clever and very convincing piece of choreography evaporated the moment crew members rushed onstage from the wings. Confused and concerned murmurs rumbled through the crowd as one of the stagehands scrambled down the ladder.

What was surely intended as a whisper to their fellow backstage crew ended up rather more of a stage whisper – easily carrying to the ears of the judges and certainly reaching at least the first few rows of the audience – because screams erupted all around the hall the moment the stagehand said, 'She's dead.'

The bottom of Addison's stomach dropped at the

stagehand's words. They were still speaking, but he couldn't make out anything else over the scraping and clattering of chairs, the shouts and the screaming of the audience. The screams themselves were not the cries and shrieks of delightfully spooked Halloween event attendees, but the deep-seated, blood-curdling, primal scream of the truly terrified.

Someone had the presence of mind to drop the main curtain, separating the stage and audience, though something apparently caught, leaving the curtain only three-quarters down, which was somehow even worse.

If Addison were the superstitious type, these latest developments would surely tip the production over into cursed status. The final nail in the coffin, so to speak.

Speaking of nails and coffins, Addison wondered if sarcophagi had nails or other means of fixing the lids in place. They were effectively just stone coffins – the real ones, anyway – so perhaps they relied solely on gravity? His only experience in this area came from the movies, and who knew how realistic they were? Addison found himself thinking about Brendan Fraser's treasure-hunting character in *The Mummy* – another film which had an outsized impact on the young and impressionable Addison – when he realised what his subconscious was doing. Something he was coming to learn about himself was that his mind, in traumatic situations, tended to defend itself with distraction, specifically wondering about inconsequential things or focusing on unimportant details – in this case, tomb raiders and scarab beetles.

Dragging his attention back from the tombs of Ancient Egyptian pharaohs to Milverton's spookily made-over town hall, Addison assessed the immediate situation.

The response from Sergeant Jake Murphy, Constable Manaia Edwards, and Constable Sean McGiffert had been much more pragmatic than his own. They had already put themselves back on duty and shifted into police mode, unwavering as they ushered a very loud and very upset audience out the front doors.

Little Red Riding Wood, Miss Candy Less, and Dame Tuck Shop were soon rejoined by Pineapple Pizzazz and Richard Coxington III, clustering together on stage right. With smeared makeup and costumes askew, they appeared as shocked about their fellow queen's abrupt end as anyone.

The crew in their stage blacks were similarly huddled, though they had now stepped a little back from the trapdoor. Some were silent, hands over mouths, unable to keep their eyes off the red heeled boot protruding from the opening. A couple couldn't bring themselves to look, wiping away tears or turned away and sobbing into their crewmates' shoulders. The final few were arguing about whether or not to pull Cilla up and out. The prevailing wisdom seemed to be you shouldn't move someone with suspected neck or back injuries in case you made it worse. The response to that – which Addison considered a very reasonable if bleak one – was that you couldn't get much worse than dead.

And on stage left, the guest judges stood behind their sarcophagus. Mabel was slowly drifting towards them, taking small steps, never taking her eyes off the trapdoor. Without a word, Addison settled her down in his vacated seat.

With the main curtain still stubbornly stuck part way open, Addison could see the hall rapidly emptying. There was a brief scramble as Jake parted the exiting crowd,

92

clearing the way for the paramedics coming in the other direction.

Addison caught sight of a pair of familiar faces – Diana and Scott, apparently never more than a few minutes away from disaster.

Carrying an emergency room's worth of equipment with them, the paramedics followed Jake up the steps and stalked across to centre stage.

Mayor Ferguson was on her feet at Addison's side, lips pressed into a line and shaking her head. 'What a mess.'

'Awful,' Addison said.

'This is the last thing we need,' she said so only he could hear. 'There's no way we'll be able to keep this out of the papers or off social media, so we need to sort it out and get through it as swiftly as possible.'

'Put our best foot forward,' Addison said, eyes fixed on Cilla Slay's airborne red heel. 'So to speak.'

'Yes, so to speak.' The mayor returned her attention from the foot of the moment to Addison. 'Otherwise any efforts to promote Milverton as a must-visit destination will be for nought.'

Addison nodded slowly, mind still reeling from the situation while the mayor – his boss, as of the coming Monday – was multiple steps ahead of him.

'You already had a tough job ahead of you next week, Addison. And this is only going to make it worse. I hope you're up for it.'

With that parting salvo, Mayor Ferguson flashed her eyes and stepped away, leaving the safety of the sarcophagus to consult with her sergeant and the paramedics.

Addison could feel himself on the edge of descending

into a stress spiral when his friend's grey-white bob and shaking hand caught his eye.

He followed her gaze to the huddle that had formed around the trapdoor's opening, blocking their view. Addison knelt at Mabel's side, laying an arm across her shoulders, and without a clue where to start, he said, 'Well…'

Mabel looked over and met his eye, nodding along in response. 'Indeed,' she said, before once again falling silent, her gaze drifting back to centre stage.

'It seems silly to ask,' Addison said next, 'but are you OK?'

Mabel patted herself down, starting to shake her head before switching back to a nod, pursing her lips then opening and closing her mouth a few times before settling on a simple, if shaky, 'Yes.'

Addison remained at her side, not interrupting as she worked through her thoughts.

'Yes, I'm OK.' Her voice had firmed up, as if she was convincing herself it was true. 'A little rattled, if I'm honest. Quite the fright when the ground disappeared from beside me.'

'I can't even imagine.'

'And then Cilla… well, one second she was there, leaning on me, and the next she was gone. You probably saw what happened better than I did?'

'It looked like she had one foot on the stage proper and the other on the trapdoor, so when it dropped away, so did she.' Addison used his hands in an attempt to recreate the scene and make sense of what happened. 'But with one foot still on the stage, she didn't fall straight down. It spun her right over and she went down head first.' Eyes wide,

94

Addison looked to his friend. 'I can't believe you didn't fall in or get dragged down too.'

Mabel let out a shuddering breath. 'It was a close-run thing. I was a bit unsteady when she toppled but I managed to right myself. Then those vines almost caught me – it's lucky I wasn't standing on any or I would've been done for.'

'You're sure you're OK?' Addison shook his head, unable to believe it.

'I'm none the worse for wear,' Mabel said, patting Addison on the arm. 'My nerves though, they're another story. It's a wonder how you bear it.'

Addison frowned, unsure what any of this had to do with him. 'How I bear what?'

'Coming face to face with death, so sudden and unexpected... You've had quite the run recently. How do you do it? What gets you out of bed in the morning?'

'Truly?'

Mabel nodded.

'My bladder,' Addison said. 'I'd rather stay in bed, but there's only so long before I'm busting for the loo.'

Mabel scoffed and offered a weak smile as she batted him on the shoulder. 'So, changing the topic? Trying not to think about it? Is that your expert advice?'

It was Addison's turn to laugh before he grew serious. 'In those situations, I think it helped knowing there was nothing I reasonably could have done to prevent it.'

'I had one job, though. My sole task was to stand there and help hold her upright. I can't help feeling at least partially responsible for—'

'No,' Addison said, cutting her off. 'Absolutely not. You were there at Cilla's request, doing exactly what was asked of you. You are not to blame, not one bit. Yes?'

Mabel equivocated and Addison widened his eyes as if daring her to disagree. 'Yes, OK, fine,' Mabel said. 'Not that that makes me feel any better about anything, not really.'

'I can understand that.' Addison thought back over his own experiences and recognised the truth in Mabel's words, and then what came next. 'Do you know what really helped? What gave me "closure" I guess you'd call it?'

'What's that, dear?'

'Getting to the bottom of what happened.'

Mabel raised an eyebrow. 'Sleuthing, you mean?'

'No need to make me sound like some clandestine cartoon detective,' Addison said with a snort. 'But yes, sleuthing. Mayor Ferguson has already made it clear she wants me on this – to figure out what happened, how it happened – for the sake of Milverton's reputation.'

'Is that what she said?'

'Well, basically.' Addison reflected on the mayor's words again. 'Or at least she wanted me ready to navigate the fallout so we could get beyond any distractions and back into clear air where we can focus on selling "Destination Milverton" again.'

'And you can't do that until whatever happened here tonight has been settled?'

'Right.'

'But you haven't even started working for her yet.'

'I know, but I'm hardly going to say "No, sorry, boss. I don't clock in until Monday."'

'No, I suppose not.'

'So,' Addison said as he pulled on his most encouraging smile. 'Considering I'm already on the case, knowing it might also help in some small way to give you peace of mind – well, that's *double* the incentive.'

Mabel's eyes flicked between centre stage and Addison at her side, shuddering as she no doubt replayed the whole thing in her head. 'You'd do that for me?'

'Of course,' Addison said without pause. 'It appears I'll already be doing it anyway. And I know how unnerving it can be to have question marks floating around, with everyone's lips flapping around you, uncertain glances in your direction.'

'You're a dear,' Mabel said, reaching a hand across herself to pat Addison on the shoulder. 'But where would you even start?'

'Everything hinges on the trapdoor, I think,' Addison said, his mind already firing in all directions. 'Someone didn't get the memo that the – uh – the "vocal voting" was only a practice round and they threw the trapdoor open anyway. Or, something down there malfunctioned. Either way, no matter the cause, it was the trapdoor opening that led to this terrible situation.'

Mabel nodded along, her frown softening as Addison spoke. They may not yet have their explanation, but he hoped having a plan went some way to assuaging Mabel's misplaced guilt.

'But before we get into that,' Addison said, 'there's something else we need to check first.'

'Oh, yes?'

'You.'

'Me?'

'While the paramedics are here' – Addison nodded over to Diana and Scott, who had by now, with assistance, hauled the body of Cilla Slay back up through the trapdoor – 'we need to get them to give you the once-over.'

'Oh, no. I don't think that's necessary. It was barely a

stumble. I am just fine.'

'I'm sure… I'm sure you think that, Mabel, and I don't want to be telling you what to do, but I think the paramedics should be the judge of that.' Addison held up a hand to forestall the protest already on Mabel's lips. '*That* is the price of my "sleuthing" services.'

Mabel's eyes narrowed. 'You are one shrewd businessman, Addison Harper.'

Addison shrugged, but didn't back down. He strongly suspected Mabel would despise having the word 'sprightly' applied to her as she was fit and healthy for someone in their seventies. Despite that, there was still no getting away from the fact she *was* in her seventies and had been knocked around a bit.

'Very well,' Mabel said with a huff before offering a small smile and an eye roll. 'If I must.'

Chapter 14

Constables Manaia Edwards and Sean McGiffert crossed the vacated hall floor, stepped up on stage, and briefly conferred with their sergeant, the mayor, and the paramedics. A moment later they were gently guiding the performers and the crew backstage while Jake – with Diana in her paramedic's uniform at his side – approached the judging panel.

Addison locked eyes with Jake, pulling his lips into a tight line and nodding almost imperceptibly, hoping to convey both 'Wow, what a situation this is,' and 'I'm OK, you focus on what you need to focus on.'

He seemed to have got enough of his message across as Jake nodded in return before switching his attention to Mabel, stopping on the far side of the sarcophagus and handing over the wig she'd lost in the fall.

'Mabel, how are—'

'I am fine.'

Jake took a beat before continuing, unconvinced and undeterred by Mabel's assurance. 'I'm glad to hear that. I've asked Diana here to check in on you, just to be sure.'

Mabel's desire to reject the suggestion was obvious, but

she only glanced at Addison, pursed her lips, and said, 'Of course.'

Jake couldn't keep the surprise off his face, having prepared himself to counter an objection. 'Right, OK. That's good.'

'I've already committed to allowing myself to be subjected to such treatment.'

'It will only take a moment,' Diana said, claiming the seat at Mabel's side.

'You sure you're—'

'Yes, off you go,' Mabel said, batting Addison away. 'You just make sure you keep up your end of the bargain.'

Addison smiled and gave her a small salute, leaving her to the paramedic's attention as he allowed Jake to lead him away after everyone else.

They were barely a step beyond the side curtain when Jake stopped and turned on Addison, pulling him into a darkened space away from the stage lighting, his hands suddenly on Addison's upper arms, his eyes raking up and down Addison's front. 'How are you?' he said, his voice low. 'Are you OK?'

Addison couldn't help the momentary lump in this throat, as if he was choking on nothing, or his tongue had swelled to block his airway. He cleared whatever had suddenly lodged itself in his oesophagus and gave Jake the wateriest of smiles. 'I'm fine, promise.'

Jake raised an eyebrow and Addison raised one right back. Jake held on for another moment then nodded, apparently satisfied. 'OK, good.' He rubbed Addison's upper arms briefly, his smile a little sheepish as he took half a step back out of Addison's personal space.

Jake nodded back the way they'd come. 'Should I ask

what that was about? With Mabel?'

'What? The "bargain"?'

'Yeah.'

'Just doing a deal with the devil – you know how it is.' Addison shrugged, his smile faltering as he did so. 'I'm worried about her. She got quite the fright.'

Jake murmured his agreement. 'She did, but she's in good hands.'

'Yeah…' Addison sighed before looking back up at Jake. 'Sorry, I thought tonight would be a fun date.'

'It's not one I'm going to forget in a hurry.' Jake let out an unexpected laugh. 'I'll let you make it up to me another time.'

Was Jake… *flirting*? Addison's neck and cheeks reddened, unable to stop his mind considering the many ways in which he might make it up to Jake. He was still working out an appropriate response when Jake cleared his throat and continued.

'Anyway, I'd better head back out there, check in with the paramedics and their patients…' He trailed off, worrying at his lip as he considered Addison, any levity in his demeanour now completely gone. 'Can I ask you to do something for me?'

Addison frowned at Jake's clearly conflicted tone. 'Yes, of course. What is it?'

'I've already asked Edwards and McGiffert to check in with the trapdoor operator, but…' Jake trailed off, as if he was thinking better of asking before he went ahead anyway. 'Could you keep an eye and an ear out while you're back there too?' Jake said, tilting his head towards where the others had gone. 'Just until we understand what went wrong tonight.'

The lines between Addison's eyebrows deepened. What was he looking and listening out for? People admitting to playing fast and loose with the health and safety rules? Was Jake pre-empting a workplace safety investigation, possible prosecution? Did that fall under his remit? If someone accidentally released the trapdoor, could this incident lead to *manslaughter* charges? Or, worse yet, did Jake think this might have been done on purpose? Was this *murder*?

That thought gave Addison serious pause. He'd been too distracted worrying about his friend's wellbeing to properly consider who had suffered the worst, and paid for it with their life.

Jake went on when Addison didn't immediately respond. 'In situations like this, a police presence can provide reassurance for some, but for others it can make them nervous, guarded. We're not trying to entrap anyone or anything, but I expect they'll be more relaxed and open around someone like you, more willing to say something they wouldn't say around the police sergeant.'

'Are you...' Addison couldn't help the smile tugging at his lips. 'Are you asking me to help find out what happened tonight? Are you asking me to participate in your investigation, Sergeant Murphy? Your *police* investigation?'

Jake made a noise that was somewhere between a grunt and a growl, clearly torn about the whole situation. 'I am only asking you to keep an eye and an ear out.' The intensity of Jake's gaze making it clear Addison shouldn't get carried away. 'I know you, Addison—'

'Do you now?'

'I know you're concerned for your friend and will want to know what's gone on tonight to give Mabel peace of mind. Perhaps the bargain has something to do with that?'

Jake said, getting it in one. 'I know you won't be able to help yourself from—'

Addison protested as if he hadn't already committed to doing what Jake was in the process of accusing him of.

'I'm sure satisfying your own curiosity will just be a nice bonus?'

Addison stopped arguing. Jake had his number, all right.

'You won't be able to keep yourself from helping, Addison. It is one of your best and also worst qualities.'

'What? How is it—'

'"Best" because it is so admirable,' Jake said, holding one hand palm up, then the other. 'And "worst" because of the trouble you've got yourself into in the past.'

Addison knew he could be trouble, but *admirable*? He didn't believe that of himself for a second, but apparently Jake did.

'You have a nose for these things, Addison. And I know you'll be nosing regardless. At least this way I might benefit from your instincts and your insights' – Jake paused, as if suddenly self-conscious – 'while also keeping you close and keeping you safe.'

Addison felt himself choking up all over again, not knowing how to react to such a statement. He dared not respond in kind, instead opting to play it cool. 'Sounds like there's a lot in this for you.' Addison smirked, expressing a cockiness he in no way felt.

'Yes, there is,' Jake said, deadly serious.

After so much sincerity, there was no way Addison could keep playing it off. Not that he wanted to anyway, he realised. 'OK, sure.'

'Just keeping an eye and an ear out, right?'

'Yes.'

'Just observation. Passive.'

'As you say' – Addison cleared his throat – 'I can do that.'

'OK, good. I'll be out here checking in with the paramedics for a minute, but Edwards and McGiffert are already backstage with the performers and the crew, so grab one of them if there are any issues.'

'Yes, yes. Don't worry about me.' Addison briefly waved a hand. 'You do what you need to do.'

'I'll be with you soon.'

Jake went to step away and hesitated, clearly torn between staying with Addison and going to do his job.

Addison leant in and gave Jake a quick kiss on the cheek. 'Go on, I'll be fine.'

Jake smiled, nodded once, and returned to the stage. Addison watched the man go, smiling to himself for a moment before he remembered he had a job to do. He turned and stalked backstage to see what he could see, hear what he could hear.

How had this Halloween Eve descended so rapidly from fun and games to horror and graves?

***

Despite their being out of uniform, Addison clocked Manaia and Sean the moment he entered the backstage area. They were off to one side and had subtly positioned themselves to maintain a clear view of the entire space, including its entrances and exits, while listening in and nodding along to a couple of crew members.

The large backstage area appeared to serve as a combined green room and communal dressing room with costumes, set pieces, equipment and all manner of *stuff* scattered about the place. Just like the physical space, the atmosphere somehow felt in disarray. Fear, sorrow, agitation, all mixed up. It made for an unsettled energy and heightened tension with no sign of relief.

The drag performers, with their oversized costumes and personalities, took up the most space. Some, still in full drag, had claimed the couches and were splayed out with drinks in hand. Others were perched at their mirrors pulling off wigs and lashes, wiping thick layers of makeup from their faces, extricating themselves from their costumes, and all-round transforming back into their everyday selves. Those who had were unrecognisable. The only way Addison could tell he was looking at the creator of Miss Candy Less, for example, was by the red-and-white striped bodysuit draped over the nearby costume rack. The wig was gone as well, revealing a head of bleached blond hair cropped short. The friendly and flirty character was gone too, replaced with someone much fiercer and apparently frustrated, judging by the way they were swiping at their face with the makeup remover pads.

Addison had found himself mesmerised by the amount of makeup coming off the surprisingly youthful face when Candy paused mid-swipe, locking eyes with Addison in the mirror. He averted his gaze, momentarily flushing with embarrassment at being caught observing the transformation.

On the other side of the costume racks the rest of the backstage crew was gathering around a trestle table laden with snacks. A few appeared to be nervously feeding a constant stream of nibbles into their mouths while others had placed a snack or two on a napkin and were now motionless, staring at nothing in particular.

One such vacant soul was a burly man, probably in his early forties, with a lush beard, and big arms, chest, and belly keeping his black crew T-shirt taut. He had cabling resting on one shoulder and looping under his arm which he seemed to have forgotten about. This did, however, suggest he might be the show's lighting or sound technician, probably in the middle of doing something when everything happened. None of that was what had caught Addison's attention though. It was his eyes – glazed over and shiny with unshed tears, threatening to spill. Percy was there, speaking quietly to the man. After a while, the assumed-technician sniffled and ran a forearm across his face to clear his eyes, shook his head, directed a weak smile down at Percy, then chucked an entire savoury into his mouth in one go.

Addison claimed a seat in a space away from the police officers, between where the performers and the crew had gathered, keeping himself a little apart from any of the others, not imposing himself on either group. The space was open, so from his vantage point he could see and hear everyone present – the perfect position to keep an eye and ear out.

Chapter 15

The only person roving between the various clusters was the driving force behind the Spooky Showcase and the man behind Lady Perry Less, Patrick Laurence. He was also currently the least mobile of them all, yet was the one doing all the moving.

Patrick seemed confident and in complete control of his crutches. In all his manoeuvring, he hadn't once put them in anyone's way or caught them on any of the many obstacles lying about. Though he was making a point of nudging detritus aside to ensure clear pathways around the room.

He was doing the rounds, lending an ear to the drag royalty, who went from upset to angry and everything in between, then the crew, who he joined for a bite to eat while he took in all they had to say.

Patrick was doing what Addison needed to be doing. If anyone could help shed light on what had happened tonight, or at least give him the insights he needed to get started, they were most likely in this room. But Jake had entrusted him with his task, more than he'd ever willingly or voluntarily done before, with instructions for him to take only a passive role in his information gathering. Patrick's approach, despite also being Addison's preferred approach, could only be considered active. He had enough self-restraint to stop himself, but even if he didn't, having Jake's constables in the room ready to report back to him was an excellent deterrent.

Addison was busy reflecting on the boundaries of what could plausibly be considered passive observation when Patrick dropped into the chair beside him. He leant his crutches against another chair before turning to Addison.

'Hey, do you mind if I sit here?'

Addison's first thought had been an unhelpful and uncharitable one, centred around the fact Patrick had already sat there, and wouldn't Addison look like a jerk if he said he did mind? Not that he minded, of course. The opposite, in fact – this was the opportunity he'd been looking for.

'No, no,' he said. 'Go ahead.'

'OK thanks. I just, you know, need a moment.'

As much as Addison wanted to launch into demanding Patrick tell him everything right that second, he knew that'd get him nowhere and would just be plain rude. He needed to work up to it. Keep it open, easy, at least to start. Be the sympathetic ear for Patrick as Patrick had been for everyone else.

'It's been a tough night, hasn't it?' Addison said.

Patrick let out a brief bark of a laugh. 'Coming after a tough couple of weeks.' He sighed, briefly lifting his casted and booted foot off the ground for emphasis. 'You'd think doing drag, we'd be used to drama but this is next level. And the emotion is all real, not just for show. I've more than had my fill.' He flashed his eyes wide and shook his head. 'I'm Patrick, by the way. We didn't get a chance to meet properly at our opposite ends of the sarcophagus. Lady Perry Less when I've got my face and my frock on, but' – he gestured to himself, running a hand from head to toe – 'just Patrick tonight.'

'I'm Addison.'

'Nice to meet you, Addison.' Patrick narrowed his eyes and tilted his head. 'Not Harper, by any chance?'

'Yes, it is, actually. How—'

'I haven't come across any other Addisons in Milverton, so it wasn't so wild of a guess. And you fit the bill – I've heard things about you…'

'Oh—'

'Good things, don't worry. Percy has talked about you a few times.'

'Has he?' Addison didn't know what the older man could have to say about him considering they barely knew each other.

Patrick nodded but didn't immediately elaborate. 'I don't mean to be rude,' he eventually said, 'but can I ask what you're doing back here?'

'Ah…' *Spying on you?* Hardly an explanation that was going to put anyone at ease. 'The police sent me back here while I'm waiting for my friend – Mabel, the magician's assistant – to be checked over by the paramedics.' Addison may have omitted plenty from his explanation, but he had been truthful – selective, but truthful. He was disproportionately pleased with his quick thinking. Perhaps the life of a spy wasn't so far-fetched for him after all…

'Oh, you're a good friend.'

'I am worried for her though, being right there like she was. It was a bit of a shock,' Addison said, recognising he might have earnt enough conversational credit now to start pushing for what he really wanted to know. 'I don't know how it all works, putting on a show, but what happened? Wasn't the voting meant to be a little practice? Was there some miscommunication? Or did someone, I don't know, accidentally pull the lever?'

Patrick breathed in and out, his nostrils flaring. 'This was no accident.'

Addison tensed, focusing all his attention on Patrick, waiting for him to go on. After a few seconds he couldn't stop himself from asking, 'What do you mean?'

'I think we're dealing with dangerous negligence here.' Patrick must have recognised Addison's need for more information, as he went on to explain. 'Opening that trapdoor is no flick of a switch – you have to put a bit of puff into it. First, there's the safety guard you have to pull back which has "Warning" plastered all over it. Then you need two hands to pull the lever itself. There's no way for someone to "accidentally" open it.'

'So, who was responsible for the trapdoor?'

'Percy was on the job tonight. It's an important job and he's very good, familiar with that old mechanism, knows how to time the opening just right. But it was only his job to *operate* the trapdoor – not to maintain or guard it or anything like that – and he wasn't scheduled to open it just yet so he wasn't in position. I could see him in the wings, waiting for the right moment to head below stage. You have to go down there to operate the trapdoor, which is a fair bit of effort – it's not in a convenient spot. No, I think it's much more likely that the trapdoor just hadn't been maintained properly and something went wrong. These old bespoke mechanisms need a lot of attention to keep running properly, safely.'

Addison nodded to show he was following but dared not interject again, not now Patrick seemed to be on a roll.

'Either someone was lazy or they didn't take enough care or didn't have enough time or money or skill to do their job properly. Or...' Patrick trailed off, holding up a finger as he subtly glanced to either side of them and lowering his voice before continuing. 'The other possibility is that someone wanted Cilla dead.'

If Addison thought he was tense before, that had nothing on now – his body reacting by tightening all sorts of muscles.

Patrick shrugged and shook his head, dismissing the thought, as if he didn't consider that at all realistic. 'Sorry, don't mind me. I'm just in a spooky Halloween frame of mind.'

Addison murmured, more than a little distracted by the possibility. 'Still, it's a chilling thought.'

'It is... and I can't help but feel responsible. If I hadn't invited Cilla here, she wouldn't have died—'

'You can't take that on yourself.' Addison may not have known Patrick, but he couldn't stand to see anyone taking on the guilt and the blame of something that wasn't their fault.

Unless it was...

What if Cilla's death had been Patrick's fault, not because of some ill-fated invitation but because he had killed her? But then why would he float the possibility of her death not being an accident? To get ahead of the narrative? A bold move, if true.

'I asked Simeon – that's Cilla Slay's boy name, by the way, Simeon Clay. I asked Simeon to come here and stand in for me tonight. I couldn't bring myself to cancel the show.

I have a bit of a following around here and I would've hated to let everyone down. I thought if I could at least call in a queen the audience would already recognise – and drag fans know Cilla Slay – then it wouldn't be too much of a disappointment. She can perform, no doubt about that. But…'

'She wasn't at her most charming tonight.'

'Yes, she had her knickers in a right twist, didn't she?' Patrick huffed, clearly unimpressed. 'So unprofessional. I should've known better. If she gets in a foul mood, there's no turning that ship around – needs a full night's sleep to reset. It was the wigs going missing this morning that did her in. We couldn't have planned for that, could we? We couldn't afford to fly her down *and* have her staying multiple nights. But it was a risk, one which didn't pay off. I was hoping we could just get through the night, at least enjoy the performances, put a spotlight on these talented acts.'

Addison couldn't help but feel Patrick was being genuine. He wanted to provide a platform for performers to show their stuff, and he wanted to give the audience a good night out. He also seemed to know a lot about Cilla Slay and the man behind the act, Simeon Clay. More than you might expect for a purely professional relationship? Was it just that the theatre community was small – and the drag performer community smaller still – so everyone knew everyone, not unlike Milverton? Or did they know each other more than that? Cilla had said something about them starting out together and being 'dear friends', but that could mean anything.

'Have you worked with Cilla before?' Addison said.

'Oh, yeah. We've known each other forever. Since theatre

school. A rocky start, I'll be the first to admit. We weren't shy to get the claws out.'

'Over what?'

'Nothing out of the ordinary. Just competitiveness, you know? And – uh – incompatible personalities? A few of her costumes and numbers, let's say, *borrowed heavily* from ideas I'd been working on. You might have noticed tonight, she performed as other people's characters – not once did she wear or do anything unique. Nothing that was pure "Cilla Slay", just rehashing what came before. Some might say she's paying homage to icons, others might say she's never had an original thought in her life.'

Patrick shrugged, but it was clear to Addison which side of the fence he thought she fell on.

He continued. 'Which is fine, of course, just different. But there are limits when it comes to recycling other people's work. No, my issue with her back in the early days, at least to begin with, was putting together our group performances. Snatching all the leading lady roles for herself. Then we were both scrabbling to build our solo careers and we clashed then too, more than a few times. But we've grown up a bit now, carved out our own spaces. I do my best to save the drama for the stage. All that drama in our past was already well behind us before tonight, water under the bridge.'

It all helped paint the picture, though not too much more than Addison had already gathered from watching them tonight. What was more telling was that while Patrick insisted the drama was all in the past, it only took the merest of nudges for him to dredge it all back up again. What Addison needed to know was how it all fitted with tonight. 'So, you two were in a good place, professionally?'

113

'Yep.'

'Which meant you could call on her at the last minute when you broke your leg? To save your show?'

Addison had hoped that last little bit might egg Patrick on, and so it did. His nostrils flared. 'I wouldn't put it quite like that. Of course, offering her the lead role was not ideal – tonight was supposed to be my baby…'

'A tough pill to swallow?'

'I gagged on it, all right. But I got it down. Good to have the option, even if it cost me.'

'Cost you… in what way?' Addison left the question open, not wanting to put words in his mouth. Did Patrick mean costly in terms of reputation, the hit to the ego, the balance of favours, or—

'In dollars, plain and simple. She charges a steep appearance fee. Which, to be fair, she earns, at least when she's at her best. And all artists deserve to be paid for their art. The grocery store doesn't accept exposure or the promise of future favours as payment, and neither should we. It seems callous to complain when someone's dead, but any profit I'd hoped to make from tonight was sunk with that unexpected cost.'

Addison tsked and hummed, as if in commiseration, but really he was wondering whether what Patrick said was still the case now that Cilla was dead. As bad as it sounded, was she still owed her fee considering she didn't finish the show? And even if she was, who would follow it up? With Cilla not around to issue invoices and collect payment, could killing her and effectively sabotaging the show help balance Patrick's books? 'I suppose now that Cilla's dead, you won't have to pay her?' Addison said, his suggestion offering the cold and calculating possibility as if it wasn't a

114

ruthless, heartless thing to do.

'What?' Patrick's mouth was open, appearing genuinely shocked. He shook his head slowly, then more emphatically. 'No. That's… no.' He looked at Addison, frowning. 'We paid her up front, and she was doing what we paid her for, right up until she couldn't. Everyone's been paid and we'll still break even. Financially I'm no better or worse off. No, that's not the issue. I'm worried about the performers I brought in, and the audience, not to mention your friend. It was supposed to be a fun, spooky night, not actually traumatic.'

'That's not on you.'

'Maybe not,' Patrick said, his shoulders sagging as he huffed out a breath. 'Sorry to unload all that.'

'No, no. That's totally fine. It's – uh – it's been a day.'

'It *has* been a day. I had just hoped we could at least put on a good show, but we didn't even manage that.'

'You had a great concept, some talented performers lined up, and I think everyone enjoyed themselves up until…'

'Yeah, "until".'

Addison recognised his moment had finally arrived. 'What went wrong, do you think?'

'Cilla Slay fell headfirst through the trapdoor is what went wrong,' Patrick said as if it could not have been more obvious.

'Yes, but…' Addison found himself at a loss for words.

'A trapdoor that should not have opened. It'd already had a workout tonight – open, close, open, close – and a fair bit of weight on and off it too. I fear it was too much for the old thing, it was probably only holding on by a thread, finally gave up the ghost, taking Cilla Slay down with it.'

'You mentioned something before about maintenance?'

'Oh yeah. There's only so much money to go around,

isn't there? And less for the arts every year. Maintaining the trapdoor probably wasn't a priority, just another nice-to-have. Tough gig for Gary, keeping this place standing and looking good.'

When Patrick didn't seem like he was about to go on, Addison had to prompt him. 'Who's Gary?'

'Gary Farnham, have you not met him? Lovely man, always wants to help, get involved. But he's forever trying to do everything, can't say no to anyone. Could do with a bit of focus, do fewer things but do them properly.'

'And he's in charge of maintenance on the town hall?'

'As far as I know. He's always "fixing" things, touching them up. Gary's a builder, carpenter, decorator, odd-jobs handyman.' Patrick flashed his eyes wide, shook his head, and lowered his voice. 'I'm surprised he still has his builder accreditation, health and safety certification, whatever it is. But what do I know? And besides, it's hard to get cross with someone when they mean well.'

Patrick pulled his lips into a line and shrugged his shoulders as if to say, 'It is how it is,' then picked up his crutches. 'I'm going to grab something to eat. You want anything?'

'No, no. Thank you, though.'

'Good chatting to you, Addison.'

'Yeah, you too.'

Addison was left alone with much to consider. He'd entered the backstage area thinking Cilla's death might have been a tragic, unavoidable accident, but Patrick's insights left him much less convinced.

He knew now other possibilities had to be considered. The first being negligence, which sadly was an all too real possibility. A death due to inadequate maintenance might still be regarded as an accident, though it'd be hard to argue it wasn't *avoidable*. Despite not yet having any evidence to back it up, Addison felt like this was the leading contender. Critically, he had a name to follow up on. Though Gary Farnham did not appear to be present and Addison doubted the man would appreciate an uninvited guest on his doorstep late on a Friday evening. Pursuing that possibility would have to wait for another day.

The second and much more sinister possibility was that someone intended to cause harm…

Everyone in Milverton Town Hall had witnessed Cilla Slay plummeting through the trapdoor to her death – the target, the method, and the result were plain to see.

But who had done it and why? Two very important questions. Because if this had indeed been done with malicious intent, they needed to uncover who was responsible, because who was to say the killer wouldn't strike again?

Chapter 16

With nothing more to go on, Addison's investigative instincts were growing increasingly restless doing laps around and around inside his head. He reckoned he'd observed all he could in this one space. Unfortunately, his promise to remain passive meant he couldn't, in good faith, roam the room asking the many questions that were building up inside him. There was no way that could be considered anything other than active.

Looking around himself for the umpteenth time, Addison couldn't even be sure what was keeping everyone in the combined green room and dressing room... Were they sticking together for the moment because that felt safer, more reassuring than dispersing and going home? Or were they in shock and so willing to follow directions, unconsciously volunteering to wait while the police and paramedics did their thing? If so, did that mean they were very quietly and politely being held by the police?

Nobody had tested that theory by trying to leave...

Addison reckoned stretching his legs a little would serve him well, a way to expend some of his pent-up energy. He wouldn't go too far, though. Just a nice, passive wander around backstage to organise his thoughts, and perhaps passively observe below stage too. He might even come across the trapdoor mechanism, see what that was about for himself.

Decision made, his next consideration was how to approach his departure. Did he stride out of the room as if he had every right to do so? Or should he assume he'd be stopped and so lead with attempting to sweet-talk his way past one of the constables?

He was still weighing up his latest conundrum when Jake appeared at the door, Mabel at his side. Addison settled himself back into his chair as if he hadn't just been working himself up to leave. A good thing too, as Jake's quick visual sweep of the room halted a moment later when his gaze landed on Addison. He was already on his way over when the rest of the room clocked the return of the sergeant and dropped into silence, everyone fixing him with their undivided attention, apparently as starved for information as Addison.

Jake stopped, no doubt feeling the weight of the room's attention and expectation on him while Mabel – still dressed as Morticia, but with wig in hand – carried on, slipping into the chair at Addison's side.

She flashed him a smile and a quick thumbs up which could've meant anything from 'The paramedics gave me a clean bill of health' to 'I escaped the quacks before they could write me off.'

Addison wasn't about to get any clarity either way as Jake had switched back into Sergeant Murphy mode to address the room. He briefly introduced himself for the benefit of the out-of-towners and thanked everyone for their patience. Then he said, 'I'm sorry to say that the paramedics have confirmed the death of Simeon Clay, who many knew as the creator of Cilla Slay. The medical team will be able to provide much more detail in due course, but in simple terms, the cause of death appears to be neck injuries sustained which are consistent with an uncontrolled fall on the head.'

The response to Sergeant Murphy's announcement was mixed…

The gasps seemed unnecessary to Addison, but considering the person involved and the fact they were in a theatre, perhaps such a reaction was fittingly dramatic. Then there were the rumblings from those who'd either figured as much or expressed variations on the theme. And one rather sarcastically expressing gratitude they had the force's best and brightest on the case.

'I can appreciate how difficult this must be for many of you who had personal or working relationships with the deceased,' Jake said, connecting with many of those present by making eye contact as he spoke. 'While I can't do anything about Simeon's death, I hope to offer you some closure and peace of mind by getting to the bottom of what happened here tonight. I would appreciate it if I could speak with each of you before you head off, just to collect initial statements.'

The formerly attentive room became suddenly restless with many checking their watches or glancing at their phone's lock-screen clock.

'I know it's getting late, so we'll keep it brief,' Jake said, having swiftly and accurately read the room. 'Constable Edwards will be assisting me so we can be sure to hear everyone as quickly as possible. And Constable McGiffert will remain with you in case you have anything you need to ask in the meantime.'

He scanned the room once more as if anticipating comments and questions, but when none immediately cropped up he nodded once and gestured for Manaia to join him. He threw an apologetic look in Addison's direction as he prepared to head off again.

Addison responded with a small, closed-mouth smile and a flash of his eyes as if to say, 'I'm fine, don't worry. Do what you need to do. I have things to tell you when you're free, though. This situation is likely more complicated than we'd initially assumed. At least, more than I'd assumed. It appears you were already a step or two ahead in asking me to keep an eye and ear out before.'

It was a lot to ask of an entirely nonverbal facial expression, but Jake lifted his head a little and twitched an eyebrow in response as if he'd got the gist.

***

The next hour involved all present being pulled out one at a time. Mabel was spared as she'd already answered Jake's questions after the paramedics had deemed her fit and well. And so Addison took the opportunity to bring her up to speed. By the time he had, Mabel was looking much more like her usual inquisitive self.

'So, I know you say it's unlikely, but just for argument's sake,' Mabel said with that familiar glint in her eye, 'assuming for the minute that this *is* foul play... Who's on your shortlist?'

'I haven't got that far, to be honest. My working theory, which I was hoping to follow up tomorrow if I can, is that we're dealing with negligence.'

Mabel thought on it for a moment. 'Do you truly believe that, dear?' she said, a patient kindness in her voice, as if she was talking to a small, upset child.

'Is that – I don't know – too hopeful of me, do you think? Just wishful thinking?'

Mabel shrugged. 'Perhaps, but it is heartening to see you with such optimism even after recent events.' She rested a hand on his forearm, seriously looking at him now as she said, 'You've clearly thought about the alternative though, haven't you?'

Addison huffed out a laugh, apparently as transparent as ever. 'Yes, I have.'

'Go on, then,' Mabel said with a nod. 'Let's hear it.'

'To start, I think it's easier to list everyone who would *not* make the list, on account of them not being below stage at the time the trapdoor opened—'

'Unless the culprit had recruited someone else to go down there, on their orders?'

'True, we can't discount that possibility. But if we find the person who pulled the lever, and if they didn't do it for their own ends then *surely* they won't keep quiet about who instructed them to do it?'

Mabel hummed in thought. 'I don't think there's anything *sure* about this whole situation. There's any number of reasons someone might do something like this for another. But yes, I agree, we need to start somewhere and can revisit this later if we need to. OK, I'm sorry, your non-suspect list...'

Addison went through his list of probable innocents, which included all of the night's performers. The two contestants who'd been knocked out of the first round had claimed spare seats near the back of the hall to enjoy the second round. Addison wouldn't have been able to say the same thing with such certainty for most other audience members, but even with the stage lighting making picking out individuals a challenge, the eliminated queen and king in full drag were unmistakable from Addison's vantage point on stage as part of the judging panel.

The three remaining contestants had been clustered in the wings to stage right after Little Red was shooed offstage, waiting to come back and receive their judgement. A clear line of sight remained between them and the judges throughout Cilla and Mabel's time together at centre stage.

For that matter, the judges – Mayor Ferguson, Patrick Laurence AKA Lady Perry Less, and himself – could also be discounted. They had each other, the contestants, and the entire audience to vouch for their presence behind the sarcophagus on stage.

'And I've already spoken with Patrick about who was in charge of operating the trapdoor mechanism tonight—'

'Oh, yes?'

'Our very own purveyor of pre-show gossip, Percy Foster.'

'Oh, no.' Mabel's gaze darted to the man across the room now in conversation with another of the backstage crew.

'No, no, don't worry. Patrick has already vouched for his whereabouts. The trapdoor wasn't scheduled to be opened for a little bit longer – not until the queens were back on stage for the round two elimination – so Percy wasn't back in position yet. He was still waiting in the wings with the queens. I noticed the queens because how could I not?'

'Dressed to impress, yes. They tend to stand out.'

'Percy, though, was in his stage blacks – not meant to be so easily seen.'

'But you say Patrick *did* see him? Even though Patrick wasn't backstage himself?'

'Yes, he did,' Addison said before trying to put himself in Patrick's shoes – or, more accurately, one shoe and one moon boot. 'I suspect he couldn't help himself from "producing", you know? Even while on the judging panel. He'd be making a point of keeping an eye out, checking people were *where* they were meant to be *when* they were meant to be there. The "Spooky Showcase" was his show, after all.'

'Yes, of course,' Mabel said. 'So, it sounds like everyone is accounted for then?'

Addison cleared his throat and looked pointedly at the black-clad folk still clustered around the snacks table. 'Except for the rest of the crew.'

'Ah, yes. They could move around anywhere unnoticed, which is the entire point of them.'

'They could, but so could anyone else I haven't already mentioned, really.'

'Who do you mean?'

'Anyone.' Addison shrugged. 'No doubt there's plenty going on when putting on a show like this, a lot of people moving around—'

'Percy said as much when we caught up with him before the show.'

'Yeah. Busy, busy. As long as you move with purpose and look like you know what you're doing, nobody's going to question you. Not when they're already too busy focusing on their own thing. This is Milverton Town Hall, hardly a high-security operation. Except for those within our lines of sight at the moment the trapdoor released, the culprit could literally be anyone.'

'So…' Mabel drew out the word as she ran lengths of Morticia's hair through her fingers, thinking through the implications. 'So, the suspect shortlist is rather more of a longlist?'

'Exactly,' Addison said, sucking air in through his teeth. 'Any number of people would have had opportunity, and if Simeon treated people in his day-to-day interactions anything like he did in character as Cilla tonight, plenty would have had sufficient motive.'

Mabel was shaking her head now. 'Quite the diva.'

'Which doesn't exactly enamour people to you, but also isn't enough to tip someone over into a murderous rage, is it?'

Mabel sighed. 'Yes, well, but you never quite know what's going on with other people, do you?'

'I guess not. Anyway, it's only a minor possibility and too far-fetched to be taken seriously, at least not while we have a more credible investigational avenue to pursue. We don't want to be shrieking at the bogeyman under the floorboards.' Addison wondered if he was perhaps more influenced by the spooky season than he'd first realised.

'Agreed,' Mabel said. 'What's next then?'

'Gary Farnham, what do you know about him?'

'Lovely man, always getting involved and helping out. You wanted to ask him about maintenance around here, didn't you?'

'Yeah. And he knows this place inside out, presumably, so he might have some ideas or possibilities we haven't even considered yet.' Addison recognised actively seeking out the man went beyond merely keeping an eye and an ear out. However, if Gary was the community-minded guy that Patrick had led him to believe, making contact with him

125

might fit within the remit of his new role in the mayor's office. So why not make that contact sooner rather than later?

'You should be able to catch Gary at the pub tomorrow, dear.'

'Tomorrow?' That was sooner than even Addison had been thinking. 'Is he a regular?'

'Oh, you know, just as much as anyone else. No, it's the annual pumpkin carving contest. They use the courtyard out the back of The Langston – easier for cleanup, I suppose? Gary normally runs it. He brings all the tools and helps the kids and their parents, makes sure nobody lops a finger off.'

'Will you be carving your own jack-o'-lantern this year?'

'Oh no. I took my Sophia last year, but she wasn't impressed with having to scoop out all the pumpkin pulp, and then she wasn't pleased with her final result either. I thought it looked wonderful, but she thought it looked ugly. So this year, I thought we'd skip that heartache and go straight for the night market and outdoor film.' Mabel turned to Addison, lifting an eyebrow. 'What about you, Addison? What are your carving skills like?'

Addison smiled and shrugged. 'I guess we're about to find out.'

Chapter 17

The following day, the weather matched Addison's mood as he sighed and stomped his way back into town. It did not bode well for Mabel's outdoor cinema later on.

He'd spent the remainder of the night and all that morning under a cloud of his own. Not even the prospect of proper coffee and a delicious pastry from Lynne's Cafe was enough to get him out of the house.

Addison had felt a little dejected, then annoyed at himself for being dejected, which only amplified the dejection cycle, building until he had a full-blown pity party going. Which was pathetic and he knew it. It wasn't like the date with Jake had been a total flop. Witnessing an abrupt death mid-date was sure to kill any romantic momentum no matter how things had been going before.

Addison recognised the state of mind he found himself in was selfish as well as pathetic. What was a less-than-ideal date night when compared to sudden death? He certainly hadn't had the worst night of all those who came through the doors of Milverton Town Hall.

Jake had joined Addison after he'd spoken to everyone, thanked them, and sent them home. He was apologetic and

Addison was understanding – that was all fine. Then they'd debriefed each other, even if Jake had suspiciously little to add after all his interviews. The only new piece of information was that each of the backstage crew members insisted they hadn't been the one to operate the trapdoor, that they knew Percy was in charge of it for the night. None had even been below stage or in sight of the trapdoor mechanism at the time of the incident.

Either everyone had clammed up when faced with a cop or Jake was back to his old tricks, keeping things from Addison. Which he probably thought was for Addison's own good or that sharing such information was not appropriate because Addison wasn't actually a police officer or some other such nonsense. Still, that was also fine.

After they'd left the hall, they'd walked to Jake's vehicle and he'd driven them to Harper House. What happened next was decidedly less fine and what had sent Addison into a funk... Jake did not come inside.

Sure, they were still at the point in their relationship where sleepovers were agreed in advance – not a major discussion or anything, just a quick check – not yet assumed as the default, though things certainly seemed to be heading that way.

In the case of the previous night, Addison thought it was safe to assume they'd both categorised the outing as a date, and certain assumptions, rightly or wrongly, came from that.

Nobody could have factored in a death on stage though, which was not only a mood-killer but also meant Jake wasn't free to be Jake, given his duties and responsibilities as sergeant.

Addison was a little disappointed, of course, but he

understood. The following morning, not even a hot shower could wash away his foul mood.

He'd pulled out some clothes and set them on the bed while the water heated up in the bathroom. Unfortunately, distracted by his thoughts, he'd forgotten to factor in one crucial detail. With his hair still dripping wet, skin warm from the hot water, and towel wrapped around his waist, Addison stepped back into the bedroom and immediately saw his error.

'Keith!'

An ear on top of the great orange lump twitched in his direction, followed by the slow turn of a head and an equally languid opening of one eye, then the other. Never one to pass up such an opportunity, the feline resident of Harper House had taken advantage of his human's pre-planning by making himself comfortable on the set-out clothes and did not appear in any hurry to give up his position.

To make matters worse, all evidence pointed to Keith, with his thick coat of vibrant ginger fur, getting a head start on his summer beach body. The calendar suggested the turn of the season was still over a month away, but with temperatures already easing up a degree or two, Keith's moulting had stepped up correspondingly.

'Get off. Come on, get off.' Addison shooed the cat without success and ended up having to lift the fluffy terror onto a clear patch of the duvet. Keith didn't resist but wasn't shy in expressing his displeasure. With a look of outrage on his face, he leapt down from the bed, flicked his tail as he turned his backside on his resident Harper, and left the room.

Once again, Addison's clothes had been subjected to

Keith's enfluffication. He should've learnt by now that no surface was safe.

The jeans had escaped with only a light coating of ginger fur, easily dealt with by a few passes of the lint roller, but the shirt had been the chosen nap location – that is, the focal point of the moulting. Addison pulled the top on and ran the lint roller back and forth across his chest. He quickly discovered it wasn't up to the task of heavy-duty cat hair removal so instead tried repeating the process with the damp towel.

Great cigars of cat hair quickly formed, rolling right off his top. Addison was soon free of the unplanned fur coat and found himself disproportionately pleased with his minor domestic success. Which reminded him that sorting through the wardrobes at Harper House remained very much on his to-do list, along with everything else. Thankful he hadn't had to resort to raiding his great-uncle's clothes for a clean shirt again, he stepped out of the house and powered towards Milverton Square on foot.

The overcast weather remained generally aligned with Addison's overcast mood, but at least Keith's antics went some way to lightening the atmosphere.

No matter how he felt, he'd promised Mabel he'd get to the bottom of the situation, and she'd even been able to point him in the right direction when it came to getting information from Gary Farnham, so he couldn't pass that up.

***

The Langston looked as inviting as ever. Its familiar panelled windows and wrought iron lanterns were set against white walls and framed by the dark timbers of its mock-Tudor frontage.

One notable difference was the hanging flower baskets that usually lined the eaves had been swapped out for carved pumpkins. Where the flowers had looked warm and inviting as they subtly swung in any light breeze, the jack-o'-lanterns looked rather creepy and ominous, the slightest movement seeming to bring them to life.

Below that was the pub's chalkboard. Today it featured what appeared to be a cartoonish ghost with bright blue eyeshadow singing 'Ghouls just wanna have rum.'

Addison couldn't help his mouth twitching up at that. If he knew a camp, spooky pun was all it took to lift himself out of the doldrums, he wouldn't have wasted so much energy worrying over it all.

Stepping through the heavy front doors, Addison found the pub to be its usual comfortable and comforting self. The dark decor, low lighting, and quiet murmur of conversation put Addison at ease. A relaxing space where it felt like you could switch off and take your time – Addison felt right at home.

Everything exactly as it always was, but just like the blackboard outside, the large mirror behind the bar had also had a Halloween makeover. It was draped in cobwebs with a few large, hairy spiders around the edges. And the special cocktail, scrawled across the mirror in neon orange marker pen, was the 'Pumpkin Spice Old Fashioned' with ingredients listed below as bourbon, pumpkin syrup, bitters, and an orange twist.

Addison could safely say he would not be having that. To be fair, it was very on-theme, considering what he was here for, but Addison didn't understand the pumpkin obsession. Were they sweet? Were they savoury? Did it matter when they didn't even taste that great to begin with?

Addison's spicy thoughts on pumpkins were interrupted by the appearance of the bear of a man that was Harry Langston.

'Good to see you, Mr Harper,' he said, nodding as he rested a forearm on the bar. 'How are you doing after last night?'

'Oh, you know…' Addison didn't know how he was doing himself so wasn't sure how he expected anyone else to know, but what else could he say?

'It's a tough one,' Harry said, shaking his head. 'Tragic. But the show must go on, as they say.'

'They do,' Addison said for want of anything worthwhile to contribute.

'Speaking of,' Harry said, drawing a hand across the bar as if drawing a line under any talk of death. 'Are you here for the pumpkin carving?'

'I am indeed.'

'Just you, is it?' Harry said, glancing behind Addison and down to his side, as if expecting to spot someone else.

'Uh, yeah. Just me.'

'Very well.' Harry smiled through his beard and clapped his hands together. 'What can I get you? Price of admission is a pint.' He rumbled with a laugh. 'Not really. But you're here, aren't you? Might as well.'

It was a bit early for a pint, wasn't it? Though it probably only felt that way to Addison because it was his first interaction of the day. It was mid-afternoon, after all. But he didn't fancy a beer…

'I can do you a pint of fizz, of course,' Harry said when Addison hadn't responded. 'If you're driving or just not drinking today. We have lemonade, cola, L&P, all that.'

'No, no – uh, can I get a gin?'

'A pint of gin?' Harry's eyes flew wide, as did his cheeks. 'I don't know about that, Mr Harper, especially if you're going to be carving. Can't have you sticking a knife through your hand, can we?'

'No, no. I—'

'One G&T coming right up,' Harry said with a smile, already reaching for a glass.

'Thanks, Harry. Oh, is the kitchen open?' Addison said, realising he hadn't really eaten anything all day and didn't want to have to resort to munching on pumpkin pulp.

'Sure is.'

'Can I get a bowl of hot chips too, please?'

'You sure can. Here's your gin, and let me give you a food order number before you head out there.'

Addison took the number and happened to glance at it. 'Thirteen? Unlucky for some.'

'On today of all days.' Harry laughed, reaching to reclaim the number. 'Hang on, let me get you a new—'

'No, no. Thirteen is fine.' Addison raised his gin as if in a toast as he peeled away from the bar, number in hand. 'I'll survive.'

Chapter 18

Addison died a little inside when he stepped through to the beer garden. The space itself was as welcoming as ever with the courtyard bounded on each side by brick walls, the pergola overhead draped in vines, and the outdoor heaters keeping it all nice and toasty.

No, it was the pumpkin carving stations that gave him pause. They'd been set up on tables throughout the courtyard, each with a large pumpkin, a set of tools, and two aprons. Many of the stations were already occupied, including a few by couples, but mostly by a young person with a parent or some other responsible adult. It was immediately obvious that this was an activity designed to be done in pairs, which made sense of Harry's question from a little earlier.

He should've roped Mabel into joining him, seeing as she was the main reason he was there.

Addison had barely a moment to stew in his newfound Nigel No-Mates status or to consider whether he might turn around and go right back the way he'd come when a voice called out.

'No need to look so terrified. We haven't started yet, and

you can make yours as scary as you like, or not. Come on, pull up a pew. This pumpkin right here has your name on it.'

The man who'd slapped a hand down on an otherwise unattended pumpkin looked to be in his late forties with scraggly tufts of hair on his head, mostly around his ears. He wore a plaid shirt tucked into light blue stonewashed jeans with a tan toolbelt encircling his waist, white sports socks, and sandals – he looked in his element, entirely comfortable with himself and ready to go. If you imagined the most stereotypical of DIY dads then you'd already be most of the way there.

'It has your name on it in spirit, anyway,' he said. 'What should we call you? For judging purposes later. I'm Gary, by the way, Gary Farnham.'

Bingo.

Addison might have been regretting not asking Mabel along today, but at least she hadn't put him wrong as far as tracking down Gary Farnham.

'Addison Harper.'

'Good to have you here, Addison. We still have a few minutes before we get underway, so you start thinking about what you're going to carve.' He gave Addison's pumpkin another quick pat before moving to welcome the latest arrivals – who appeared to be a father-daughter duo.

Addison hadn't given any thought to what he was going to carve…

The classic jack-o'-lantern face with the triangular eye holes and the jagged grin was an obvious choice?

Or he could go for something a bit more local? This was a local contest, after all. What was something distinctly Milverton? A landscape in silhouette showing the mountain ranges behind town, wind turbines dotted across their slopes? That'd be nice, maybe a little too sedate? And potentially fiddly, likely beyond Addison's as-yet untested carving abilities.

Perhaps a bat would be better? That was spooky, and relatively straightforward shape-wise.

Or could he carve Keith's likeness? A cat wouldn't be too tricky. That look of disdain and impatience on his furry little face when his bowl was empty and he believed it ought to be otherwise… Now *that* would be terrifying.

'Hey, Addison.'

Harry's son appeared at Addison's table, breaking into his thoughts as he set down a bowl of heavily salted, triple-cooked chips that were still steaming with heat.

'Hey, Ben. These look amazing, as always,' Addison said, and he meant it too. This was not the almost mandatory pleasantry offered when accepting food. This was acknowledging potato at its finest. He tore his gaze away from the hot chips as Ben set down a small caddy of condiments, cutlery, and serviettes. 'How's uni? Are you back home to help out for the weekend?'

'Yeah,' Ben said, holding the now-empty serving tray loosely at his side, infinitely more relaxed than when they'd first met only weeks earlier. 'Saturdays are busy on a normal weekend, and with everything going on in town today, it'll be even busier.'

'You mean this pumpkin carving contest and the – uh – the show last night?'

'And the Halloween market tonight. That's always fun, and they have the outdoor cinema in the square too.'

'Oh, yeah. I did hear about that. Do you know what the movie is going to be?'

'There's two. A kids' movie first, then an adult one later.'

Addison raised an eyebrow. '"Adult"? That's a bit racy for the town square, isn't it?'

'Oh!' Ben's eyes went wide and his cheeks went redder than even Addison thought he could manage. 'Not *adult* adult. No, like, umm, not for children, for grown-ups, I mean.'

'I'm sorry,' Addison said with a smile, feeling as if he needed to apologise for causing such horror. 'Don't worry, I knew what you meant. What are they showing?'

'The earlier one is *The Nightmare Before Christmas*, I think. But it was when I heard the late movie was going to be *Sleepy Hollow* this year that I knew I had to come back.'

'Oh, cool. I haven't seen *Sleepy Hollow* in years. I remember when I was little getting up after being sent to bed and sneaking back into the living room to watch it.' He'd forgotten about that and couldn't help smiling at the thought.

'Yeah, it's pretty vintage. I wasn't even born yet when it first came out. It's cool though.'

Addison's smile froze in place – he had never felt so old as he did at that moment. Objectively, he knew Ben must be a full decade younger than him, but it was still a shock to realise they were of different generations, and that Addison was of the *older* generation.

'Anyway,' Ben said when Addison was too busy screaming internally to respond. 'I promised Dad I'd help out this afternoon and through dinner. But a couple of friends came up with me from Wellington for the weekend and I'm joining them later for the movie.'

'That sounds great,' Addison said, and meant it. He may have suffered the sudden death of his self-perceived youth, but he'd swiftly moved through the stages of grief to the inevitable, begrudging acceptance. He was genuinely pleased to hear Ben was finding his people, and to see he'd already grown in confidence in the few short weeks since they'd first met.

'It'll be fun,' Ben said with a smile. 'Anyway, anything else?'

'No, no, I'm good. Thanks, Ben. And thanks for the outdoor cinema tip – I might have a look into that later too.'

'Sweet, might see you there, then.'

Addison was idly sticking chips into his mouth – delicious, by the way – and wondering if Jake might be up for a date do-over – curled up under a blanket together, watching a spooky movie, feeding each other popcorn. He could already see himself overthinking the whole thing and talking himself out of it despite his initial thought that it was a fantastic idea, something he would very much enjoy. So, before he could embark on any second-guessing, Addison fired off a quick message to Jake suggesting the movie, leaving out any thoughts regarding blankets or popcorn.

It had been at least three seconds since Addison had sent the message and set his phone face down on the table when he reached for it again. There was no way Jake could've responded already, but he couldn't help himself.

Luckily, Gary Farnham took that moment to interrupt Addison's angsting after the fact.

'All right, folks,' Gary said as he stood on a spare chair in the corner and turned, speaking loudly for all in the courtyard to hear. 'Haere mai, welcome to Milverton's annual pumpkin carving contest.' His announcement was delivered with some fanfare and was met with cheers and a smattering of applause. 'Now, it's all a bit back-to-front, isn't it? Pumpkins are planted in spring, harvested in autumn. So carving pumpkins for Halloween makes sense for the northern hemisphere, but here it's still springtime and we've barely planted the things. So, how did we get these full-sized pumpkins? Any guesses?'

Gary looked around the space, nodding one by one at each of the children with their arms in the air, fidgeting in place as if they were barely able to contain their thoughts.

'Extra smelly manure? Like, really stinky? Because that's good for plants.'

'Magic seeds? Or does that only work for beans?'

'Did these pumpkins eat all of their breakfast? Mum says if I eat *all* of my breakfast then I will grow big.'

'Did you forgot to pick them last time?'

'This clever young person is *very* close, well done,' Gary said, looking proud as Punch. 'At the last harvest, we didn't forget them, but we did set them aside especially for today. Good thing they keep so well, don't you think?'

'It's all a bit of a waste though, isn't it?' That was one of the grown-ups. 'All this perfectly good food that we're just playing with?'

'Ah! Another excellent point. Now, the fun they bring us today surely means they're not a waste?' Gary held up a finger to halt any attempted protest. 'But also, all the pulp we scoop out today, and all the offcuts? Yep, they'll be going straight to a local pig farm. And once the spooky season is over and our creations start to shrivel up, they'll make their way to the pigs too. Think of all that pumpkin they'll get to eat – what a feast!'

This received a few appreciative nods from the adults and an equal number of groans or disgusted expressions from the younger participants.

'Next up, before we start, a bit of health and safety.' This time it was the adults' turn to groan. 'Yes, yes. We have to do it, so bear with...' Gary went on to cover an exhaustive list of potential risks alongside techniques to eliminate, isolate, or minimise those risks. The relevant points included ensuring pumpkin debris made it into the buckets, using knives appropriately, and having at least one grown-up per young person. 'You might like to take turns with the knife? Our young people could do the *big* bits, and our grown-ups could do the tricky, boring bits. Deal?'

Everyone was on board with that. Overall, it seemed like their host had everything under control. Gary Farnham came across as thorough, thoughtful, and competent – a far cry from the haphazard, stretched-too-thin, dangerously negligent person Addison had been led to expect.

This man may not have been the slapdash killer Addison thought he'd been looking into, but even the most organised and fastidious person could make mistakes. Besides, he was here now and so might as well see what this man of many roles – builder, carpenter, decorator, designer, odd-jobs handyman, pumpkin carving contest organiser and host – had to say for himself. The likeliness of his culpability may have dropped in Addison's eyes, but he might still have valuable insights to share.

'You should have everything you need,' Gary said. 'A permanent marker to draw your designs on your pumpkin, a knife to cut the holes, and a spoon to scoop out the goop. Yes?'

The contestants in the courtyard rumbled their agreement.

'All right. Now, no rushing. Take your time. We don't want any accidents. But also, you have one hour. Have fun!'

Marker in hand, Addison faced his blank pumpkin. Where did he even start?

He had to at least pretend to participate. If he focused on interrogating Gary and not carving his pumpkin then Gary might start questioning what he was doing there.

Feeling rather like he was cheating, Addison snuck a glance at a neighbouring table. The grown-up had already cut out a circular lid around their pumpkin stem and their young person was enthusiastically scooping out pulp barehanded.

Of course. Addison went to do the same but found the pumpkin's shell – or was it skin or rind? – much too tough. The incision was less of a cut and more of a stab, with more violence required to pierce the outer layer than he'd anticipated. Addison almost felt like he needed a grown-up with him too. He bet Jake would've had no trouble but immediately scolded himself, reckoning no good would come of such wistful, purposeless thinking. Besides, Addison didn't need a man to help him cut a vegetable.

Pumpkin successfully stabbed, Addison hacked a rough circle around the stem and pulled off the lid with a pulpy, stringy squelch. With spoon in hand, he started scooping out the pulp and depositing it into the bucket, as instructed.

Meanwhile, Addison kept half an eye on Gary, who was doing a quick lap of the courtyard to check everyone was happy. He also tried to cast his mind back, pick up what he'd been thinking of carving before Ben had arrived with hot chips. Could he carve something from *Sleepy Hollow*? Maybe, but his recollection of the film was murky at best. The classic 1993 animated family film *The Nightmare Before Christmas* was another story – Addison had practically worn out that videotape growing up. He could do Jack

Skellington, the Pumpkin King of Halloween Town? His bony skull was almost a variation on the classic jack-o'-lantern, but with rounder eyes, and a stitched mouth instead of a jagged one – practically designed to be carved into a pumpkin.

With that settled and his pumpkin successfully hollowed out, Addison made quick work of marking it up. Satisfied his design looked at least vaguely recognisable, Addison made the first cut of consequence.

He was working on the second eye hole when he noticed his target – one Gary Farnham – had embarked on a second, slower lap of the courtyard. He spent time with each contestant, offering suggestions and encouragement and all-round taking his sweet time. Based on Gary's pattern of movement, Addison reckoned he was next, and he was ready.

Chapter 19

'And what do we have here?' Gary said, dropping into the seat next to Addison.

'Ah, this is, well it's meant to be, it's going to be Jack Skellington from *The Nightmare Before Christmas*?'

Gary raised an eyebrow. 'Are you asking me or telling me?'

'I am telling you,' Addison said, adopting the time-honoured 'fake it till you make it' approach.

'Excellent.' Gary turned from Addison to face the partially carved pumpkin. He squinted and tilted his head, which didn't fill Addison with confidence. 'Oh yes, I see it. He has a stitched-up kind of mouth, doesn't he?'

'He does. I'm going to have a go at that next.'

'Very good. You are well on your way, Addison,' Gary said, slapping his hands on his thighs as if preparing to get up. 'Even without an assistant, it looks like you have everything under control. Unless you had something you wanted a hand with while I'm here? I have two going spare.' Gary lifted his hands up and shook them, as if giving Addison the ol' razzle dazzle.

'Ah, yes, actually. While I've got you, Gary,' Addison

said, pointedly putting his carving knife down. 'There's something else I might need a hand with.'

'Oh yes, what's that?' Gary fully turned, giving Addison his undivided attention, faint frown lines appearing between his eyebrows.

Addison doubted he'd get the information he wanted by launching in head-first with 'I hear you did a slapdash job on maintaining the town hall which led to last night's shocking death, what say you?' Instead, he'd given a little advance thought to how he might broach the subject and had come up with a plan. 'You're a builder, is that right?' Addison said, easing in with a simple question to which he already knew the answer. 'At least when you're not hosting pumpkin carving competitions.'

'That is correct. Builder by trade, designer by dream. Nothing quite as satisfying as a job well done, is there? Except maybe trying my hand at something a little creative.' Gary gestured around them, indicating they were in the middle of one such example. 'Not quite so predictable though, is it?'

'What's that?'

'What's what?'

'What's not quite so predictable?'

'Oh! Creativity, of course,' Gary said. 'Sometimes it works out, sometimes it doesn't. When I'm doing my building work, I prefer to take a more conservative approach – belt and braces, right?'

'Right.'

'But creatively, I do like to push the envelope a little bit, otherwise what's it all for?'

'Absolutely,' Addison said. 'The thing is, I'm thinking about doing some work on Harper House – definitely some redecorating, but also maybe some renovations – it's early days yet, so nothing set in stone. Someone with a foot in both camps might be just what I need...'

'Oh yeah?'

'But I'm worried I might already be getting ahead of myself, jumping straight to the fun bit. I'm thinking it might be worth getting a builder's report done first? Make sure there aren't any major fixes required before I start unintentionally papering over any problems.'

'Quite literally. Yes, I see your point. A prudent and admirable approach. Any dampness or leaks?'

'Not that I've noticed.'

'Jammed doors or windows?'

'No, no, nothing like that.'

'That's a good start,' Gary said, nodding along. 'You're planning on living in it then?'

'Yeah, that's the plan.'

'Good. And it sounds like you want to do a proper job. None of this slapping on a fresh coat of paint, staging it with some trendy furniture, and then flicking it on to some poor sucker for a premium. Yes, our older buildings need plenty of love and care if we don't want them falling down around us.'

Addison couldn't have steered this conversation better if he'd tried. 'You have experience dealing with older buildings, then? Knowing what to look for in identifying issues, putting together maintenance plans, dealing with unusual or bespoke features, all that?'

'You bet. It's often a challenge, of course, but that's all part of the fun.'

'Is there much work for you doing this kind of thing?'

'Plenty, don't you worry about that. There are a couple

of us that do most of the work around here. Too much for any one outfit, anyway. I pick up work on places like yours, as and when. Then there's my regular work for the council, which I do a fair bit of, helping maintain a bunch of the civic buildings in town.'

'Oh, nice. Milverton has some beautiful old buildings—'

'Doesn't she just?'

'What about the town hall? Is that part of your rounds?' Another question to which Addison already knew the answer, but he could feel himself getting very close to the ones he'd come here to ask.

'Yes. Lovely building – a real asset for Milverton. But oh' – Gary's face fell – 'did you hear about last night?'

'Yes, I was there, actually.'

'Terrible, just terrible. Were you really? Terrible.' Gary shook his head, appearing entirely genuine. 'I would've loved to see the show, but my boy had a basketball game over in Palmerston North, and I wasn't going to miss *that*. I helped out with a couple of the set pieces, so it would've been great to see them in action.'

'What do you mean?'

'Oh, I built them. The sarcophagus and the crypt wall were my handiwork – the construction anyway. I had help with the painting though, so I can't take full credit for that.'

'I didn't know that was your handiwork,' Addison said slowly, wondering at Patrick's omission of this very relevant little detail. 'They looked great, by the way. And sturdy.'

'Well, thank you very much. Anyway, I was lucky enough to see a bit of the rehearsal, a couple of the acts, but it would've been fantastic to see it all come together on the night. At least, until…' Gary flashed his eyes wide and shook his head once more.

'Yes, until the trapdoor unexpectedly flung open.' Addison dropped the comment and left it there, a familiar tactic that once again bore fruit mere moments later.

'That trapdoor mechanism is quite unique, as far as I know,' Gary said. 'I gave it an extra going over just last week when I heard they'd be using it for the show – just to be sure, you know? Better safe than sorry. All in perfect working order, no worries. I've been running through the incident in my head ever since I heard what happened. But no...' Gary sighed, deflating. 'An awful case of miscommunication if ever there was one. Have you been below stage at the town hall?'

Addison had not. He'd intended to go last night, but between observing the performers and crew backstage, talking to Patrick and Mabel and Jake, then being driven home, he hadn't had the chance. 'No, I haven't.'

'You can't see the stage from the lever itself, so your channels of communication have to be working well to operate that trapdoor safely. There's been talk of sealing it off in the past, for those very safety reasons, but it was never a priority.'

He'd have to take Gary's word for it regarding sightlines and the layout below stage, at least for the time being. He couldn't see any reason the man would have to lie, and it would be something Addison could verify easily enough, which was a reason *not* to lie.

He was still thinking through it all when Gary said, 'Unless...'

That caught Addison's attention. He liked the sound of that, and despite the almost overwhelming urge to shake the words out of the man, Addison held his tongue. Thankfully, his patience was rewarded.

'Unless...' Gary said again. 'At least, as horrible as it sounds, I *hope* that's what happened.'

'What else could have happened though?' Addison knew precisely what else, but he didn't want to put thoughts in the man's head or words in his mouth. Gary was someone who wasn't actually present on the night but he had been involved in the overall production in a small yet important way. Addison wanted to hear what niggling thought was preying on his mind – or his conscience, perhaps?

'Accidents, mistakes, miscommunications – everything is done to avoid them, but they happen, of course. This production, though, plagued with the blasted things... Last-minute venue change, that was the first drama. Then poor Theo almost loses a finger. Then Patrick breaks a leg, meaning his Lady Perry Less couldn't host. Replacement hostess loses her wigs – I heard about that too. Then during the production itself, a trapdoor flings itself open.'

'Seems like a serious run of awfully bad luck,' Addison said slowly. '*Implausibly* bad luck?'

Gary pinched his lips together and flashed his eyes wide. 'I'm inclined to agree,' he said before lowering his voice, leaning in ever so slightly. 'Now, I don't know about the incidents outside the theatre, but at least when it comes to the backstage operations and the *technical* aspects of the production, I know who I'd be looking into.'

Addison wondered how accurate his reading between the lines was – he didn't want to assume, had to be sure. In an equally low voice, he said, 'Are you talking about the sound and lighting technician?'

'I am indeed.' Gary nodded once. 'Kieran Nash is his name. He tends to take on more than just the sound and lighting though, as is the way with smaller productions.

During the show, he'll be the one keeping tabs on the mechanical bits and bobs too, such as the trapdoor. I hate to point fingers, but if there was even a whiff of doubt about this being just a terrible accident – and I think there is, for what that's worth – then, well…'

It was compelling stuff, though thinking back to the night before, Addison was wary of getting carried away. 'Kieran would've already been interviewed by the police, along with everyone else. I'm sure they'll have him in mind if there's anything there.' The truth was, though, he wasn't so sure. As Jake had said himself, people could find themselves clamming up around the cops – unintentionally or otherwise. They might be inclined to convey only things they knew for certain. Or, another angle to consider: if they were safe and comfortable knowing they were in no way culpable, would they be *more* or *less* likely to freely speculate about possibilities, share rumours, offer gossip?

'These kinds of things shouldn't be happening though, should they? It's like we're in a cartoon. I'm surprised we didn't have stage lights or anvils dropping from the ceiling,' Gary said with a shrug. 'Anyway, couple the technical mishap with Kieran's history with the victim, and I think it'd be worth having a word with the guy.'

'Yeah…' Addison frowned, his mind playing catch up. 'What? His history? What history?'

'Oh, poor Theo Robinson was helping me with the set pieces – I am glad his finger is going to be OK, I should've known better.' Gary tutted. 'Anyway, Theo was telling me that Cilla Slay – who was she when she wasn't in drag?'

'Simeon Clay.'

'Yes, that's right. Simeon Clay and Kieran Nash used to date back in the day, when they were going through theatre school, or something.'

'Percy did mention they had exes working together backstage last night,' Addison said, thinking back. 'I'd just assumed he meant a couple of the crew members, not our hostess.'

'Quite a fiery relationship, to hear Theo tell it, and it didn't end on the best of terms. I'm not throwing accusations or anything like that, but understandable if Kieran was a bit distracted with his ex in town. And on his stage, no less. But if there was still bad blood there' – Gary's eyes went wide – 'last night would've been the perfect chance to get one back.'

'That's…' Addison didn't know where to start. 'Well, that's a wildly public and fatal bit of revenge.'

'True,' Gary said. 'But he might not have meant it to be fatal, just a fright on stage.'

'Right. Yes, of course.'

'Kieran has a bit of a mean streak when he's stressed or doesn't get his way. From what I hear, Simeon was much the same.'

'So, not just something he put on when in character as Cilla Slay?'

Gary shook his head slowly. 'Would've made for an explosive relationship, I expect.'

'I'll bet,' Addison said, already considering the possibilities this new information provided.

'Anyway,' Gary said, once again slapping his hands on his thighs before looking about himself, as if resurfacing from their discussion back into the pub garden's courtyard. 'Very good talking to you, Addison, but I've been neglecting the other contestants. I'd better see if anyone else needs a hand and let you get back to your carving.'

'Absolutely, thanks for your thoughts. Good to get a better understanding of what's going on.'

'No worries at all. And don't forget to give me a bell next week, will you? We'll tee up a bit of a health check for Harper House, see how the old girl is doing. Sound good?'

'Yep, that sounds great. Will do.'

Addison watched as Gary Farnham continued his rounds. When Patrick had presented the man's character and work habits, the fact that Gary had constructed the very sturdy Spooky Showcase set pieces felt like a pertinent piece of information. As was Kieran's dating history with Simeon Clay. Both key details Addison would've expected to be mentioned. Things just weren't adding up...

Had someone made a mistake – perhaps intending a bit of light revenge but it got out of hand – and were now hiding it? An understandable reaction when the direct consequence of your action was someone's death.

Or had someone killed Simeon Clay, AKA Cilla Slay, very much on purpose?

Either way, it appeared the death was due to someone's actions and not their *inaction*. No matter whether it was accidental or intentional, it was becoming clear that Cilla Slay had been killed.

Mind churning, Addison picked up his carving knife and got back to work.

Chapter 20

Addison did not win the pumpkin carving contest. Nor did he score second or third place. And that was as it should be, considering some of the other pumpkins that were held up for judging. One featured a spider on a web and was so fine and intricate that Addison didn't know how it hadn't collapsed. One played for nostalgia with their entry showing Goodnight Kiwi and Cat tucked into bed up a television satellite tower. Another had the same idea as Addison for a local scene with the mountain range dotted with wind turbines, though he suspected they'd pulled it off more successfully than he ever could. The bronze winner – a wide-eyed owl – was a particular favourite of Addison's.

Meanwhile, with only half a mind on his carving at most, Addison was really just relieved that his efforts had resulted in something vaguely recognisable. His interpretation of Jack Skellington, the Pumpkin King of Halloween Town, didn't look at all out of place amongst the other entries now decorating the pub's beer garden.

Better yet, chatting with Gary and completing his carving had wiped any thought of obsessively checking his phone from his mind. So, by the time he'd finished, Addison was very pleasantly surprised to find Jake had not only responded but that he thought the outdoor movie was a great idea. He was working and had a few things to finish off but would be free to join Addison by nine, which worked out perfectly.

Addison may not have won the pumpkin carving contest, but he had won a hot date with Milverton's top cop. All was well with the world.

Addison stepped out of The Langston to find that with the cloud cover now lifted, the sky blazed red in the last of the sun's light.

Milverton Square bustled with the ghoulish, the grotesque, and sometimes even the glamorous. The square itself had been given a spooky makeover, appearing more like a Victorian cemetery than a comforting and pleasant town square. Flickering lights had been laced through the trees, with bats hanging from the branches. Tombstones thrust from the lawns and amongst the rose bushes. The stone clocktower and oversized duck sculpture had been ominously underlit, making them appear colossal and almost oppressive.

Scattered throughout were market stalls, food trucks, caravans, and various carnival amusements. Addison was passing the fortune teller's tent when he spotted a familiar dark mistress hand in hand with an amorphous green blob.

'If it isn't Morticia Addams, once again,' Addison said, approaching Mabel and then dutifully kissing the back of her proffered hand. She was fully done up, just like the night before, but had swapped her black handbag for a black tote bag.

'Well Morticia gets to be Morticia every day, why not me? Get my money's worth out of this costume hire.

Besides, plenty of people here tonight won't have had the chance to see me last night.' Mabel emphasised her point by taking a step back and striking a dramatic pose.

'Yes, I completely agree.'

'I have done away with the heels though,' Mabel said, putting out a foot to show her black trainers. 'That'd be asking for trouble on this grass. I've opted for my walking shoes, much more comfortable for spending time on my feet.'

'Yes, very sensible—'

'As are you, apparently,' Mabel said, eyes wide as she pointedly looked Addison up and down. 'I see you've pulled out all the stops with your costume tonight.'

Addison had left the house thinking of interviewing a potential suspect and entering a pumpkin carving contest, with the vague notion of an outdoor movie. Dressing up hadn't even occurred to him. To draw attention away from his lack of spooky spirit, he turned to the green, shiny, gloopy, shapeless being that was Mabel's granddaughter. 'And who – or what – are you tonight, Sophia?'

'I am a ball of snot,' Sophia said without missing a beat.

Addison goldfished for a moment before smiling. 'Brilliant.'

'Because snot is gross and makes people scream, so it's scary too.'

'I'm impressed, Sophia. Inspired, and very well reasoned. I am wonderfully disgusted.'

'Thank you,' she said simply. 'But why aren't you dressed up?'

'Yes, Addison. Why aren't you dressed up?' Mabel said.

So much for drawing attention from himself. Addison had many excuses, none of which were likely to pass muster.

'You should get your face painted,' Sophia said, 'so you don't feel left out.'

'That is very kind and thoughtful of you.'

'Yes,' Mabel said. 'And we wouldn't want such thoughtful kindness to go unheeded.'

'The face painting lady is just over there.' Sophia helpfully pointed her out.

'Thank you, Sophia,' Addison said, following the determined ball of snot and her grinning grandmother.

Soon seated in a rickety collapsible chair, Addison talked them down from a full-face skull to a small cartoon skull and crossbones on his cheek which the face painting lady whipped up in minutes.

'That's better,' Sophia said. 'Isn't it?'

Addison agreed that indeed it was, and with that situation under control, they could continue their wander around the square.

'Good to see everyone's getting into the spirit of Halloween,' Mabel said, biting down on her smile.

'Yes, yes.' Despite his protests, Addison couldn't help smiling to himself and shaking his head. 'I still find the whole thing deeply strange.'

'What's that?'

'Oh, you know, encouraging children to visit strangers' houses in the dark. And extort sweets from them under threat of egging their house and toilet papering their front garden.'

Mabel murmured thoughtfully. 'I take your point. We don't really go in for the whole trick-or-treat thing here.'

'I suppose not. You see it in the movies plenty, though.'

'It's big in the States, I believe, so that makes sense.'

'I wonder what the ancient pagans would've thought of all this,' Addison said as they wandered past a candy apple stall and candy floss cart – which were both firm favourites, if the swarm of costumed children was anything to go by.

They were approaching the hall of mirrors when Addison spotted Constables McGiffert and Edwards patrolling the square.

Normally, dressed in their blues as they were, they'd stand out in a crowd. Here though, with so many emergency services members apparently represented, the real officers' presence was less obvious.

Some of the more grown-up participants had opted for their own interpretations of the uniforms, interpretations that were rather more form-fitting or featured rather less fabric.

Though seeing the constables had got Addison thinking again. 'Have you heard any more updates about what happened last night...' Addison trailed off, shifting his attention from Mabel to Sophia then back again. 'Shall we discuss later?'

Mabel considered it for a moment before agreeing that it was probably for the best. 'Maybe when we don't have so many ears around.'

Sophia immediately informed them that she knew they were talking about her and that she was mature for her age, as her teachers had said, so they should feel free to talk about whatever grown-up things they liked.

Addison and Mabel smiled at each other, but didn't take Sophia up on her offer, at least for the most part.

'All this,' Addison said, gesturing around them. 'Considering – uh – very recent events... is it not in poor taste? You know, a bit morbid?'

'Rather fits with the theme, doesn't it?' Mabel said before waving her glib comment away. 'No, we may not fully understand what happened, at least not yet. But we can't let that stop us or we'd never get anything done.'

Addison nodded, recognising the truth in the words. 'The show must go on.'

'Just so.'

'Speaking of,' Addison said, struggling to stop the smile from completely taking over his face. 'Jake is joining me later to watch *Sleepy Hollow*.'

'Wonderful. I am very happy to hear that.' Mabel patted him on the arm, smiling right back at him. 'A bit of a date do-over, is it?'

'Exactly my thinking.'

'You're in hot demand tonight, dear. It's kind of you to accompany an old lady and her granddaughter for a turn around the square.'

'Don't be silly, I'm having a great time.'

'Well, thank you for letting me help fill in time until your proper date.'

They passed a chocolate fountain that had been set up for fondue, and a pick-and-mix sweets station – both surely food safety disasters waiting to happen. Then a stall featuring cupcakes sporting all manner of iced spookiness – ghosts, pumpkins, spiders, eyeballs, bats, black cats, moons, owls, and witches' hats.

It all looked amazing, but much too sweet – he could even taste the sugar in the air. Addison realised he needed something a little more substantial, at least to start. And that's when they came across what he considered the 'proper' food stalls – burgers, kebabs, rice dishes, fried chicken, noodles, hāngī, curries, fish and chips, hot dogs, and so much more – all of it mouth-watering.

Addison wanted it all, and was on the verge of decision paralysis when he spotted the dumpling truck and realised that was exactly what he wanted. Something tasty and filling but not too heavy in the stomach.

Pleased with his choice, Addison returned with his steaming tray of dumplings – pork and chives, delicious – to find Mabel had ordered arancini from the cheese caravan. The cheesy stuffed Italian rice balls coated in breadcrumbs looked divine. Mabel must have recognised his food envy as she offered to swap one of her arancini for one of his dumplings, a trade which Addison gladly accepted.

Sophia chose a hotdog on a stick. And a 'tornado potato', which was a new one for Addison, also coming on a stick. It appeared to be one potato sliced in a continuous cut around and around, then stretched out like a coil spring and deep-fried. Sophia alternated between the two, taking a bite from one then the other.

They each devoured their food in minutes before continuing their wander around. They passed on the merry-go-round, with none confident they could keep their dinner down. But that would've been nothing on what they came across next.

It was another carnival staple, the obscenely creepy open-mouthed clown heads rotating back and forth, waiting for plastic balls to be tossed into their gobs. They were about to skip past that one too when Sophia spotted one of her friends walking away in triumph with an oversized stuffed monkey.

The friend was dressed as Oogie Boogie from *The Nightmare Before Christmas*, sporting a head-to-toe, roughly sewn hessian sack. And the parents were dressed as the film's protagonists, Jack and Sally.

Addison didn't have to dust off his investigative skills to deduce they might be going to the outdoor cinema's first screening of the night. Mabel had a similar thought, and it was the work of mere seconds for her to check in about Sophia watching the movie with her friend.

Mabel reminded Sophia to stay with the group and not wander off before thanking the parents and promising she'd retrieve her granddaughter at the end of the movie.

Mabel led Addison away.

'So, what—'

'I love my granddaughter, I do,' Mabel said, 'but I have already seen that movie more times than I care for. So please don't judge me for seeing the opportunity and taking it.'

'I would never,' Addison said, his smile wide. 'Shall we get a drink?'

'You read my mind.'

Chapter 21

Now that impressionable young minds were otherwise occupied, Addison brought Mabel up to speed with what he'd learnt as they made their way over to the bar area.

He told her how, according to the interviews Jake had conducted the night before, none of the backstage crew had operated the trapdoor the time that killed Cilla Slay, nor had they seen who had.

He shared his impression of Gary Farnham as a competent man who did solid work. That he was unlikely to be responsible for shoddy workmanship or half-baked maintenance, as had been suggested previously.

And he relayed Gary's thoughts on the situation. That it might have been a terrible case of miscommunication, another incident in a run of bad luck, or Kieran Nash getting one back.

'Kieran Nash,' Mabel said slowly. 'Now why does that name ring a bell?'

'He was the show's lighting and sound technician—'

Mabel clicked her taloned, bejewelled fingers. 'That's the one. He's often helping out with all that technical guff, making our talented stars shine. Important work – the shows wouldn't be the same without it. Yes, Kieran. I knew I knew the name.'

'Yes, but Kieran Nash is also Cilla Slay's – well, Simeon Clay's, I guess – ex-boyfriend.'

'*Really*? Now that I didn't know. Opens up all sorts of possibilities,' Mabel said slowly, already thinking it all through. 'Well, it seems like you're making real progress.'

'Yeah, it does and it doesn't. It's just a whole lot of personalities and personal histories at this point. I'm starting to build a picture, but I only have the faintest idea of the smallest corner of it…'

'Still, it's something.'

'Hardly—'

'I appreciate you doing this – you know that, don't you?'

'Oh, it's nothing. I—'

'No, Addison. It's not nothing,' Mabel said, her voice stern. 'I didn't have the best sleep last night, if I'm honest. Nothing to be done about what happened, but getting a clear answer for how or why it happened… I think that'll go a way to putting my mind at ease. And even if nothing comes of it, I appreciate you trying.'

Addison went to say something a few times but couldn't settle on what. Instead he frowned and nodded, more determined than ever, and eventually said, 'I'll do my best.'

'I know you will. You know what your next step is, don't you?'

'I need to speak to Kieran Nash,' Addison said.

At the very same time, Mabel said, 'You need to speak to Sergeant Murphy.'

'Ah, yes.' Addison winced. 'You're probably right.'

'Of course I am, dear.' Mabel smiled and patted him on the arm.

'Jake has already spoken to Kieran, so he might already know they'd dated and just hasn't shared that with me, because—'

'Because, officially, he is the investigator.'

'Yes.'

'Not you.'

'No,' Addison said, thinking about his role in all of this, officially. 'Last night, while he was pulling people aside to talk, Jake asked me to keep an eye and an ear out. He didn't say anything about keeping me in the loop. This arrangement only goes in one direction.'

'And that's fine, dear. The more information the police have, the sooner they'll be able to get to the bottom of this.'

'It is my responsibility to tell Jake what else I've seen and heard.'

'A model citizen—'

'I will *continue* to keep an eye and an ear out,' Addison said, nodding along to himself. 'I need to speak – and listen, of course – to others involved in the production, not necessarily just those directly involved. Those on the fringes might have some good insights too, might even be able to see things more clearly, not being in it themselves. And then I will share any details that might be relevant to Cilla's death. Meanwhile, if I happen to make my own progress in getting to the bottom of this, then so be it.'

'Astonishing.'

'Huh? What is?'

'Your mental acrobatics, Addison,' Mabel said, looking very amused. 'Too clever by half. Your ability to justify your actions... I suspect such things have got many a man into trouble before.'

Momentarily speechless, Addison was tempted to justify

162

the justification of his actions.

He was doing it for Mabel, though in a roundabout way he was also getting a head start on his new role with the mayor. Then there was the small matter of satisfying his own morbid curiosity. Primarily, however, he was doing it for Mabel.

He didn't want to get into any of that reasoning and certainly didn't want to be the poster boy for men dubiously rationalising their actions. Instead he simply said, 'My intentions are good.'

Mabel's smile widened. 'Yes, I know they are. I'm just having you on. Let me get you a drink.'

Addison shook his head, but smiled right along with her. 'I'll allow it.'

He may have spent the afternoon at the pub, but his drink had been rather secondary to the activity and the questioning. He'd also since had hot chips, dumplings, and arancini, wandered around the square, and been subjected to a face painting. His gin and tonic was but a distant memory as he stepped up to the temporary bar.

Paul Stewart, owner and head distiller of the Milverton Distilling Company, was only in his sixties and as well dressed as ever with his signature sprig of botanicals pinned to his suit jacket's lapel. He was adjusting a small, free-standing chalkboard when he looked up, a charming smile spreading beneath his tidy moustache the moment he noticed their arrival.

'Well, now. If it isn't two of my favourite and most discerning customers.' Paul said with a subtle wink in Mabel's direction.

'Oh, you,' Mabel said, a slight rosiness appearing across her cheeks despite all the powder.

'It is *always* a pleasure to see you, Mabel. Or should I say, Morticia?'

'Tonight I answer to both, so whichever takes your fancy.'

'Very well. But yes, as I was saying, always a pleasure, especially after that recent kerfuffle up at the distillery. And of course Addison – nothing gets past you, my boy.' Paul cleared his throat, shook his head and pinned his smile back in place. 'Yes, lovely to see you both again. But let's hope all the drama tonight is limited to the big screen.'

'Indeed, indeed,' Mabel said, any coquettishness now completely replaced with a tone of genuine concern. 'How are you doing, Paul, truly?'

'Oh, you know how it is.'

'Not really, no, if I'm being honest.'

'No, I suppose not.' Paul leant on the bar, letting out a long breath. 'Well, we've been doing a bit of reflection, rejigging plans, all that, but we keep trucking along. And I've been looking forward to tonight, something a bit different.' Paul pulled on a smile, his grave expression shifting to something more familiar – relaxed, affable, and clearly indicating he was ready to move on to other things. 'And I suppose you'll be needing a drink?'

'You suppose correctly.'

'Very well.' Paul clapped his hands once and rubbed them together. 'May I draw your attention to tonight's selection? I do enjoy a classic cocktail – they have become staples for a reason, haven't they? – but it's always a bit of fun doing a twist on a classic, or dusting off a less common recipe for a themed cocktail night.'

Across the top of the chalkboard, the distiller had written 'Paul's Killer Cocktails' before filling the space with the night's offerings. Addison couldn't help thinking it was all a bit soon, but it was Halloween so he also thought he might be able to let it slide.

'First up we have the Corpse Reviver Number 2—'

'Gosh, what a name!' Mabel said.

'Tart and bracing – perfect for a hangover, hence the name. We're making it with our very own Milverton gin, of course, and lemon juice, Cointreau, Lillet Blanc, and then the real kicker: absinthe.'

Addison felt his throat close up involuntarily at the mention of the final ingredient. 'A bit much to start, I think.'

'Perhaps you're more interested in being mesmerised by a Vampire's Kiss?'

Mabel snorted. 'I think he's more interested in—'

'I think I might know what I'm more interested in,' Addison said, cutting her off before she could no doubt raise the topic of his love life. 'And I think I would like to hear what makes up a Vampire's Kiss.'

'This one's vodka-based, with raspberry liqueur and frozen raspberries, topped up with bubbles, and rimmed with red sugar.'

'Oh yes,' Mabel said, 'I do enjoy a nice rim.'

Addison choked, drawing concerned looks from Paul and Mabel which he waved away.

'Sweet, floral, and a bit sparkly,' Paul said with accompanying jazz hands, still keeping an eye on Addison as he did so.

'Delicious,' Mabel said. 'I think that might be my drink tonight.'

'Very well,' Paul said. 'But don't decide just yet, Mabel. I have a few more options that might appeal. Next up we have the Witch's Heart – blackberry liqueur, apple juice, lemon juice, simple syrup, grenadine – giving a blend of berry sweetness and green apple tartness.'

Addison thought that sounded like a bit of him, more balanced than the first two options.

'One more on tonight's theme, sort of.' Paul's eyes sparkled with a glint of mischief. 'The Green Fairy.'

Mabel oohed. 'That sounds—'

'Hard no,' Addison said. 'No way. Not a chance.'

'Oh, why not?'

'It's just absinthe, Mabel. Like fennel-flavoured petrol. Awful going down, and chances you'll bring up your dinner again later in the night are not low.'

'Yes, absinthe,' Paul said, 'but it also calls for freshly squeezed lemon juice, simple syrup, bitters, an egg white, and a splash of water.'

'Egg?'

'Oh yes,' Paul said. 'Gives it that rich, smooth texture, and a bit of froth on top.'

Mabel hummed. 'Still, I think perhaps not. No, I'll have—'

Paul held up a hand, apparently not yet finished. 'One more. Of course, I couldn't do an event without offering my specialty: the Milverton Martini.'

Mabel and Addison glanced at each other.

'A "killer cocktail" indeed,' Addison said.

'No *extra* ingredients, I promise,' Paul said, clearing his throat and holding his hands up as if in surrender. 'Just the gin and dry vermouth of your classic martini, then the karaka liqueur to bring in the hint of sweetness, and then a dash of orange bitters to take the edge off that sweetness. All foraged and crafted just minutes from this very spot, the Milverton Martini is absolutely the taste of Milverton.'

'It does sound good…' Addison said slowly, reminded again why he'd been intrigued to try it a couple of times before, not that he'd managed a taste just yet.

'And that's it for tonight,' Paul said with a single, conclusive clap.

'May I have a Vampire's Kiss?' Mabel said without missing a beat. 'Thank you, Paul.'

'Decisive, I like it. And certainly, you may,' he said with a nod before turning to Addison. 'And for you?'

'I'd like to try the Witch's Heart, please.' He'd seriously considered ordering a Milverton Martini, but realised he wasn't ready quite yet, not after the drama at Penshaw Hall.

Paul clapped his hands once and rubbed them together. 'Coming right up.'

Addison knew it was silly, but he couldn't help watching as the master mixologist prepared the cocktails – to be sure nothing unexpected found its way into their drinks. He felt a smidge less silly when he noticed Mabel was doing the same, though doing her best not to be obvious about it.

'Actually, Mabel, I have a small job for you, if you don't mind?'

Mabel flinched a little, briefly thinking she'd been caught supervising. 'Certainly.'

'Wonderful! This might sound a little strange, but all will become clear soon enough, I promise,' Paul said with a smile, handing over a small pair of metal tongs with flat, paddle-like ends. 'I would like you to hold the ends between your hands, bring them up to your body temperature.'

Mabel frowned but did as instructed, hands clasped together around the tongs.

Paul continued preparing their cocktails, and after only a few moments of silence, Mabel said, 'Did you know New

Zealand's only native land mammal is a bat?'

Apparently the lack of chat had been so awkward for Mabel that she'd felt the need to throw out a random fun fact to fill the air. It appeared to come out of nowhere until Addison remembered the square was full of its rubbery, plasticky brethren serving as spooky decorations. Still, not Mabel's smoothest conversation starter.

'I did indeed,' Paul said, pouring a succession of ingredients – each clearly labelled – into the cocktail shaker. 'But at least we have two species of them: the long-tailed bat and the lesser short-tailed bat. There's also the *greater* short-tailed bat, but that was last spotted in the sixties, so chances they're still going aren't looking great.'

'Poor, hideous creatures,' Mabel said. 'With a name as uninspired as that, they probably died of boredom.'

'Not a fan of bats then, I take it?' Addison said, surprised at the bitterness in her tone.

'They're just…' Mabel pulled her lips back over her teeth and made grabby gestures with her fake claws. 'Not nice.'

'Didn't one of them win "Bird of the Year" once, not that long ago?' Addison was sure he'd read something about that.

Paul paused his cocktail shaking to say, 'It did indeed – the long-tailed bat.'

'How did it win "Bird of the Year"? It's not even a bird.'

'Close enough,' Paul said with a shrug before honeying the rim of Mabel's martini glass, rolling it through a small tray of red sugar, and pouring in the contents of the shaker. 'They're only little fellas, like thumbs with wings.'

'And we're talking about them, aren't we?' Addison said, watching closely as Paul set Mabel's cocktail on what appeared to be a wet silver platter before starting on the second cocktail. 'The "Bird of the Year" campaign is all about raising awareness for conservation efforts.'

'Conservation efforts? Bats?'

'Yes.'

'Bats are something we want to conserve...' Mabel trailed off, as if originally intending the comment as another question before registering Addison and Paul's reactions and so switching it to a statement.

'That's right,' Addison said.

'Yes, it is,' Mabel said, quickly rallying despite her apparent distaste for the animal. 'Who cares if they're not a bird? What's a little controversy?'

'Exactly.'

'It can do wonders when it comes to nabbing headlines,' Paul said, pouring Addison's cocktail into the second martini glass before adding a dash of grenadine, the red liquid bleeding through the drink, and finally resting three raspberries skewered on a toothpick across the top of the glass.

Mabel nudged Addison. 'You wouldn't happen to know anything about scoring a front-page feature, would you?'

Addison was weighing up whether to defend himself or just ignore the jab when Paul saved him from agonising. 'Māori folklore associates bats with the mythical hōkioi, a large bird of prey which lived in the heavens, only descending to Earth after dark. Never seen, only heard.' Paul lowered his voice and leant in. 'Which you hoped you never did.'

'What? Why?' Mabel responded in equally hushed tones.

Paul's eyes flashed as he set Addison's cocktail alongside Mabel's on the wet platter. 'I could not have timed this better if I'd tried. Thank you, Mabel,' Paul said, holding out a hand for the tongs. He then produced a faintly wisping plastic bag and set it on the bar, holding the tongs just over its opening, a terrible expression on his face. 'You hoped you never heard the bird, because its cry foretold death and disaster.'

Paul plunged the tongs into the bag, pulling out a small cube which *shrieked* at the contact with the body-temperature tongs, like souls scrabbling to escape the underworld, sending a chill through Addison's body and raising the hairs on his arms. He also let out an involuntary 'Ooh.'

Mabel gasped, her taloned fingers over her lips, as Paul then dropped the cube onto the wet tray, setting off a swirling and spooky fog effect that curled around their glasses.

'Bravo, Paul. Bravo!' Mabel clapped in appreciation, quickly joined by Addison.

'What a show.'

'That was wonderful,' Mabel said, her tone one of awe. 'How did you do that?

'Just a little dry ice. The warmth of the metal vibrates so rapidly against the freezing cold ice that it sets off that bone-chilling, blood-curdling scream. And then there's the fog created from contact with water.'

'I hadn't anticipated the mini biology and chemistry masterclasses when I came out tonight,' Addison said with a chuckle. 'But I'm here for it.'

Paul beamed, gracing them with a small bow. 'Supposedly dry ice chips can go *in* the drinks.'

'What? Doesn't dry ice burn to touch?'

'It does – hence the tongs. I'd have to warn customers not to touch it or swallow it or get it on their tongue. Because, as you say, it'll burn whatever it touches. I'd have to tell people to be careful to sip only from the edge, and so on and so forth. I think the health and safety spiel would put a real damper on the fun. Hard to enjoy a drink when all you can think about is your throat burning up from the inside.'

'That's awful,' Mabel said, her hand at her throat.

'I agree. Better, I think, just to put on a bit of a show for the oohs and the ahhs.'

'You may consider us appropriately oohed and ahhed,' Mabel said, reaching for her glass.

Addison did likewise, holding his glass aloft. 'What shall we toast to?'

'To good intentions.'

Addison laughed. 'All right, then. To good intentions.'

They smiled and clinked glasses.

Mabel expressed her pleasure the moment she'd taken a sip. 'Delicious, Paul. Delicious.'

'Agreed, just what I felt like.' Addison had enjoyed the dry ice spectacle, but when it came to the drink itself, his Witch's Heart was a winner.

'So,' Paul said, clasping his hands and rubbing them together, satisfied his concoctions had been well received. 'What's next on your Halloween hit list, folks?'

Mabel raised her glass again. 'Getting a drink was as far ahead as we'd planned for the moment.'

'Well, success,' Paul said, motioning an oversized tick mark in the air. 'But if you wanted something more to *ooh* and *ahh* over, have you seen Brodie Seatter-Dent's latest – uh – art installation?'

'I don't think we have?'

'Oh, you'd remember if you had – it's just on the other side of the square. He's called it *Reflections in a Gazebo* or something like that. Interesting to look at, but I'll be the first to admit I didn't really "get" it. Brodie gave me the spiel but I was none the wiser. A bit highfalutin for me. He's clearly put a lot of thought into it, perhaps too much? I could go on all day about my gin, the botanicals, everything to do with the distillation. But when it comes to art, I am a man of simple tastes.' Paul's lips twitched into a smile as he gestured to Addison. 'I can see you appreciate the arts, though.'

Initially confused, Addison then realised the man referred to the cartoonish skull and crossbones painted on Addison's cheek, which he'd all but forgotten about.

Addison groused. 'I was bullied into it.'

'Yes,' Mabel said, 'by a small child and a little old lady.'

'They were vicious.' Addison shook his head in mock seriousness. 'You mustn't let appearances deceive you, Paul.'

The distiller only laughed.

'Shall we go and check it out, Mabel?'

'We shall.'

Chapter 22

Careful not to spill their drinks, Addison and Mabel made their way slowly through the milling crowd. It was now made up primarily of adults and teenagers, with the younger ghouls and vampires having been drawn to the night's first film, which Addison caught snatches of over the sounds of the market.

Addison politely turned down the clown manning the ring toss stall before turning to Mabel. 'I forgot to mention that I ran into Brodie last night during the interval.'

'You did? Have you met before?'

'No, I mean, I *literally* ran into him. Spilt my wine down his top.'

Mabel gasped. 'You didn't?'

'I did. He wasn't impressed.'

'Naturally.'

'Yeah,' Addison said with a sigh. 'I tried offering to pick up the dry cleaning bill but he wasn't interested. He was in a rush for the bar – dismissed me, told me to get out of the way.'

'How rude.'

'To be fair to him, I had just tipped red wine down his

front, so I get it.'

Mabel blew a raspberry. 'He only wears black anyway, and so many layers – you wouldn't even notice it.'

'Let's hope he's as relaxed about it now, but I doubt it.' Addison shrugged. 'Anyway, he's an artist... would you say, could he possibly be on the fringes of Milverton's theatre crowd?'

'Are you thinking...'

'He might have an insight into what happened last night?'

Mabel hummed, considering the suggestion before she finally said, 'A long shot.'

'But also... worth a shot?'

'I don't see why not.'

Paul's directions had not been particularly clear or specific, but Addison and Mabel suspected they'd found what they were looking for.

A large black portable gazebo frame – just the frame, no fabric – with solar garden lights piercing the ground at each of the four corners. The soft white spotlights pointed diagonally upwards, illuminating the installation. An eclectic range of objects appeared to float in midair, though Addison didn't have to dust off his deductive powers to speculate fishing line or something similar was involved. There were ornate mirrors; scraps of paper scrawled with text and diagrams; and a range of photographic, illustrated, and painted self-portraits, each encased in its own cage. The suspended objects slowly rotated as people passed by or the wind caught them.

'What does it make you think? How does it make you feel?'

Addison screamed at the unexpected voice, the hairs on

the back of his neck leaping to attention as he squirmed away. It had felt to him as if the words had been channelled directly into his ear, such was the proximity of the speaker. However, the words themselves had been uttered languidly, as if it were an effort that was so far beneath the speaker.

It was Brodie Seatter-Dent.

Which made sense, considering this was his work. Still, he'd appeared as if out of nowhere. Apparently his entire wardrobe consisted of drapey black garments that faded into the darkness.

Addison didn't know if it was the low lighting, or just the atmosphere of the evening, but Brodie appeared pale and waiflike, as if partially incorporeal, like a ghoul. He was dressed much the same as the night before – black from head to toe, with so much drapery that Addison didn't know where one garment ended and the next began. Based on what he'd seen so far, Addison wouldn't have been surprised if everything Brodie owned was at least Halloween-adjacent.

'Sorry, you gave me a fright—'

'Oh, it's *you*,' Brodie said, eyeing Addison's cocktail and taking a pointed step back.

'Yeah, I'm sorry again—'

'What's done is done,' Brodie said, his words clipped, making it clear he didn't want to dwell on what had happened the night before.

Addison scrabbled around for something else to say that might get them through this awkwardness. He didn't have anything, certainly anything the creator of the piece might be receptive to. 'Uh... what do you call it? Your installation?'

'I call it *Reflections of the Self*.'

'Paul was close,' Mabel said.

175

'Hmm?'

Addison interceded before Mabel could comment on portable garden gazebos or solar garden lights, which he suspected were not the point of the work. 'Can you tell me what inspired you to create this piece?'

Addison hadn't wanted to ask, knew better than to ask, but what else was he to do?

'Oh, everything and nothing. That's the beauty and the horror of it,' Brodie said with many pauses, as if he hadn't practised it endless times while standing before one of the slowly rotating mirrors. 'But that doesn't help you, does it? Doesn't answer your query? No. More specifically, *Reflections of the Self* is a meditative unravelment of a thinker void of conscious thought, forever entrapped in the foyer of life, a liminal space of mirrors and memory and moments that are somehow both everlasting yet also gone too soon. An exposition of reality, identity, love, and loss. If the self is intangible, then how does one hold on?'

Addison realised that, despite his best efforts, he'd tuned out part way through. The sudden expectant silence signalled to Addison that Brodie had reached the end of his answer.

'Extraordinary,' he said while attempting to maintain an expression of serious consideration.

'Yes. It will be a one-person show, one day,' Brodie said with utmost conviction. 'Conceived, written, directed, and produced by me. And starring myself, of course. The perfect expression of me could involve no other. Tonight's display' – Brodie jerked his chin at the gazebo and everything hanging from it – 'is a mere amuse-bouche.'

Addison managed to catch all of the artist's response that time, but now couldn't help also noticing a slight tension in the way he held himself. A jumpiness in response to abrupt sounds and movements around them. An apparent nervousness which seemed to belie the complete confidence of his words.

And the blinking. Addison didn't tend to notice people's blinking – like breathing, it was just a thing that happened. But something about the way Brodie blinked drew attention to itself. Was it slightly more often than most, or a little uneven?

A little twitchy.

And then Addison immediately felt bad for noticing such a thing – that was probably just how Brodie blinked.

Mabel jumped in when Addison didn't have a follow-up comment ready to go. 'How do you find the time?'

Brodie murmured, subtly shaking his head. 'Do you not make time for what is important?'

'So true, so true,' Addison said quickly. He'd heard enough. It was time to start steering the conversation, and he had an idea. 'You must have such a supportive and understanding boss. What is it you do for work?'

That was a big swing and Addison knew it. Asking a presumably full-time creative what they 'do for work', as if their creative work isn't worthy in its own right and couldn't possibly draw the income required to sustain a person. He hoped it might rile the artist up a little, nudge him into saying something he might have otherwise kept close to his chest. Addison was fishing – for what, he did not know. He wasn't proud of the tactic but hoped Brodie would take the bait nonetheless.

'What do I *do for work*?'

'Yeah, your nine-to-five,' Addison said as if blithely unaware of the impact of his words. 'When you're not preparing or putting on your latest project?'

'What I do is not work, no mere job. This is everything. It is my life.'

'Oh, you're able to do this full-time? That's great, but… how?' Addison gestured to the installation around them. 'You're displaying your work, free of charge.'

'Yes, creative funding grants have supported some of my projects in the past,' Brodie said, grinding out the words, his frustration with Addison apparently warring with his need to explain. 'But now I am grateful to the generous and clear-sighted support of those who fund my artistic pursuits: my patrons—'

A loud and manic cackle erupted nearby, causing Brodie to shy away.

'Sorry,' Addison said. 'I didn't catch that last bit. What did you say?'

'He said his parents fund his artistic pursuits.' That was Mabel, ever helpful.

'My *patrons* do, actually,' Brodie said, quick to set the record straight. 'Though, yes, my parents' annual contribution is significant – the majority of my current funding, in fact. But great art is not cheap – it takes time and money – which I do gently remind them of on occasion.'

'Absolutely.' Addison nodded, gesturing to the art installation around them once again, as if highlighting a prime example. 'You mentioned creative funding grants you'd received previously. Did they – uh – not come to the party for this recent work of yours?'

'No, they didn't share my vision for my latest project,' Brodie said, and in such a way that made it clear what he thought of that. 'Though apparently they were willing to put funds into last night's farce…'

After much patient ego stroking, Addison was relieved to find they finally appeared to be approaching what they'd come for.

'Oh, yes. What did you think of the show?' Addison said.

Brodie sighed, huffing out a great, dramatic breath as if he himself was performing on stage that very second – though the effect was undercut a little by his persistent, low-level twitchiness. 'I am a strong supporter of the arts in all their many wonderful, important, ground-breaking forms. So I went. But last night... how can I say this?' Brodie looked skyward, hunting for inspiration. 'Derivative, to put it kindly.'

'No, it's not everyone's cup of tea, is it?'

'And art shouldn't be. If you try to please everyone then you'll end up pleasing no one. But calling last night's efforts "art"? No. Not even close.'

'Still, it's a shame you didn't enjoy it,' Addison said. 'Did – uh – did those you were with enjoy the show, at least?' Which was his way of asking if anyone could vouch for Brodie's whereabouts throughout the Spooky Showcase, provide him an alibi.

'Is anyone ever with anyone else, *really*?' Brodie said, staring off into nowhere. 'Our paths may intersect on occasion, but we move through this world entirely alone...'

Addison went to clarify but Brodie held a hand up in his face to interrupt any comment. He rummaged through his layers before eventually pulling out a small, dark leather-bound notebook, unwound the wrap-around strap, and quickly scrawled something inside, presumably his latest philosophical utterance.

Brodie surfaced from his note-taking. 'What was I saying? Yes, my thoughts on the "art" of drag are no secret.

179

Copycat, derivative, lacking any integrity, it is not *important*. Who cares if it's entertaining, fun, supposedly joyful and welcoming? The only real, truthful part of the show was that impromptu finale. Inspired. Though it's a shame it took an accident to create any real art.'

Such breathtaking callousness. Addison was too shocked to respond to the idea that apparently the loss of someone's life was hardly worth mentioning. Surely *that* was the real shame here.

'Though should we be surprised? It was inevitable.'

Brodie may have been dropping bomb after hateful bomb, but that last comment caught Addison's attention. He glanced at Mabel, whose eyebrow was already raised, clearly having caught it herself.

'Inevitable?' Mabel said. 'Why do you say that?'

'Setting aside any discussions around creative merit,' Brodie said, though it clearly pained him to do so, 'the whole production was unprofessional, unsafe. I was helping out in the lead-up to the show – supporting the community, you know, we all do our bit. But in the end, I just couldn't be associated with such a thing. Cut finger, broken leg – that's before the show even started. Then on the night itself they had a malfunctioning trapdoor. As I say, inevitable.'

'I didn't know you'd helped out—'

Brodie held up a hand. 'Early on, yes. But it didn't take me long to see the show was unsalvageable. Patrick didn't want to hear it, of course. Didn't appreciate my insights. He just wanted to pull on that ridiculous character of his, Lady Perry Less, and flounce about on stage. No regard for artistry or health and safety. If you ask me, well, it should've been the captain going down with his ship.'

'Right, yeah…' Addison absently nodded along, his

mind firing. He needed to keep Brodie talking while he organised his thoughts, in case he found he had more questions he wanted to ask. Addison brought the conversation back to what he suspected was Brodie's favourite topic: himself.

'You mentioned before that tonight was a little teaser of what's to come. So, when can we look forward to seeing your show?'

'Creatively, it is ready. Practically, there are a few minor details to iron out. All dependent on other people.' Brodie tsked, shaking his head. 'There's procuring technical support, and a venue in which to stage my production, ticketing, and other such minutiae. Then there's the need for additional patronage to fund the necessary evil that is promotion – an indictment on society, truly, but it is the society in which we live. I am yet to secure patrons with the necessary vision to take this on, my most ambitious project yet.'

'Your current *patrons* aren't willing to invest further?'

'They are not. They will be kicking themselves once they experience the final result – a *proper* show – wishing they'd had the vision to follow through when it counted most, which is right now.' Brodie paused, looking Addison up and down, as if for the first time. 'You're not from around here, are you?'

'Ah, no. Not until fairly recently,' Addison said. 'An unexpected inheritance brought me up from Wellington.'

Brodie's former dismissiveness suddenly turned attentive. 'An inheritance? Based on your interest this evening, you seem like someone with an eye for meaningful, important art. I think I would be willing to allow you to become a patron of mine, for the right sum.'

Chapter 23

It took a while, but Addison and Mabel managed to extricate themselves from their conversation with Brodie. It had been painful to witness – the desperation for funding battling with his apparent need to appear as if he remained above it all.

'What a piece of work,' Addison said the moment they were clear.

'The art or the artist?'

Addison scoffed. 'Both.'

'He has a real chip on his shoulder, doesn't he?'

Addison and Mabel took their time completing a circuit of the Halloween night market, debriefing as they went. The conclusion they reached was that, setting aside Brodie's lofty and spiteful attitude, his comments had added to the growing picture of a slapdash stance on health and safety backstage.

They caught the last few minutes of *The Nightmare Before Christmas*, standing at the back behind the lawn full of moviegoers sprawled on picnic blankets or seated in low-slung, portable camping chairs. The credits rolled and at least half the audience packed themselves up and headed home, with more than a few small children already partially or fully asleep, clutching onto their parents.

Mabel collected a sleepy Sophia from her friend's family before turning back to Addison. 'I take it from your lack of any bags that you haven't brought anything to sit on for your movie?'

'Ah, no.' Addison winced. 'I hadn't planned to be here when I left the house earlier. I wonder if any of the stallholders are selling—'

Mabel unshouldered the black tote bag she'd been carrying around all evening and handed it to Addison. 'You can borrow mine.'

He started to protest but she cut him off.

'Consider it my thanks for keeping me company this evening,' she said, 'and for your part in saving me from watching that movie yet again.'

'Well, when you put it like that.'

'Now, there's a picnic blanket in there with a waterproof underside, and a woollen blanket for on top.'

'Mabel, my saviour.'

'I wouldn't want you boys catching a chill, now, would I? The temperature has dropped a bit. I hope it's enough – if not, you'll just have to cosy up a bit.' Mabel's final comment was accompanied by a sly wink.

Addison felt the heat already shooting up his neck and across his cheeks. He bit back a smile and said, 'I'm sure we'll manage.'

'I'm sure you will.' Mabel smiled and turned to her granddaughter. 'Ready to go?'

Sophia nodded and Mabel waved over her shoulder as they walked off.

Addison hadn't had a chance to say, but he'd been glad

of her company too – it saved him from working himself into a tizzy counting down the minutes until his date do-over. Even so, in the thirty seconds he'd been by himself, he'd already found something to agonise over. Should he claim a spot and set up camp, or wait until Jake arrived in case he wanted to have a wander around the night market too?

He glanced up at the clocktower – just about nine o'clock, so half an hour until the scheduled screening of *Sleepy Hollow* – and when he looked back down again he spotted someone he was very pleased to see.

Walking towards him was Sergeant Jake Murphy, looking as handsome as ever and smiling the moment he spotted Addison. He wasn't in uniform, nor was he in costume – just regular clothes. Addison walked over to meet him, and before he even had a chance to say a word, Jake had leant in for a quick kiss before wrapping his arms around Addison, giving him a brief squeeze before stepping back and smiling once more. 'Hi.'

Addison smiled right back. 'Hi,' he said, deciding this was an excellent start to their date do-over.

'I hope I didn't keep you waiting long?'

'Oh, all of a minute.'

'OK, good.'

'Busy day?'

'Yeah, it was. Just finished and I came straight over here…' Jake looked at the crowd around them, with more than a few full-on costumes and the majority of attendees having at least made a token effort. 'As you can see, I have come out tonight as an undercover plain-clothes police officer.'

'Ah yes, a classic Halloween costume,' Addison said even

as his mind ran away from him, cherry-picking Jake's words and considering them in a different light, fixating instead on getting 'under' the 'cover' of his 'clothes'. He quickly reined things in, deciding it was best he kept those thoughts to himself, at least while they were in public. 'And as you can see,' Addison said, gesturing to his face painting, 'I am a pirate.'

'Arrr.' The heartiness of Jake's pirate snarl matched the effort Addison had put into his pirate makeover.

'I'll have you walking the plank if you don't watch out.'

Jake's eyes brightened, clearly amused. 'I'd like to see you try,' he said, before looking around them. 'But in the meantime, shall we have a wander around, unless you've already had your fill?'

'I'm very happy to go again.'

And so they did. Addison noticed the demographic had shifted, with the kids having been scooped up and returned home to bed. Now it was just hordes of teenagers either loudly showing off or pretending like they weren't lapping it all up, and then pairs or small groups of adults.

He could have easily spent the evening with Jake and not once raised Cilla Slay's untimely demise, but he had promised Mabel he would speak to him about it. Better to dispense with that early, so the need didn't niggle at the back of his consciousness all night. Get it out of the way so he could focus on enjoying himself and, more importantly, enjoying Jake.

As they did a leisurely lap of the stalls and amusements, Addison quickly brought Jake up to date with all he'd learnt since the previous night, including information he'd gleaned from Gary Farnham, Paul Stewart, and Brodie Seatter-Dent.

Jake seemed a little distracted, but Addison assumed he

was just processing the new information, seeing how it fitted in with what he already knew.

Eventually Jake said he'd follow up with the lighting and sound technician, Kieran Nash, as he hadn't volunteered his dating history when Jake had interviewed him the night before. Addison wanted to speak to Kieran himself, but also recognised that this wasn't his investigation and he was not in charge. More importantly, Jake seemed more open to Addison's involvement this time, willing to consider him an asset in the inquiry as opposed to an impediment, or worse, a danger to himself. Addison didn't want to overreach and ruin that.

'I forgot to ask last night,' Addison said. 'Did you get a chance to look at the trapdoor mechanism?'

'Yeah, I did. It all looked to be in working order, operated as expected. No sign of distress on the components, no evidence of tampering.'

'Right, OK,' Addison said slowly, thinking over the implications. He was at least pleased to finally have the trapdoor mechanism's fitness confirmed, even though he hadn't had a chance to check it out for himself. He also felt relieved to have dealt with his duties and followed through on his promises, leaving the evening wide open for... well, for whatever it might bring.

'The movie will be on soon,' Jake said, apparently recognising the quick debrief had concluded, and possibly even trying to nudge the conversation away from what for him was work chat. 'Shall we get some snacks?'

'That sounds great,' Addison said, very willing to shift the topic.

'I saw a popcorn cart just over there?'

'Oh, yeah—'

Jake had quietly slipped his hand into Addison's, wiping any thoughts from his mind and words from his mouth, before leading them back the way they'd come.

Addison was too shocked, delightfully so, to say anything or do anything other than accompany Jake. His hand was warm, somehow soft and smooth yet rough and firm at the same time, and just very nice overall. Addison tightened his grip ever so slightly.

Jake held Addison's hand as they bought movie snacks – Addison getting an ice cream and Jake a bucket of popcorn.

Addison eyed up a few other sweet treats he'd quite like, but buying anything else would mean giving something up. One hand held the ice cream he'd just bought, the tote bag over that shoulder. The other hand was currently holding Jake's, and he wasn't about to relinquish that.

He held on until it was time to spread out their blankets – the one with the waterproof base below, the cosy woollen one above, with Addison and Jake comfortably sandwiched in between.

Tucked up, Addison soon finished his ice cream. He briefly mourned the end of something so delicious, but immediately realised he now had *two* free hands. With one hand, Addison helped himself to Jake's popcorn, and with the other, he reclaimed Jake's hand in time for the movie to start.

Chapter 24

Far from the dread apparently experienced by many come Monday morning, Addison tended to feel the opposite. It was arbitrary, really, but a new week meant a fresh start.

Despite yet another unexpected dead body in his life, Addison was feeling good about things. He and Jake may have had one date end rather abruptly, to say the least, but they'd quickly followed it up with one that was infinitely more successful.

They'd both enjoyed *Sleepy Hollow* on Saturday night, then returned to Harper House, where Jake had stayed over. Neither was in any rush to get out of bed the next morning either, both luxuriating in a lazy start to their Sunday. However, soon enough Jake had to head off, saying he had things to sort out at his place.

Addison always enjoyed spending time with Jake, so hated to see him go.

Keith, on the other hand, seemed pleased with this development. The fiery ginger feline had been furious about his overnight bedroom eviction. Addison had spent Sunday assuaging his own guilt by offering cat treats, which Keith pretended he didn't care about but pounced on regardless.

It was for the best, though. If Jake had spent the day, Addison knew he wouldn't have been able to concentrate on sorting himself out for the following day – that is, the first day of his new job.

Addison had ironed a shirt and gone through – once again – the limited information he had about his new role.

He even had time to quiz himself on the road code in preparation for his upcoming learner driver licence test – unrelated to the new role, but also important. It was only a theory test, but who knew there were so many road rules, any one of which he could be tested on?

Addison had kept quiet about his road code studying and the fact he'd booked himself in to sit the test – he wanted to surprise Jake with it.

But first, he had a job to do.

Before that, though: coffee.

The brief walk into town was much the same as it always was except for the sudden appearance of fireworks for sale. Signs had been cable-tied to street lights, A-frame signs had popped up on footpaths, and a shipping container had materialised in what was an otherwise vacant lot normally used for overflow car parking. The signage all featured explosive, eye-catching imagery and much urgent language making it clear fireworks would only be sold for four days.

It was all a bit much.

However, one place Addison could take refuge until he was sufficiently caffeinated to face the world was Lynne's Cafe, often described by Lynne as her 'cosy little corner on the square'.

The bell tinkled overhead as Addison stepped inside and Lynne beamed as he approached the counter. She sported yet another new apron from her apparently inexhaustible supply. This one featured an image of fireworks exploding from a coffee cup above text that read 'Unsupervised children will be given an espresso and a box of firecrackers.'

'That's quite the threat,' Addison said with a smile, nodding to the apron.

Lynne chuckled, clearly delighted. 'Oh, I wouldn't really,' she said before quickly narrowing her eyes and pinning Addison with a look. 'Or would I?' Lynne held the look for all of a second before her expression softened and she laughed again, smoothing down her apron. 'I like to keep it topical sometimes. It's that time of year again, isn't it? Halloween over the weekend – though from what I hear, it all got a bit too real. Just terrible.' Lynne sighed and shook her head. 'But now that's done and we're right into Guy Fawkes – only a few days until Bonfire Night.'

'Yeah, I saw the posters on my way in.'

'That'll keep our fire and police departments busy, I'm sure. It's always a bit of fun, but I hope nobody gets too silly this year.' Lynne tsked, hand on a hip. 'Anyway, how are you, love?'

'Yeah, good.'

'Now, what day is it?' she said, her eyes widening as she finally clocked his appearance. He'd erred on the slightly dressier side of 'corporate casual' – that being the specified dress code, whatever that meant. 'Is it today? It is, isn't it? Your big first day in the mayor's office?'

'It is indeed. HR asked me to come in at ten so they could get a few things sorted before I arrived.'

'That's good, easing in to your first day,' she said as she moved behind the coffee machine, already very familiar with Addison's order.

'It'll be strange, being back in an office.'

'Don't you worry, they'll look after you over there. Speaking of, how's our sergeant? Is he looking after you?'

Addison felt his cheeks warming at the thought of how Jake had looked after him over the weekend, but cleared his throat and managed to at least repeat his response from earlier. 'Yeah, good. He's good.'

'Has he sorted out a place then?'

That was an odd thing to say and an odd way to say it, the confusion effective in dousing any over-excited reminiscing. Lynne was busy back there, so only fair if she said something a bit wonky – Addison knew what she meant. She did have her finger on Milverton's pulse, so much so that she apparently knew Jake was sorting out things around his place.

'Um, I don't know if he's finished,' Addison said, 'but he was working on it at his place yesterday.'

'Ah yes, certainly not a one-day job, is it? It's amazing how much *stuff* you can accumulate in only a year or two.'

Addison murmured his agreement, though he was more confused than ever.

'Moving house is a big job, and only gets bigger each time, I swear.'

Lynne banged and crashed around behind the coffee machine, so she couldn't see the look of shock no doubt plastered all over Addison's face, nor could she hear the uncertainty in his voice. 'Moving house...'

'It's pretty bold of a landlord to boot the police sergeant out of his rental. Not that our Sergeant Murphy would give him a hard time because of it, of course. He's too much of a professional for that.'

'Booted out...?'

'Oh, you know what I mean. Not letting the fixed-term

tenancy roll over into another year. Apparently the landlord wants the property back so a cousin or a niece or someone can rent the place. The sergeant has enough on his plate without having to go hunting for a new place to live. Anyway, one oat flat white and what can I get you from the cabinet today?'

Addison normally took such delight in poring over the day's baked treat offerings, giving serious consideration to making his selection. Today however, he stared through the glass, not registering a thing. Eventually his eyes landed on the brownie and he said that's what he'd like, thank you.

'And one square of chocolate brownie dusted with icing sugar. Perfect.' Lynne set down Addison's coffee and brownie. 'There you are. You get those down you. You're looking a little peaky, love – I hope you don't mind me saying. Caffeine and sugar, that'll put you right.'

'Thanks, Lynne,' Addison said.

Then, on autopilot, he went to pay but Lynne waved him away.

'It's on me. Good luck today. You'll do great.'

Addison made for the nearest available table – near the front window, facing the square – and sat with his order, stunned. Jake hadn't breathed a word of his imminent eviction. Why hadn't he mentioned it – at least, more than some vague passing comments about sorting something out with his place?

He'd had plenty of opportunities to bring it up over the weekend – at the show, the night market, after the movie, at any time when they were back at Harper House that night or the following morning.

Harper House, the vast old homestead with her many rooms. Addison couldn't help thinking there was plenty of space for any of the aforementioned *stuff* Jake may have accumulated. Plenty of space for Jake.

Decent-sized beds too, not that they needed more than one. One was certainly enough for both him and Jake, and Harper House's resident feline to curl up at the foot – later on, of course – if that's what Keith wanted.

It hadn't even been two months since they'd first laid eyes on each other, and the time they'd been dating was best measured in *weeks*. Asking Jake to move in... it was too much, too soon.

Addison could absolutely understand why Jake wouldn't ask to move in.

But why wouldn't he even bring up that he was having to find a new place to live? Was he worried it would sound desperate? Like he wasn't capable of looking after himself? Or that Addison would think he was fishing for an invitation, that Addison would feel obligated to offer one? Leading to potential feelings of claustrophobia and the inevitable resentment? Killing any chance at a relationship dead in its tracks before it even had a chance to really get going?

What if... could Addison offer? Would that come across as desperate or needy, invasive or presumptuous, like he wanted to lock Jake down or make him dependent? Or some unholy combination of the lot? Addison didn't want to give off any of that.

Setting aside potential perceptions – from either side, rightly or wrongly – did he want to live with Jake? Did he want them to move in together, despite knowing each other for barely more than five minutes?

That was an easy question to answer.

The answer was yes.

No self-reflection or internal interrogation required.

Yes.

What was the alternative? Jake would move temporarily into a short-term let, lugging his stuff around town and living out of boxes and suitcases. He'd either be doing that or, if he could find something suitable quickly, jumping straight into a long-term let. That would mean at least a year.

They might not have known each other long, but Addison was optimistic. He already knew he would rather not be living apart from Jake for that long, keeping connected only with dates and sleepovers.

But how to broach the subject.

'I don't mean to kick you out, love,' Lynne said, calling out from behind the counter. 'But didn't you say you were starting at ten?'

Addison shot a look out the window at the clocktower.

Two minutes to ten and he hadn't touched his flat white or his brownie. He downed the now-cold coffee, inhaled the baked treat, and flew out the door, hand raised in farewell and thanks, the overhead bell banging instead of its usual tinkling as he did so.

Chapter 25

Addison had never given much thought to the council offices. He'd only been in them once, when interviewing for the job that he was now about to start.

The building was situated behind the town hall and the library, the opposite side to the square. Which was probably for the best as it wasn't the most attractive building. Brutalist was the word that came to mind. Not that he was any kind of architectural scholar, but Addison was pretty sure that was the word. Blocky, concrete, and overwhelmingly grey. Something from the sixties or seventies, maybe? It looked functional, with not even a cent wasted on decoration. The most notable thing about it was that it was *big*. It fronted onto Victoria Street and ran the entire block from Wyndham Street to Ruahine Street.

Addison only had a moment to consider such things before he arrived at the entrance, with brass letters picking out 'Civic Administration Building' above the door, and stepped through.

Today's receptionist – Jordan, according to their name badge, with pronouns listed below as they/them – was very polite and friendly but apparently had not been expecting him. They repositioned their rounded, wire frame glasses, consulted their screen, clicked a few times, tapped on the keyboard, clicked some more, and then returned their gaze to Addison, looking none the wiser. 'Would you like to take a seat while I make a call?'

Addison did so, and three calls later the receptionist escorted him to the mayor's office.

'Addison?'

'Yes?'

'Um, you have' – they looked him in the eye and wiped under their nose – 'icing sugar or something.'

Eyes wide, Addison shot his hand up and wiped the white dusting from his top lip, then again off his shirt front where it landed next. 'Thank you,' he said. 'Chocolate brownie topped with icing sugar from Lynne's.'

Jordan only smiled and left. Addison was grateful they'd said something, saving him from any further embarrassment, but more importantly, he hoped they believed him about the origin of the white powder. It wouldn't do to have rumours bouncing around the council building, especially not on day one.

The mayor's office wasn't vast, but it also wasn't cramped – modest was the word. It was filled with everything you might expect of such a space. All practical, nothing too flashy.

Nearest the door sat an armchair, a two-seater couch, and a low coffee table with a couple of newspapers – one local and one national, both current, Addison noticed. This setup suggested those invited to take a seat there were in for a more relaxed, friendly meeting with Milverton's mayor.

At the opposite end of the office was the mayor's desk with a closed laptop at its centre, files and documents stacked to left and right, a wheelie desk chair on the far side, and two visitors' chairs facing. Much more businesslike, though this impression was softened by the shelving that covered the entire wall behind the desk, running from floor to ceiling and wall to wall. Yes, it was stacked with ring binders and file boxes, but also biographies and novels, framed photographs, and various ornaments too eclectic to be one person's choice of decor, so presumably gifts.

After some internal deliberation, Addison opted for one of the chairs facing the mayor's desk, deciding he didn't want to appear to be making himself too comfortable.

He was starting to reassess his decision once he'd been there for a good ten minutes. His eyes had drifted to the ceremonial robes and chain of office draped over a coat rack in the corner – wondering if he might get away with trying them on – when Harriet Ferguson, Her Worship the Mayor of Milverton, blew in.

'There you are, Addison. Excellent,' the mayor said, waving him back down into his seat as she took hers behind the desk. 'We'll be working closely, you and I, so please just call me Harriet. You'll be reporting directly to me. A little unusual, but we need to be fleet-footed on this. Helping with my vision for Milverton, but also taking the initiative and responding swiftly as things come up. Which you have already proven yourself very capable of in recent weeks.'

The mayor suddenly stopped her spiel and now appeared to be waiting for a response.

'Ah, thank you,' Addison said. 'I'm looking forward to getting into it.'

'That's what I like to hear. Now, I haven't gone and hired you – someone with initiative, intuition, motivation – to then go and tell you what to do every minute of every day. I will be leaving the job up to you, Addison. However, what I ask is that you get your face out there and talk to residents, business owners, organisation representatives, visitors – anyone and everyone. Find out what they want, what they think Milverton needs. Listen to their ideas. We can take the temperature of the town, and an added bonus is it makes us look *proactive*. That is what I need you to do but how you go about it is entirely up to you. Yes?'

'Sure thing, sounds great.'

'But not today,' Harriet said, looking down and tapping her finger on the desk as if running through a list in her head. 'Today, we need to introduce you to the team, get you logged into the system, get you started on the onboarding materials, induction videos, all that. What else? Oh, you'll be based just out there – I've commandeered a space for you.'

'I'll have my own desk?'

'Of course.' Harriet looked at him briefly as if he'd said something ridiculous before she launched herself out of her chair. 'Anyway, come on, let's meet the team.'

The mayor took him on a quick lap of the open-plan area, introducing him to everyone, not that Addison remembered any of their names by the time he'd been deposited back at his very own desk.

He'd grown accustomed to a flexible working arrangement, hot-desking, whatever they wanted to call it this week. And it very much seemed to be the way everywhere was going. However, here in Milverton, everyone still had their own assigned desk – with paper folders, files, photos, and knick-knacks – but most importantly for Addison in this moment, they had little name plaques. The bronze-coloured rectangles were affixed to the edges of everyone's cubicle walls and also featured their pronouns – always helpful, and any way to minimise potential faux pas put Addison's anxious mind at ease. Forgetting someone's name or accidentally misgendering them was never not uncomfortable for all involved.

'One last thing,' the mayor said. 'An occupational health and safety investigator will be arriving shortly on account of the incident we had at the town hall on Friday night. The regulators seem to think our people have been rather too relaxed when it comes to health and safety. I have an initial meeting with this investigator now which I need to get to. And from what I'm hearing, I'm anticipating a very quick turnaround on the report. Now, Addison, I want you to start thinking about how we might package and present the initial findings – whatever they may be – at least until we can get on top of any actual problems identified. We can't have locals and visitors thinking Milverton is some deathtrap town.'

'Right, yes, sure. I should probably join you in—'

'No, no. No point in both of us sitting through that. I'll set up a meeting to discuss once I have the findings in hand. That'll be our first bit of work together but not just yet. Right now, I'll let you get your feet under the table. There's your laptop and your induction pack' – Harriet patted a glossy folder on Addison's desk with Milverton branding on the front – 'which you'll need to get through or you'll be hounded by the HR and Accounts departments to complete forms and things. And as your direct manager, I will be hounded too, so please finish them. *Please*, for my sanity and yours.'

'Will do.'

'Quick as you can. With the fallout I'm anticipating after the death on the weekend, I'll need you properly on board as soon as possible.'

'Yes, of course.'

'Right, I'll see you later.'

After his whirlwind introduction, Addison was left to get on with the familiar paperwork endured by all new employees.

Unfortunately, he couldn't. Addison might have a work laptop, but he had no way of getting into it. He quickly flicked through the induction pack, then went through more slowly for a second time, concluding that he hadn't been provided any login details to access the system. Either someone had forgotten to note that down for him or IT hadn't set up his account yet. He couldn't call IT either because he didn't know their phone number, and couldn't log into his laptop to search for the number either.

He didn't want to disturb his new colleagues, or look too clueless in front of them all of five minutes after being introduced. However, there was one person he'd looked a little silly in front of already...

Jordan, the receptionist, very patiently gave Addison instructions on where to find the IT department.

A few floors and corridors later, Addison dinged a Dalek-shaped desk bell on an unattended service counter.

After many seconds and much groaning, the most put-upon person Addison had ever laid eyes on shuffled into view.

Addison politely and succinctly outlined his situation, to which the IT person responded by advising Addison that he would need to lodge a help request ticket through the online system, all while tapping a laminated sign taped to the counter next to the desk bell that said the exact same thing.

Addison responded by saying that he was unable to do

so because of the aforementioned situation – that is, he didn't have access to the online system, so could not, in fact, lodge a help request ticket.

The most tediously circular conversation Addison had ever experienced continued until the IT person eventually, reluctantly, 'this time only', agreed to lodge a help request ticket on Addison's behalf.

Addison ground out a thank you before he left with a promise his access should be live within 'a couple of hours'.

After a few deep breaths to calm his frustration, Addison read the printouts in the induction folder and otherwise did everything he could which didn't require access to the system.

He also noticed his name plaque holder was empty, so grabbed a sticky note to fill the space for the time being. He wrote 'Addison Harper (he/him)' and stuck it up.

***

Anxious to get started on the proper work, Addison flew through his induction tasks. Over his first two days, he powered through endless forms, blitzed emails, and watched the mandatory induction videos at double speed. Supposedly there was enough material to fill his entire first week, but that seemed like overkill, so for his own sanity he tried to get through them with a bit more pace.

Even so, the dryness of the content meant he needed to get up from his desk plenty, which his new boss had encouraged – 'Loiter around the kitchenette, meet people. Liaising with colleagues from various departments will be a big part of your work, so best you get to know everyone as soon as possible.'

Addison continued to be bombarded with names and faces, ninety percent of which he immediately forgot. Luckily, until such things had lodged themselves in his brain, all it took was a quick lap of the office while glancing at name plaques to refresh his memory.

One other aspect of working in an office environment he'd forgotten about in the time he'd been working from home, or had become desensitised to at his previous workplace, was the proliferation of laminated posters. There was, of course, the one at the IT help desk, but Addison had also been politely reminded to hold the handrail, to think twice before printing, to wash his hands, to put dirty mugs directly into the dishwasher, to mind his step, to refrain from reheating fish dishes in the microwave, to leave meeting rooms as he found them, and to keep his staff ID card on him at all times, among many, many more.

Addison was looking forward to getting into the job properly, meeting more Milvertonians, and getting word out there about all the fun and fascinating things happening in Milverton. The mayor's great charm offensive would involve him working with newspapers, magazines, radio stations, businesses, and online content creators; designing, printing, and distributing posters; developing social media content and creating online ad campaigns; attending events, and even possibly getting involved in organising them. Moral of the story: lots of interesting and varied things which Addison couldn't wait to get stuck into.

***

Wednesday morning – day three of his new employment – there was a light rain over Milverton. Not for the first time,

202

Addison wondered why he was surprised, considering how green the town and the surrounding district were. The brisk walk in his waterproof jacket meant he arrived at the office a little overheated and proportionately irritated.

His suspicions that he looked a bit bedraggled were confirmed by the faint eyebrow raise from Jordan as Addison passed reception. However, silver linings and all that, the briskness of the walk meant he'd arrived a few minutes early, with enough time spare to shake off the rain and get his hair looking less like the haphazard bird's nest he knew it must be.

Addison had dropped his bag at his desk and was one step into his mission to the bathroom mirror when he heard his name being called.

It was the mayor, his boss, calling from her office.

He might not be looking his best, but he reasoned she'd be less concerned about that than she would if one of her subordinates immediately walked away from her after she'd just summoned them.

Addison made do with running a hand through his hair and otherwise embraced his lightly drowned rat aesthetic. He grabbed a pen and notepad before stepping through his boss's office door.

Behind the desk was the mayor herself, waving him in. And in one of the visitor's chairs, eyes widening at Addison's appearance, was Sergeant Jake Murphy.

Chapter 26

Addison had told himself that he was being good, restraining himself, keeping out of the police's way, allowing them to do their work. But really, he'd been so focused on making a solid first impression at work that he'd had little brain space to puzzle over the untimely death of Cilla Slay.

As far as that situation went, his job was to help manage the narrative and control the damage to Milverton's reputation. That was his job, the one he'd been employed to do and which he was being paid to do. Plenty enough to be getting on with without actively working to resolve Cilla's unexplained death, though it could be argued that doing so went hand in hand with Addison's official role.

Even if it didn't, he still owed it to his friend to swing a spotlight onto the situation, so to speak. He wanted to give Mabel the peace of mind that she hadn't been in any way at fault. When it came to that side of things, Addison's ongoing involvement was much less official.

He had already passed on everything he knew to the police – via one Sergeant Jake Murphy – but now had nothing new to go on. Addison knew what he *could* do… He could start casting a wider net, knocking on the doors of people even more tenuously connected to Cilla Slay specifically and the Spooky Showcase in general. However, with his new job, he just didn't have the time or the flexibility for that kind of approach. Even if he did, he expected asking such questions would get people asking who he thought he was sticking his nose into their business, and that would be a very valid question.

Instead, Addison had been anticipating getting information by other means... Not that he had any expectation of officials reporting to him, but he also expected that he'd hear something some way or another. There was the mayor – also his boss – with the preliminary results of the health and safety investigation and then there was the sergeant – also the man he was seeing – with developments of the police investigation.

Addison hadn't known when he might catch wind of such things, but now it appeared he might be about to hear both.

'Come in, come in. Don't just stand there. Join us,' the mayor said. 'Perfect timing.'

'Sorry, I didn't realise we had a meeting.'

'We didn't, but now we do. I've only just put it in our calendars.'

Probably for the best that Addison hadn't had any advance warning or he might've worked himself into a state.

Addison took the spare visitor's chair beside Jake.

'It's good to see you, Addison,' Jake said, a small smile playing on his lips.

'You too,' Addison said, unable to help himself from smiling back.

The mayor tsked and rolled her eyes. 'The pair of you,'

she said, snapping her fingers. 'We have much too much to cover for you two to be making cow eyes at each other.' She followed up the admonishment with a snort of amusement which took any real sting out of the words. 'In saying that, I am very happy for you both, but it's not going to get in the way, is it?'

'Oh, no. No, no. It's – uh – no,' Addison said with little eloquence and much fluster.

Jake damped down his own smile. 'No, Mayor Ferguson.'

This meeting was the first time Addison and Jake had spoken or seen each other in person since they'd had breakfast together at Harper House on Sunday morning. Or more pertinently, since Addison had found out from Lynne that Jake was being evicted from his place.

They'd exchanged a few brief messages over the past couple of days, but Jake hadn't mentioned anything about it and Addison hadn't wanted to ask via text message. And now he wasn't about to ask in front of Harriet – he would wait until they were alone together.

Even then, they hadn't known each other long – had been dating only a few weeks, with plenty going on in that time – so it was probably unreasonable to expect Jake to share such important and personal things. Logically, Addison knew this, but emotionally it was a touch more difficult to convince himself…

In that moment, Addison committed to getting through the first week at his new job and allowing Jake to get through his latest investigation. Perhaps *then* he might ask about Jake's living situation.

For now, all he had to do to arrest any errant smiles was think about Jake not confiding in him. That was the position

Addison adopted, hoping it would put him in good stead for getting through this professional, very not personal, meeting.

'Excellent,' Mayor Ferguson said. 'Now, it's that time of year again, so before we get into what I called you both in here for, I want to quickly discuss fireworks.'

'We've had a busy couple of days since they went on sale,' Jake said. 'But it's roughly in line with what we'd expected based on incidents and callouts – for us and the fire department – from the past couple of years.'

'That's good, I suppose. Or at least not bad,' Harriet said. 'But what's this I heard about last night? A literal bin fire?'

'Ah, yes. A bunch of high school students. One of them got their older brother to buy a few strings of firecrackers and a couple of big shells and missiles. All was going fine apparently until they decided to light one and drop it in a recycling wheelie bin, slamming the lid closed before it reached the end of the fuse.'

'Now why on Earth would they want to do that?' the mayor said, shaking her head.

'They said they wanted to see what would happen.'

'I can blimmin' well tell them what would happen.'

'They reckoned it was educational, a science experiment. Not that anyone was buying that, of course.'

'I should hope not,' Harriet said. 'Did someone suggest for their next experiment that they might like to hop in the bin themselves too, see what happened then?'

Jake huffed out an amused breath. 'We didn't want to give them any more ideas.'

'Probably for the best. We don't know what these soft-headed little pyromaniacs might be capable of. Anyway, what was the damage?'

'The bin caught fire, melting the plastic, and setting the rubbish in the bin next to it alight – more fuel for the flames. It's lucky we've had a bit of rain lately and with more forecast today, it stopped things getting further out of hand before the fire department could put it out.'

'Lucky indeed, fingers crossed it'll dampen their enthusiasm for venturing outside to let more off in the coming days. The public sale ban can't come soon enough – it'll happen, mark my words. The council puts on a safe, professional display that looks ten times better than what Joe Public can buy from those pop-up stores anyway. And then there's the bonfire too – well attended every year.' Harriet was shaking her head again. 'Anyway, this is the backdrop we're working with while we have our friendly health and safety investigator prowling around town. Speaking of, this landed in my inbox late last night,' she said, shaking the printout in her hand. 'The investigator's preliminary findings.'

The mayor had wanted to believe Cilla Slay's death was just a terrible, unavoidable accident, but the investigator had other ideas. She summarised the investigator's notes, which plainly said they'd found the health and safety culture within the theatre company to be fatally lacking. They then went on to relay an exhaustive list of the most minor, inconsequential issues. Harriet scoffed before sharing a few of her favourites: a sprinkling of glitter on the floor backstage creating a slip hazard; a dirty coffee cup left on a makeup table being a potential hygiene issue; and gaffer tape holding down cables scuffed at the edges forming a trip hazard.

'It's a load of nonsense, nothing I've seen here suggests "fatally lacking" to me,' Harriet said, slapping the printout in disgust. 'I'm sure there are health and safety improvements to be made, and likely always will be. But if this is all they have to point to, then the theatre company and the town hall are in better shape than even this office. Anyway, apparently we can look forward to their full report, including recommendations, within two weeks. I expect it will be much the same, just in more tedious detail.'

'Two weeks?' Jake said. 'I don't think we can wait around for that, not when we're still open to so many *other* outstanding possibilities.'

'I quite agree,' Harriet said. 'One of those possibilities being a terrible accident, of course. But until we can confidently confirm that's the case, which I fully expect it will be, then we must continue to investigate. Do you have any updates for me, Sergeant?'

Just as the mayor had brought them up to speed on the investigator's preliminary results, Jake summarised his follow-up interview with the lighting and sound technician, Kieran Nash, after Addison had discovered his former romantic relationship with the victim. Kieran's excuse for not mentioning it was that, in his words, 'that was ancient history,' and he thought saying anything about it would only make him look bad.

Addison scoffed. 'It looks worse *not* saying anything about it.'

'Agreed,' Jake said with a nod. 'But no matter how it looks, at the time of death he was stationed at the tech booth – where all the show's lights and sound are controlled from – an alibi which I have already been able to verify.'

Addison's immediate reaction was disappointment. He felt no particular ill will towards Kieran Nash and he hadn't expected his lead to point to the smoking gun just like that, but he had hoped his input might've helped Jake progress the investigation in some small way. He felt like they were no closer to the truth than they'd been when Cilla Slay fell head-first through the open trapdoor. 'So,' he said, 'a dead end then?'

'Oh, no. Kieran had a lot to say for himself.' Jake briefly flashed his eyes wide at Addison. 'He was much more open and willing to volunteer his own thoughts and suggestions this time.'

'I suspect that having the police's undivided attention might *encourage* someone to be more helpful, especially if it might shift the police's attention onto someone else?' Harriet said.

Jake nodded. 'I suspect you're right. So, if he was just saying these things to hurry us off his doorstep, we have to take what he says with a grain of salt.' Jake pulled out and flipped open a small notepad. 'Kieran offered potential motives for Spooky Showcase producer and Lady Perry Less creator Patrick Laurence; carpenter, odd-jobs man, and set builder Gary Farnham; a few names of those responsible for the show's ticketing; backstage crew; other actors and musicians; and a number of contemporaries from the theatre school Simeon Clay – AKA Cilla Slay – attended.'

Addison shouldn't have been so quick to despair – it sounded like they had plenty to be getting on with.

Harriet drew her lips into a tight line. 'That is a lot of names.'

'Yes, a rather long list I'm working my way through.' Jake briefly glanced at Addison. 'There was one other name that cropped up.'

'Who was that?' Harriet said.

Jake looked in Addison's direction again and so he was

fully expecting his name to be the next out of Jake's mouth. Instead he said, 'Johanna van Niekerk.'

Addison frowned, feeling like he'd heard the name recently but couldn't remember when or where. 'Who's that?'

'She runs a costume shop here in town,' Harriet said, murmuring as she thought it over.

'Ah, right.' Addison nodded. 'Cilla was dragging her wigs during the show – "hideous", "nasty", and "cheap" were the words I think she used.'

Harriet tutted. 'Johanna was certainly not best pleased to hear that.'

'I was wondering if, well…' Jake said before trailing off.

Harriet picked up his half-finished thought. 'You were wondering if Addison might be better placed to ask Johanna a few questions?'

Meanwhile Addison was wondering why he might be better placed. He was also wondering if this might just be a case of throwing him a bone so he kept his nose out of other, more important business.

'Yes,' Jake said, 'but perhaps that wouldn't be—'

The mayor held up a hand. 'An excellent idea. The sooner we can resolve this, the better. It's all hands on deck. By your own admission, you have plenty to be getting on with. And, from what I hear, Johanna's more likely to speak to someone not in a police uniform at the moment anyway.'

Addison looked between the mayor and the sergeant. 'Uh… why's that?' He was very happy to help, but the fact this woman apparently had beef with the police was surely a cause for concern. On the other hand, Jake may have held back certain things from Addison but he knew Jake would never suggest sending him into a dodgy or dangerous situation.

Jake sighed and shook his head. 'We had to suspend her driver's licence recently. Too many speeding fines. She was never over the limit by much, but still managed to accumulate enough demerit points within two years to get a three-month suspension. That was only the other week, and she's not too happy about it.'

'So she's unlikely to be any more helpful with police matters than she's legally required to be at the moment,' Harriet said, receiving a nod of confirmation from Jake before she turned to Addison. 'It's probably worth you stopping into her shop anyway, in your new official capacity. I'm sure she'll have plenty to say.'

They wrapped up the meeting soon after that and Addison returned to his desk. He was about to take a seat when Jake appeared at his side.

'Hey.'

'Hey.'

'How are you doing?' Jake said, keeping his voice low to avoid being overheard by too many of Addison's desk neighbours.

'Yeah, good.'

'Thanks for taking on one of the follow-ups.'

'Of course.'

'Sorry I've been so busy—'

'That's fine, no worries,' Addison said, and he meant it. At least as far as Jake's work and the investigation were concerned.

'Did you want to do lunch today?' Jake said. 'It'd be good to see you properly, hear how your first couple of days have gone?'

'That would've been great, but I – uh – have an

appointment over my lunch break,' Addison said.

Jake didn't immediately respond, as if waiting for the elaboration that was not offered. 'OK,' Jake said, his smile a little strained. 'Another day?'

'Sure thing.'

Chapter 27

Addison had struck up conversation in the kitchenette while waiting for his tea to brew, but his heart wasn't in it. Small talk was never particularly inspiring, but after the meeting in the mayor's office – not to mention his distant and rather awkward parting with Jake – it was even more difficult to engage in weather chat.

He returned to his induction to-do list, picking off a few more items, completing and submitting the mandated 'Workstation Ergonomics Self-Assessment' as he finished his cup of tea.

A quick glance at the clock confirmed Addison still had time before his scheduled learner driver test over his lunch break but he realised he couldn't quite bring himself to embark on yet another task that promised to be just as stimulating as the last. He also refused to sit idle as that would inevitably mean stewing on Jake.

Why not get a jump on his introductory tour of Milverton's businesses and do his designated questioning while at it? No time like the present.

Addison logged off, grabbed his jacket, and left the building.

Johanna's Costume Closet and Prop Emporium – commonly referred to as Jojo's Co Clo, according to Mabel – was located through a nondescript door at the end of a street-art-painted alleyway that started next to the betting shop.

Initially dubious, Addison then spotted the haphazardly outfitted mannequin positioned under a rainbow umbrella beside the door and knew this must be the place.

From the outside, he'd expected a cupboard-sized shop poked in behind the nearby shops, but what he stepped into was truly cavernous. The equivalent of two or three storeys in height, the only light came from the windows in the roof and the strip lighting hanging between them. No windows on the walls at all, which suggested this warehouse space filled the entire block behind the backs of the smaller, street-facing shops on all sides.

The space was far from empty, with rows of racks extending well overhead storing and presenting an obscene range of items, everything you could feasibly need to put together a costume – wigs, hats, crowns, fascinators, shirts, trousers, dresses, capes, jewellery, presumably fake weaponry, amongst so much else. Such was the extent of the items that ladders leant against many of the racks to access everything out of reach.

If he'd known such a place existed, he might have put a little more effort into his outfits over the weekend. Addison was still gawping, taking everything in as he slowly wandered up one of the aisles, when he heard his name being called.

'Addison Harper!'

The voice's owner stalked towards him, carrying herself with a confidence and grace that anyone would envy, a brightly coloured shawl streaming in her wake. The way she moved, Addison would've picked her as a dancer.

'Ah, hi,' he said. They'd never met but Mabel had pointed her out on Friday night, and perhaps someone had done the same for him in reverse? 'And you must be Johanna?'

'That's me, or Jojo if you prefer,' Johanna said as she reached him, putting out a hand for a firm handshake. 'I was in the audience on Friday night, with my crew. Saw you up on stage.'

Addison didn't want to volunteer that he too had seen her, clearly fired up during the interval when speaking to the mayor. 'Yes,' he said instead. 'I didn't expect to be up there on the judging panel.'

'And you were chatting with Mabel Zhou before the show, weren't you?' she said. 'Yes, I noticed her. Wanted to see how her Morticia Addams turned out. Perfect, just as I knew it would.'

'Yes, Mabel looked amazing,' Addison said while absently wondering at Johanna's strong South African accent, the decades in New Zealand having barely scuffed even the edges off it.

'That Cilla Slay though,' Johanna said before pulling a face like she'd just caught a whiff of a fresh dog turd.

Addison had intended to discuss his new role in working with the mayor to market Milverton, and had been working up a few ways he might slowly and subtly broach the subject of Cilla Slay's untimely death. It turned out he needn't be coy about it – they were going straight in.

'She looked great too,' Addison said, conscious that Cilla had been wearing some of Johanna's products. 'But wow, she was… unpleasant.'

'"Unpleasant" would not be the word I would use to

describe her, much too gentle. But yes, *unpleasant*. She called all this' – Johanna spread an arm wide, waving it around the space with a flourish – 'a "tacky little shop" as if I was running some cheap dollar store. Excuse her very much.'

'Oh yes, that was quite nasty.'

'Yes, that's a better word. She called my wigs nasty, well I call *her* nasty. I idolised her, I did. Watched her on TV – the costumes, the reveals, I thought she was wonderful.' Johanna scoffed. 'Then she goes and has a go at me, about my supposedly poor-quality products. She wasn't shy in telling everyone either, wanted them to know she didn't have her actual wigs with her, which she's very proud of and precious about. Understandable, but no need to tear me and my business down just because she couldn't keep track of her luggage...'

Johanna had trailed off, appearing as if she might be about to wrap up her tirade, shake her head to dismiss all that drama, and ask what she could do for Addison today. He hated to prod a sore spot, but he couldn't have her changing the topic until he'd had a chance to ask his questions. 'Cilla made a real point of mentioning it, didn't she?' he said. 'And in the opening number too.'

Apparently that was all it took to fire her up again. 'Oh! I could not believe it when I heard that,' Johanna said, sufficiently re-engaged. 'I try to help her out at the last minute and that's the thanks I get? Now, do you know what was most galling?'

She paused, apparently awaiting Addison's input.

'What?' he said, playing along.

'The accusations of poor quality. I'm an upholsterer by trade, so I know how to sew things together that won't be coming apart in a hurry, don't you worry. These costumes need to be sturdy so they last, especially when you have queens tucking themselves into them. Don't want any wardrobe malfunctions on stage, nothing bursting out mid-performance, do we?' Johanna huffed, clearly agitated, scrabbling around for more evidence to defend herself. 'Ah! My dance crew's costumes? We're all different shapes and sizes and I've made every single one of them – no issues, no complaints. And we look *fabulous*, I don't mind saying so.'

Addison barely had to say a thing. Johanna was bold and loud and had no apparent filter. Instead he focused on wearing his most attentive, understanding, open face. Nodding and murmuring agreement and outrage at all the right points, but otherwise leaving Johanna to it.

Also, not that it mattered for the situation at hand, but he was quietly pleased he'd picked that Johanna was a dancer.

'No, I'm glad Cilla bit the boards,' Johanna said. Addison couldn't help his eyes widening at the statement, but he said nothing, leaving Johanna to continue. 'That's what she gets for swooping in here thinking she's Little Miss Muckety Muck. I know queens spend big on their wigs, perfected and personalised for each look. I have good stuff, I stand by it, but nothing bespoke. What did she expect me to put together in *one afternoon*? And the day before Halloween no less? I have a lot of great stuff for hire, and despite already supplying half of Milverton it felt like, I had a lot left to offer the day before Halloween. Still, it was *the day before Halloween*.'

'A busy week, I assume?'

Johanna scoffed. 'Do bears you-know-what in the woods? You bet. The busiest week in my entire year. I run a costume hire shop, and Cilla rubbished me and my business – which I've built up over twenty years and I'm very proud of. And she rubbished my team. We were in the audience – me and my team from here at the shop, and some of my dance crew too. We thought it would be a nice night out, enjoy someone else performing for us for a change. But then we get *that*.'

Addison felt for Johanna, but his key takeaway from her latest rant update was that it sounded like she had an alibi. 'She was not a gracious hostess,' Addison said for want of anything more insightful to contribute.

'Addison Harper, you have quite the knack for understatement,' Johanna said with a laugh. 'Yes, and if that wasn't bad enough, talk about dying on stage. But then to *literally* die like that. Wouldn't wish it on anyone, but if it had to happen to someone, well, shall we just say Cilla Slay earnt her spot on that shortlist.' Johanna flashed her eyes wide as she pulled her brightly coloured shawl in around her.

'You didn't, you know…' Addison said with a quick shuffle of his eyebrows, leaning in conspiratorially. 'You didn't have a hand in bumping her to the top of the shortlist? Bumping her *off* that shortlist, even.'

'Oh, no.' Johanna's tone made it clear she thought the notion preposterous.

'Wouldn't blame you if you did.'

'If only. But, well, I suppose if someone else hadn't got to her, I might have – I was fuming. No, I don't mean that. I was fuming, all right, but no, I wouldn't have killed her. No way, not literally.' Johanna paused, considering her next comment. 'Professionally, yes. I would have destroyed her. I have my contacts up and down the country, in all the costume and prop hire places. One word from me and Cilla Slay wouldn't have even been able to hire a basic plastic sword, let alone a glamorous, show-stopping costume.'

'That'd sure be one way to kill a career.'

Johanna nodded. 'Those performers would do well to recognise that.'

'Because what's the alternative? Make everything themselves?'

'Some do, yes. That's a lot of work, and takes a lot of talent. Not too many who can pull it off.'

'What about your competitors? Those dollar stores? They sell costumes. Must be eating into your business?' Addison knew he was stirring the pot with that one.

'No, business is strong, those cheap dollar shops can't compete, their costumes fall apart if you look at them funny.'

Addison didn't quite believe her. 'Those cheap, mass-produced costumes might not have the quality, but would they serve well enough for a one-off fancy dress up?'

'Oh, sure. And I suppose you turn up to dinner parties without so much as a bottle of wine for the hosts? Good luck getting invited back again next time, you cheapskate.'

'Touché,' Addison said with a smile, before slowly tilting his head. 'So then, if we assume for a moment it wasn't a terrible accident... who do you reckon?'

'Who do I reckon what?'

'You know, did away with Cilla Slay?' Addison said before listing all the people Jake would be interviewing, each name thrown out there as if it had just come to him.

'For starters, it wasn't our Patrick, not the type. I've known him and his wonderful Lady Perry Less forever. Not the ticketing or backstage crew either, nonsense – I suspect they'd fade into the background as far as Cilla is concerned, beneath her notice, not in her crosshairs, so not burning to get their revenge. No, it had to be one of those other drama queens.' Johanna said it so dismissively, as if it should be obvious. 'Someone didn't get what they wanted and decided someone else needed to pay for it. Unfortunately for Cilla, that someone else was her.'

'Really?'

'A lot of drama in the dramatic arts. It's in the name. Should we be surprised? I am one small, but important cog in the great theatrical machine,' Johanna said as she once again threw out an arm for emphasis, her shawl fluttering in response. 'I don't like to get myself involved too much in the drama or it'd never end. Some of them, though, they do not know when to stop. They take the drama with them, don't leave it on the stage. Too involved, can't see anything beyond, nor can they put the latest drama in perspective. So what if you have fewer lines than your co-lead, is anyone going to notice? No! Get a grip. Mark my words, one of those queens – or the king – got their panties in a bunch and then took things way, way too far. Cilla had rubbed them the wrong way one too many times, they'd lost all sense and been driven to do this.'

An interesting perspective, but Johanna offered nothing in particular for Addison to latch on to. Except for the final comment about being driven... A quick glance at the time confirmed he was almost due at the testing office.

Confident there was nothing more to be gained from his visit to Johanna's Costume Closet and Prop Emporium, Addison wrapped up the conversation, thanked Johanna for the chat, and said that now he'd seen her shop he promised he'd be back in again very soon.

Chapter 28

Addison suffered for his determination to avoid sitting idle in the time between his morning meeting and his learner driver licence theory test.

He'd been so busy with work, but also bored out of his brain from all the induction material. With his head full of new things, as well as thoughts about Cilla Slay's death and Jake's living situation, he only hoped he'd retained enough of his road code study to pass the test.

What had he been thinking last week when he booked in this test slot? He had to keep telling himself that the majority of adults in New Zealand had their driver licence. Not to big himself up too much, but if they could do it then so could he.

Things started off well. He'd arrived with minutes to spare, filled in the form, provided proof of identity, passed the eye test, had the person take his photo and record his signature, and paid the application fee.

So far, so good.

Then he had to actually sit the test: thirty-five multi-choice questions assessing his knowledge of the road rules and safe driving principles. Going in he knew he had to get at least thirty-two correct. This was far above the usual fifty percent required for a passing grade, only allowing for three incorrect answers. Though, probably for the best, considering controlling multiple tonnes of steel, glass, and rubber at great speed – while dodging other multi-tonne machines also travelling at great speed, not to mention pedestrians, cyclists, trees, and other such obstacles – was rather more life-and-death than your typical high school English test.

Addison second-guessed more than a few of his answers – did anyone truly know precisely how close you're allowed to park to an intersection? – but submitted his completed test with moderate to high confidence.

Turned out, he needed all three wrong answers as leeway, scraping in with just thirty-two out of thirty-five, but a pass was a pass!

Addison proudly accepted his temporary paper licence, bought a pair of bright yellow 'L' plates to stick in the front and rear windows, then left the testing office with the promise that his permanent learner licence card would soon arrive in the post.

With that step done, the next was actually learning to drive – putting theory into practice. Addison was torn about who to ask to be his 'qualified driver' in the passenger seat – as required by law for those on their learner licence.

Jake had already offered when he subtly-unsubtly gifted Addison the copy of the road code. It was an exposing, vulnerable thing to do, and somehow he felt as if it would be coming on too strong to ask Jake to teach him to drive. But more importantly, he didn't want Jake to see him presumably at his worst. Addison didn't have the audacity to assume he'd be a natural.

He'd heard it said that driving was like riding a bike, which was preposterous. Sure, he'd long ago learnt to ride a bike, so for him riding a bike was literally 'like riding a bike' as the saying goes – a skill he could tap into even if he hadn't practised in a long time. Driving was a different story – he'd never learnt, never practised, so had nothing to tap into.

He wanted Jake to think of him as competent and capable. He wondered if Mabel might truly be willing? At least until he had the basics sorted.

Addison still had a bit of time before he had to get back to the office, so he stopped in at Milverton's visitor centre.

This counted as community engagement, surely? Getting his face out there, talking to residents? The visitor centre was certainly a focal point for Milverton – at least for its visitors and visitor-focused businesses.

A plausible explanation, but not why he was there. The reason for his visit popped up from behind the counter, her grey-white bob the first thing to catch his eye.

'I was expecting to see Morticia Addams,' Addison said as he made his way over. 'She's not here, is she?'

'Unfortunately not. One weekend only. You'll have to make do with little old Mabel Zhou, I'm afraid.'

'Good thing she's who I came to see,' Addison said before proudly presenting his temporary paper licence.

'Oh, well done, dear. I am very proud of you.'

'Thank you.'

'Only, what, fifteen years late?'

'Good things take time.'

'Oh, don't you start,' Mabel said, laughing. 'We are not trotting out all those time-related cliches again. But yes, I mean it, well done.'

'Thank you, again.' Addison paused, wondering if he was going to ask and then deciding yes, why not? If he didn't ask, he wouldn't know. If he did ask, the worst she could say was no. 'Mabel, I wonder if – and you can absolutely say no – if you might be willing to act as my "qualified driver" when I'm driving, as legally required while on my learner licence?'

'Of course, dear,' Mabel said, smiling as she patted his arm. 'It would be my pleasure.'

'You're sure?'

'Of course. I have a few years' experience—'

'And the rest.'

'Cheeky. Do you want my help or not?'

'Sorry, yes, I do.'

'Though, you know what some people are like,' Mabel said, raising an eyebrow. 'I'm an elderly Asian woman, a driving triple threat according to some.'

Addison's jaw dropped. 'Well yes, according to the ageist racist sexists. But we don't listen to ageist racist sexists, do we, Mabel?'

'No we don't.'

'They're not our people, so they don't count.'

'Quite right.'

'Besides,' Addison said, 'I'm now a learner driver. My lack of skill or experience is officially recognised by this very piece of paper. I am legitimately not good at driving.'

'I have the experience. And you're right up to date with all the finicky little rules—'

'Most of them.'

'Most?'

'Thirty-two out of thirty-five, just as an example proportion.'

225

'Well that's all right. Between my experience and your up-to-date knowledge, we'd make the perfect driver.'

'So, you'll really help me get going?'

'Yes, of course. Any time. You let me know when and we'll take my new car for a spin.'

'You are very brave, Mabel.'

'Thank you.'

'I didn't really mean that as a compliment—'

'Why haven't you asked our sergeant, Addison? I'm sure he'd be more than willing to help.'

'Ah. I'm sure he would be too. But…'

Mabel let out a breath, shook her head and patted his arm again. 'Yes, I understand. Don't worry, dear, you can fail as much as you like in front of little old me and I won't think any less of you.'

'Thank you, Mabel.'

'I'm sure your Jake would say the same thing.'

'Yes, I know that too. But…'

'Yes, yes.' Mabel shook her head and rolled her eyes. 'Men. You two are as bad as the rest.' She laughed. 'Anyway, what else is new?'

'Just this morning I caught up with Johanna of—'

'Of Johanna's Costume Closet and Prop Emporium, yes?'

'Yes, and—'

'Hold that thought,' Mabel said, already bustling away. 'I'm going to get a pot brewing so we can do this properly. You watch the desk.'

Addison did as instructed but didn't have to wait long before Mabel returned with two mugs and the visitor centre teapot wrapped in its bright orange knitted tea cosy with pompom on top.

Addison waited until everything appeared to be in place.

'Ready?'

Mabel nodded. 'Ready.'

Addison quickly recapped what he'd learnt from, and about, Patrick Laurence AKA Lady Perry Less, Gary Farnham, Brodie Seatter-Dent, Johanna van Niekerk AKA Jojo, and Kieran Nash, via his conversation with Harriet and Jake.

'So many names,' Addison said as a final aside. 'Some with multiple identities, nicknames, or just double-barrelled surnames.'

Mabel murmured her agreement as she poured their tea, adding a drop of milk to each and two teaspoons of sugar to hers. 'It is a fair bit to keep track of.'

'Stepping back for a second, though,' Addison said. 'Everyone I've spoken to was involved in putting on the production, or supplying things they needed, but none of the actual performers themselves.'

'What about Lady Perry Less? No, I suppose with the broken leg she wasn't performing on the night. It was just Patrick, purely in his capacity as producer, not performer.'

'I don't know if this is just because it's fresh in my mind, but I'm thinking back over what Johanna said. She's very much on the fringes, looking in, so more likely to be able to be objective?'

'Putting aside the fact her business was torn apart live on stage?'

'Well, yes,' Addison said, admitting that was rather a big concession to make. 'Still, Johanna wasn't worried about the production crew. She was only interested in the performers.'

'But the performers were all accounted for, right? Two watching with the audience, three in the wings ready to return to the stage.'

'Right.'

'So,' Mabel said, 'where does that leave us?'

'At a dead end, again. Which is just so frustrating. Aren't these investigations supposed to follow a nice, tidy narrative arc? A few suspects, a few red herrings to distract our lovable sleuth, but ultimately a big build-up to a satisfying conclusion?'

'Oh, Addison. You've been reading too many mystery novels. Real life is rarely so tidy.'

Addison sighed, as if his physical and emotional deflation were in lockstep. 'I know, I know. What do we have? Other than a bunch of he said, she said, they said?'

'Don't beat yourself up, dear. You're doing wonderfully. I know, between you and that sergeant of yours, you'll get to the bottom of this.' Mabel nodded once with finality as if drawing a line under the conversation. 'Anyway, do you think you'll be coming to the bonfire tomorrow night?'

'Uh, yeah, I guess so. Another event in Milverton's stacked social calendar... I probably should, would be good to see what's what for work – what's working well, what's not so much – ready for future events.'

'It's a funny one, isn't it?'

'What's that?'

'Guy Fawkes. Bonfire Night. Another northern hemisphere import,' Mabel said. 'Halloween has its origins in pagan traditions, but what we see tends to have a strong American, family-friendly flavour now, doesn't it?'

'Sweets, costumes, haunted houses – it's all good fun.'

'Exactly. But that was last week, and this week we have the British. Commemorating a failed attempt to blow up the House of Lords? We don't even have a House of Lords here.'

'Elected members only.'

'Hear, hear.'

'Again,' Addison said, 'it's all too much fun to give up completely though, isn't it?'

'Bonfires, fireworks, marshmallows, burning effigies…'

Addison found himself reflecting on some of the other celebrations throughout the year. 'At least we *also* have the likes of the Lantern Festival and Diwali.'

'Art Deco Weekend in Napier.'

'And Matariki, of course.'

'Yes, Matariki. Celebrating the Māori New Year makes much more sense. But we're not going to start taking away festivals, are we?' Mabel flashed her eyes wide. 'Who would dare be that grinch?'

'You could say farewell to any future prospects in politics,' Addison said, tipping back the last of his tea. 'Anyway, we have well and truly digressed. Thank you for this, but I'd better get back to work.'

The rain was starting to ease up so Addison decided to take the long way around the block, pulling out his phone to make a call.

No matter what might be on his mind regarding Jake – the handsome man he was currently seeing – he had to tell Sergeant Jake Murphy – the officer in charge of the investigation – what he'd heard from Johanna.

Jake had taken a chance on involving Addison in this investigation. No matter his ultimate reason for doing so, Addison would prove his worth, and that started by not being any tardier in his reporting than he already was. And while he was on the phone, if the vibe was right, he might even subtly, casually, easy-breezily ask if Jake had any dinner plans later.

Jake picked up on the third ring, greeting Addison

warmly, though with what Addison registered as a slightly harassed edge to his tone. Suspecting he'd caught Jake in the middle of something, he quickly summarised what Johanna had to say for herself including the fact, he now realised, that she hadn't once mentioned her driver licence suspension. And why would she? That was apparently a major reason Addison had been sent in Jake's stead.

He was warming himself up to broaching the topic of dinner plans when Jake thanked him for the update and expressed regret that they hadn't been able to see much of each other since the weekend. 'We've been working with the fire department, and we're expecting tonight to be another busy night. Since the bin fire that the mayor mentioned we've had a few minor issues, mainly just guys getting a bit excited and shooting off their fireworks prematurely.'

Addison laughed despite the fact it was partially responsible for keeping Jake from him. 'That's totally fine,' he said, which he knew was the correct response even if he didn't quite believe it himself.

'It's always like this in the week leading up to Guy Fawkes Night.' Jake breathed heavily down the line. 'I've been putting in more than my fair share of hours but I've lined things up to have a clear evening tomorrow. Would you like to come to the bonfire with me?'

'Ah, yeah, that sounds good.' Not what Addison had been angling for when he'd made the call, but he was pleased nonetheless.

If Addison's reasoning for going to the bonfire was mere embers before, now it was a happily crackling blaze.

Chapter 29

It continued to rain on and off throughout the day and into the evening, but apparently that hadn't dampened the enthusiasm of Milverton's budding pyromaniacs.

Addison heard the fireworks more than he saw them – screeching, sizzling, soaring into the air before bursting, banging, popping and then fizzling, sparkling, and drifting slowly back down again.

Not that he was itching to join in the fun. It had been years since Addison had started a new job and he'd forgotten how much it took out of you. Meeting new people, learning new things, all while being sure to be 'on' and putting your best foot forward.

A quiet night in with Keith was just what Addison needed and quite possibly what Keith needed too. The poor cat hadn't received nearly as much attention lately as he'd been getting in the weeks previous.

Addison had this thought as he crunched his way up the driveway under the cover of the overarching trees. That thought was reinforced the moment he stepped through the front door of Harper House and shed his damp jacket only to find Keith ready and waiting. The resident feline had taken up position on the staircase, sitting on precisely the correct step to bring him to Addison's eye level.

'Hi, Keith,' Addison said, injecting cheeriness into his voice in an attempt to counter the cat's unnerving gaze. He rambled about his day, asking Keith what he'd been up to and otherwise filling the air with verbal nonsense as he dropped his bag and made his way to the kitchen.

The cat said nothing, but he did follow, sitting just inside the kitchen door.

'Treats?'

Keith's tail flicked in response but he otherwise did not acknowledge the offer, seeing the blatant attempt at bribery for what it was.

Regardless, Addison set down some treats, replenished Keith's bowls with his regular dinner food, then got on with whipping up something for himself. Nothing special, just a basic, boring weekday meal for one, something that hit the key food groups and staved off scurvy and rickets and other such ailments.

He couldn't help noticing Keith maintained his watch from just inside the kitchen door, pointedly ignoring the treats, until Addison turned around at one point to find Keith in the same position, but the treats miraculously missing.

Addison didn't want to embarrass the cat by calling him out, but couldn't help his lip twitching in amusement.

The cat had been fed, as had he himself, and the dishes were done. Addison rested his hip against the kitchen bench, the wide-open evening looming ahead of him...

With no more intensive studying of the road rules to do, his contributions to the investigation at a dead end, and any romantic developments temporarily on pause, what was a guy to do?

He *could* go to bed, get an early night. Mentally he was drained, but physically it was like he had ants in his pants, as his mother would say. And going to bed at this hour – how sad would that be? On a more practical note, he knew if he nodded off now he'd be wide awake again by three or four in the morning.

Was this his life now?

With his new job only just begun, Addison could no longer pretend – even to himself – that he wasn't committing to staying in Milverton.

Beyond the job, what did *commitment* look like? What was something tangible he could do to prove to himself he wasn't just temporarily camped out at Harper House?

His gaze drifted around the kitchen and landed on the pantry doors. He'd been meaning to do a proper clear-out for a while. Who knew what was lurking back there in the deep, dark recesses? Though, as satisfying as that would be, it hardly proclaimed, 'I am here and here is where I intend to stay.' That's what he needed for himself.

Addison realised what he needed to do, what would make a real difference.

He climbed the staircase and once he hit the landing, instead of turning towards the guest bedroom as he usually did, he turned the opposite way.

In previous weeks he'd ducked his head into the main bedroom a couple of times but hadn't spent any real time in there – it had felt like too much of an invasion of his great-uncle Herbert's privacy. Harper House was his now, as his great-uncle had wanted. And that meant the main bedroom was his too.

The decor had the same more-is-more 1960s aesthetic as

the rest of the house – the warm, golden wood panelling and groovy carpet with psychedelic swirls, flowers and spots in riots of browns and oranges.

The bed itself looked much more modern, thankfully, with maybe a king-sized mattress. The headboard backed on to the wall that separated the bedroom from the landing, with bedside tables and lamps sitting to either side. The room had large windows to the front and side of the house which took up much of the external walls, with low chests of drawers beneath them. On the fourth and final wall were two free-standing wardrobes, so reminiscent of the portal to Narnia that Addison half-expected he would meet Mr Tumnus if he ventured through.

It was a good-sized bedroom, certainly more spacious than the guest bedroom. And more than any one person might need. Addison couldn't help thinking the room would accommodate Jake too, if he wanted…

That would solve Jake's issue of needing to suddenly find a new place. But considering Jake didn't think they were at the point of their relationship where he could share that he was likely going to have to temporarily move into a motel or short-term accommodation – because sorting out a new, longer-term tenancy was always a challenge, and often not quickly resolved – Addison doubted Jake would be willing to move in with him and Keith.

To Addison it felt like they'd barely seen each other lately, which was fine, that happened when people got busy. It was more difficult to line up time to spend together. However, that wouldn't be an issue if they lived together and he had Jake coming home to him after every shift.

He was still leaning against the doorframe and surveying the space when Keith appeared at his side, his little tongue swiping around his whiskers, clearly having demolished his dinner the moment Addison left the kitchen.

'We're moving into the big bedroom, Keith. What do you reckon?'

Keith said nothing, but he did slink into the room, languidly leap onto the bed, curl into a ball, and promptly go to sleep.

Addison snorted but couldn't help smiling. 'Make yourself at home, buddy. I'll take that as your endorsement of the move then, shall I?'

Keith didn't offer even a flicker of an ear or twitch of the tail in acknowledgement, but that was all right. Addison stepped into the room and started with the wardrobes. After he'd confirmed their back walls did not in fact open up into a wintery forest on another world, he started hauling out his great-uncle's coats, jackets, and shirts, transferring them to the guest bedroom, where he laid them out on the bed. Next up was moving the line of shoes from their former home at the base of the wardrobes and arraying them in a corresponding line against the wall in the other room.

Addison was pleasantly surprised to discover everything was relatively fresh, with not a dusty, fusty mothball in sight. He had even spotted a few things he was considering putting back where they'd come from, and so merging them into his own wardrobe, but most were destined for a charity shop.

Sometimes it felt like he was checking one item off his to-do list only to add two more.

Next Addison moved on to the low chests of drawers for socks, undies, shorts, trousers, and T-shirts. It was at this point – with all the banging and crashing of doors and drawers, huffing and puffing as Addison got down on his knees then back upright again – that Keith had engaged loaf mode on the corner of the bed in order to keep a watchful eye on the comings and goings.

Addison chanced a pat on one of his passes, and Keith dutifully accepted.

With the clothing and footwear all relocated to the guest bedroom for future sorting, the only furniture Addison hadn't yet investigated was the bedside tables.

He had to do it, knowing there was no way he'd drift off to sleep that night if his subconscious was left wondering what might be hidden within. His mind conjured up all manner of possibilities, from the sentimental to the salacious, but all very *private*.

Determined to power through no matter what he might discover, Addison wrenched open the drawers and immediately realised he needn't have worried. There were a couple of books, reading glasses, a stick of lip balm, a tube of hand cream, and a couple of small bottles of prescription medication, all of which he placed in a small box and set down in the guest bedroom.

One item though certainly did meet the criteria for sentimental: a photo album. Well worn, the hefty tome had clearly been flicked through many times. Unable to curb his curiosity, Addison opened the album and slowly turned the pages.

Each photo was in its own clear, plasticky slip, holding it in place. The images in the earlier pages showed their age – partially faded, with warmer tones, a little washed out – but they grew brighter and sharper as the pages went on.

Addison recognised his great-uncle Herbert in many of the photos. He recognised Percy too, a regular subject through the decades. They were seen together as well, mostly in group shots, but some just the two of them – at the beach, on walks in the bush, in Wellington and Auckland, and quite a few on stage.

As Addison neared the end of the filled pages, Keith started making regular appearances in photos taken in and around Harper House. Just a shock of ginger fur to start, he quickly grew into the full-sized feline Addison could now see stationed at the end of the bed.

A small wad of loose photos had been jammed in just after the last page of properly arranged photos.

They all looked like they'd been taken within the last year or so, and his great-uncle Herbert hadn't got around to putting them in properly. Apparently to-do lists never went away...

Addison picked up where his great-uncle had left off, taking his time to slip the most recent photos into place.

One in particular caught Addison's eye. His great-uncle beamed from centre stage with two thumbs up. He was dressed in a circus ringmaster's costume with black top hat, bright red tailcoat and bowtie, golden waistcoat, and black trousers and boots. Figures stood to either side wearing form-fitting bodysuits and the biggest, brightest wigs.

The figure to stage left was dressed as a human cannonball, in a shiny red bodysuit with matching cape and a motorbike helmet perched on top that served more as a fascinator than anything that might protect the wearer's head. Addison was surprised to find he recognised the performer, even under all the makeup, as Patrick Laurence AKA Lady Perry Less.

And the figure to stage right, of course, was her drag daughter, Miss Candy Less. Addison had seen this same costume just days earlier – the bold red-and-white-striped bodysuit with bursts of black lace at the ankles, wrists, and neck that had put him in mind of a gothic candy cane.

Addison stared at the photo, his mind jumping back to Candy's most recent performance, then her waiting in the wings during Little Red's magic show and then what came after.

He thought about how all the performers had been accounted for at all the times that truly mattered, how they were in full sight of Addison and the judges at the time of the incident... But were they?

Addison interrogated his own memory. He'd disregarded the second round's contestants because he'd seen them clustered in the wings as Little Red wrapped up her performance, but how long had it been before he'd next glanced over there? It wasn't until after the incident, at least. For the most part, his attention had been on the show, where the action was happening. He'd been focused on Cilla and Mabel at centre stage in those final moments, then his attention had been locked on the open trapdoor, also at centre stage.

For how long?

At least until all those on stage had gathered in their mutual shock, until the crew member had clambered down and declared Cilla Slay dead. And how long had *that* been? Thirty seconds? A minute, even? Two? Had he looked over even once in all that time?

He couldn't be sure that he had.

There was a gap – or at least the potential for one – in the alibis he'd assumed. Little Red Riding Wood had barely left the stage after her magic performance, assisted by Mabel, when Cilla dropped headfirst. But Miss Candy Less – she might have been there, as Addison had always assumed, but she might also have been *anywhere else*. Considering how much her costume stood out, he'd expect to have a positive recollection of her presence, which he did not. Could Candy have ducked away and returned to the wings before anyone noticed her absence? Or was she simply standing to the back, behind the other queens, momentarily out of Addison's direct line of sight? He wasn't actively keeping tabs on everyone's movements – why would he?

He slid the photo into place, closed the photo album, and put it back in the bedside table's drawer.

Addison knew who he needed to speak to next.

Chapter 30

Word on the street – or, more accurately, at Lynne's Cafe, as prompted by a subtle enquiry while ordering a coffee and croissant the following morning – was that the person behind Miss Candy Less conveniently had a public-facing day job just around the corner.

Addison had already heard they worked in a charity shop or second-hand clothing boutique or something, but not exactly what or where. However, the moment the shop was described to him, he realised he knew exactly where, had even sort of been there before.

After seeing the photo and making the connection the night before, Addison hadn't had the time or energy to do a full sort through of his great-uncle's clothes. Exhausted, mentally and physically, Addison had laboured through putting a fresh set of sheets on the bed, brushed his teeth, and then collapsed, immediately dropping off to sleep. So that morning he'd picked out a few items from the pile on the guest bed that he could never imagine bringing himself to wear, folded them nicely, dropped them in a tote bag, and brought them with him into town.

With this bag in hand, he strode alongside a parade of

blue, red, and white flags lining the street, the text on them alternating between 'Cars' and 'Sale'. He turned off the footpath, a clear avenue with shining cars to either side led to a glass-fronted shop to the rear of the car yard with an enormous sign above it that read 'Vroom Vroom Vehicles'. Tacked onto the end as if an afterthought was what Addison had previously thought might be an old barn door. Upon closer inspection he could confirm it was indeed an old barn door. But most important were the roughly painted brush strokes that read 'and Vintage Clothing'.

That was his destination.

It turned out to be an old lightweight prefabricated building – perhaps more accurately described as a shack – presumably the car yard's former office before they'd upgraded to their oversized and very modern glass-fronted space. The building had been shunted to the far corner, with a narrow walkway running along the very edge of the car yard from the street, behind the final row of cars, all the way to the shack.

Just as with Jojo's Co Clo, Addison reasoned his visit here today could be explained away as another stop on his introductory tour of local businesses, but to be doubly sure, he also had his few items to donate or sell or trade or whatever it was they did here.

He stepped up onto the small timber deck and through the creaking front door.

He had anticipated a typical charity shop, with mountains of knick-knacks and bric-a-brac; racks of clothing groaning under the weight of mismatched hangers and polyester blouses; sets of cutlery, crockery, and glassware, each with one or two items missing; and bookshelves overrun with multiple copies of each of the blockbuster bestselling thrillers from twenty years ago.

This shop was not that.

It featured a mid-century aesthetic, not dissimilar to Harper House. And it was very much *curated*.

Where a typical second-hand shop might have rammed ten or fifteen racks of clothes into the space, this one had five. The restrained selection was reflected in the pricing too. Addison turned over a couple of price tags as he passed, seeing numbers that were, if anything, higher than he might have expected to pay if buying new.

The nearest rack was labelled 'New Arrivals' and featured only three items: a psychedelic maxi dress with a label pinned to the front which read 'Vintage 70s vibes'; a faded olive green trench coat with brass buttons and a tag indicating it was 'Authentic military wear'; and a drapey, layered black top with a label reading 'Tiny tear, still stunning'. Addison couldn't help thinking the general spookiness of the last item might have been perfect for the weekend just gone, but he was not here to shop.

He approached the only other person present, a lithe figure with bleached blond hair cropped short, probably in his early twenties at most, perched on a high stool in the corner and flicking absently through their phone.

'Hi, I was told Miss Candy Less works here.'

The thumb stopped scrolling and the eyes below the bleached blond hair slowly raked up Addison's front until they met his eyes. 'That's me.'

Addison's jaw slackened. 'Wow, what a transformation.' And he wasn't just saying that. He'd been able to pick out Patrick's features from the photo of Lady Perry Less, but he couldn't see Candy at all in this person's features. 'I didn't recognise you.'

'That's the whole idea, honey. But I'm in boy mode, not in character, so it's Andrew Leigh. Call me Andy.'

'Andy... and your drag persona is Candy?'

'Yes, I know – Andy to Candy, Leigh to Less – not stretching the imagination too far, was I? But when my drag mother, Lady Perry Less, is already using "Less", what better way to pay homage? But where she's all danger, I'm all sweetness and scandal.' Andy added an unconvincing smile in a poor attempt to underscore his point, clearly not fully in character.

Addison was a little relieved. As far as double identities went, having them both sound so similar would surely be easier to keep track of.

'Your drag mother?'

'Yeah, she got me started. Helping with the wigs, the heels, the lashes, and everything in between,' Andy said, emphasising each word with a gesture. 'I am her protégé, if you like. But for how much longer, who knows?'

'What do you mean?'

'Well, you know. I love her to bits, respect her utterly – the makeup, the dresses, the choreography, the ability to captivate a room. But there always comes a time when the student becomes the master and it's time to step aside. Out with the old, in with the new. Especially when she can't even perform.'

Addison realised that by coming in here asking for Miss Candy Less, he'd started the conversation on the desired topic; neither of his backup excuses for being there was even required.

'Why? What happened?' he said, exaggerating his tone, eyes wide, as if lapping up the gossip.

Just as he'd hoped, Andy leapt at the opportunity to

share. 'Well, you know.' A shrug, a tilt of the head. 'I thought of myself as her understudy, and then she broke her leg which was awful for her, but I couldn't help thinking that this was my chance to step up, take the lead, but no, she called in an outsider at the eleventh hour. Left me to perform along with everyone else. Which was fine. No, who am I kidding? I was furious, complained about not getting the chance, but turns out that was for the good. Glad I wasn't tapped for the top job.'

'Oh, yes,' Addison said. 'I'm sorry about last Friday night.'

'You heard about that, then?'

Addison realised Andy didn't recognise him. When in character as Miss Candy Less, was Andy so dedicated and concentrated on the performance that he didn't have spare capacity to notice anything around him? Or was it because he was so self-centred and self-involved that it didn't register as being worth his attention?

In the normal run of things, Addison wouldn't have been so self-centred himself as to think that everyone would have remembered him being there. But he was quite literally on stage, under the stage lights, in full view of all in Milverton Town Hall. One of only three judges. And he wasn't even disguised in a costume, just a little dressed up for the theme, so that wasn't to blame either.

Addison decided not to correct him, reasoning Andy might speak more openly if he thought he was the one entirely in control of the recollection, not knowing that Addison would be ready and waiting to catch him in a lie.

And so, Addison simply nodded to confirm that yes, he had heard about last Friday night. The nod also served to encourage further gossip, as if he was so excited to hear that he was lost for words.

'Oh, the *drama*,' Andy said, really drawing out the vowels. Eyes alight, absolutely unable to hide that this kind of thing was what he lived for, what he thrived on, both in and out of character. 'I hate to say it, and I'd deny it if anyone said I'd said it, but wow, *good job*. Couldn't have happened to a more deserving person.'

The spite was strong with this one, but in a gleeful kind of way.

'Did you see it happen?' Addison said. 'First-hand?'

'Did I see it happen? Front-row seats, pretty much.'

Addison didn't recognise it immediately, but Andy actually sounded *proud* to have witnessed Cilla Slay's downfall. 'Really?' he said. 'Were you in the audience at that point?'

'No, no. I was in the wings. Even better than the front row. Saw the entire thing unfold.'

This was the crux of what Addison had come here to get to the bottom of: was Miss Candy Less really in the wings, or had she slipped away for a moment? Just long enough to activate the trapdoor mechanism and scurry back into position?

'What was it like, watching from the wings?' Addison kept the question open, giving Andy plenty of rope to work with, so to speak.

'I was a bit annoyed with Little Red, if I'm honest. She kept asking me to help with that ridiculous box of hers. Did she not see my heels and my costume? Not designed to be dragging great big lumps of carpentry around the place. If she couldn't manage it herself – getting it going on stage, then helping shunt it out of the way afterwards – then she should've done something else.'

Addison nodded along enthusiastically, making all the right noises.

'I wasn't standing in the wings just so I could lend a helping hand to anyone who didn't have their act together. I was ready and waiting to be called back for the judging, wasn't I? I didn't want to be getting distracted or called away for anything. Wasn't going to risk having our hostess call my name, "Miss Candy Less!" and me not being right there, ready to go. She would've had to make some joke at my expense or something to fill the time while I got my sweet little self up there again. No, I was right there the entire time, getting in Little Red's way whether she liked it or not.'

It would be easy enough for Addison to check in with Little Red. Which he would do, of course, but that just felt like a bit of a formality – dotting i's, crossing t's. Andy seemed too genuinely wrapped up in himself to be making things up, covering his tracks, keeping his story straight.

'Anyway,' Andy said, shaking his head. 'I saw the whole thing, even if I couldn't enjoy it properly with Little Red getting in my way.'

'Oh yeah, that must've been such a pain,' Addison said. 'So, what happened next?'

Andy then described everything exactly as Addison himself remembered it, crashing through the retelling, gesticulating the entire time. No inaccuracies, no pausing for thought – for example, to remember the lie or the story he'd fabricated.

All up, Andy was far from the most likeable person, with little in the way of generosity of spirit, but he was not a liar.

'Wow,' Addison said once the retelling appeared to draw to a close, before humming to himself as if something didn't quite add up. 'But, after all that, are you not glad to be rid of Cilla?'

'What? Why?' Andy said, appearing genuinely confused. 'How does that help me? The Spooky Showcase was *one night only*. I wasn't going to be hostess for the next performance because there was no next performance. If I was to benefit from Cilla's death, then I would've needed someone to off her *before* the show, wouldn't I? Then, with it being very last minute, Patrick, in his role as producer, would've had no choice but to give me the tap for hostess duties. Cilla's no good to me dying mid-performance.'

Addison couldn't help the quick burst of laughter – the logic was flawless.

Andy laughed too. 'Right?'

'So, it's Patrick you hold the grudge against then, for not giving you the tap in the first place?'

'Not at all,' Andy said, waving the suggestion away, though the response felt more forced than anything he'd said earlier. 'I respect my drag mother. She decided I wasn't ready to take the reins – which was her call and I respect that. Doesn't mean I have to like it. Cilla was a good choice business-wise. But...' Andy trailed off, thoughtful.

Addison raised an encouraging eyebrow. 'But...'

'Well, all I'll say is that if someone else had the arts funding' – Andy waved his fingers with a flourish, making it clear he thought that someone else ought to be him – 'Patrick scored for the Spooky Showcase, then we might have all enjoyed a *proper show* last Friday night. I would *kill* for that kind of funding.'

Addison raised an eyebrow.

'Oh, not *literally*,' Andy said, rolling his eyes. 'You know what I mean.'

'Sure.' He did know what Andy meant, but still, what a choice of words… 'Anyway, if you had the funding, what would you have done differently?' Addison reasoned many enjoyed reflecting on the errors of others from the safety of the future, knowing any alternatives they proposed could never be tested and were therefore perfect.

And so it was, with Andy being more than happy to share his thoughts on the music, lighting, decor, set design, programming, promotion, seating, and anything else he could think of. Apparently no stone would be left unturned. 'But if I was in charge, I would've made sure everything was done *properly*. Too late now,' Andy said with a shrug, as if it was of no real consequence. 'Next time Lady Perry Less breaks a leg, she'd better not come crying to me thinking I'll save the day. I mean, I *would* save the day – not for her, but for the show.'

Addison nodded and murmured, as if that was as it should be. 'The show must go on.'

Andy flourished his hand once more, acknowledging the sentiment, before sucking in a quick breath and letting it out again. 'Anyway, you didn't come in here to listen to me, I'm sure.'

That was, in fact, precisely why Addison had come in here, not that he said so.

'What's in your tote bag? Did you bring in something you were hoping to add to my collection?'

'Oh no,' Addison said, recognising he'd be laughed out of the shop if he presented Andy with three of the least appealing items he'd semi-randomly plucked from his great-uncle's wardrobe. 'These are just some things for a friend. No, I've just started a new role in the mayor's office.' Addison launched into his spiel, thankful he'd prepared a second backup reason for being there, but he was no more than ten seconds in when he saw the shopkeeper's eyes glaze over.

No matter, Addison had already got what he'd come for. So he swiftly wrapped it up, said he was looking forward to working together to market Milverton, and saw himself out.

The short walk to the office gave Addison the time and space to order his thoughts.

The headline: Andy Leigh, performing as Miss Candy Less, was not the killer. He really thought he'd had something there – a real *aha* moment. All it ended up being was a reassessment of his own poor assumptions.

Andy was just all spite and hot air. Immature, a real drama queen. Addison suspected that murder required more dedication and stability of purpose to pull off than Andy could muster.

On the one hand, Addison felt like he was back to having no clear direction or prospects, but on the other hand, the answer felt so very close. It was *right there*, he could feel it, just couldn't quite put his finger on it.

They'd been through everyone. The culprit either had to have come in entirely unseen, or their presence was just not noteworthy because they were so often present. Who could move around like that? It didn't help that so many people had been getting dressed up all week, so effectively everyone was in disguise…

Addison huffed out a sigh, entirely unsatisfied with his progress, such as it wasn't.

He'd spoken to Patrick and Mabel backstage, Gary at the pub, Brodie at the night market, Mayor Ferguson and Jake at the office, Johanna at the costume hire shop, and Andy at the vintage clothing shop. Every time he thought he might be onto something, he was quickly proven wrong.

Addison realised he couldn't rely on getting the information he needed from others. He'd exhausted that approach and now he needed to *do* something. What that might be, he didn't know, but he reckoned revisiting the scene might be a good start. He'd heard what it was like below stage but there was nothing quite like seeing something for yourself.

Doing so, Addison hoped, might spark an idea or jog a memory or give him cause to reassess a prior assumption. He wouldn't know until he had a look.

Chapter 31

On his walk back to the office, Addison called Mabel and outlined his thoughts before asking who he might talk to about getting access to Milverton Town Hall, specifically below stage.

'Percy has a key,' she said. 'He'd love to show you around, I'm sure. I'll give him a call and ask him to phone you, shall I?'

'Oh, yes. That'd be great—'

'OK, I'll do that now. Let me just hang up on you first.'

'Doesn't have to be right now,' Addison said. 'Just when you get a chance...' He trailed off as he pulled the phone away from his ear and saw she'd already done as she said she would and hung up on him.

Right, no mucking about. Mabel meant business. Addison couldn't help but agree – the faster this could be resolved, the better.

It would be good to get below stage and have a look around soon. Ideally tomorrow, if Percy could swing it. Addison didn't know the man's availability, nor what might be required to get access, so he didn't know how likely getting in so soon might be. He realised there was no point waiting and wondering, so had transitioned from mulling over his chances to considering what he might get himself for lunch. He was almost back at the office when an unfamiliar number popped up on his phone.

Absently, he took the call. 'Kia ora, Addison speaking.'

'I hear you wanted to have a nosy?' A man's voice, but not one Addison immediately recognised.

'Sorry, who is...' Addison started saying before he registered who was calling. 'Percy?'

'Of course, who else?' Percy laughed. 'I thought you were expecting my call?'

'Yes, sorry, yes I was.' Addison laughed too, momentarily taken aback. 'Just – uh – just not so soon.'

'Is now not a good time?'

'No, no. Now's fine. Thanks for getting back to me, Percy.'

'All right, then. About that nosy?'

'Well—'

'See what we can see?'

'Yeah, if you had a bit of time and were happy to show me around, I'd really appreciate—'

'How's two minutes?'

'Um,' Addison said, uncertain, thinking he might need a little more than two minutes to have a decent look around but not wanting to take up too much of the man's time. 'Any amount of time you have would be a great help.'

'Oh! No, my boy,' Percy said, laughing down the line again. 'I'll be there in two minutes. I'll meet you out the front. Ta-ra.'

Once again Addison found his phone call abruptly terminated. First Mabel, now Percy – what was it about these two? He smiled and shook his head before pivoting on the spot and heading around to the other side of the block.

Addison arrived to find Percy already waiting at the entrance to Milverton Town Hall, a wide smile on his face.

'I was at Lynne's finishing up a raspberry lamington when you called,' he said. 'She does them just how I like them – the sponge, the coconutty coating, and the layer of cream she puts through the middle. Proper cream too, as it should be.'

'I couldn't agree more,' Addison said, never not disappointed if he discovered mock cream when biting into what had promised to be a delicious treat. 'You've convinced me – I'll have to try one some time.'

'Oh, blast,' Percy said, shaking his head. 'I should've grabbed an extra to bring with me. I'll just pop back—'

'No, no. That's all right. I've already interrupted your day enough. And besides, I'm at Lynne's practically every day, plenty of opportunity to grab one myself next time I'm in.'

'In that case, I shall look forward to hearing your report,' Percy said with a smile. 'Now, I'm very happy to help but I'm not sure why you've asked *me*.'

'Mabel said you had a key?'

'Oh, I do.' Percy pulled a key ring from his jacket pocket before unlocking the large front door and pushing it open. 'But so do you, young Master Harper.'

'No, I don't have a key. Why would—'

'On your great-uncle Herbert's great big ring of keys.'

Addison hadn't figured out even a tenth of the keys on that key ring yet, unlabelled as they all were. 'Even if I knew which one it was, I'm not about to let myself into the town hall.'

'Why not?'

'Because, well, you can't do that?'

'Of course you can. You have a key, so you have permission. You're a Harper.'

Addison wasn't going to argue with the man, at least not right now, not when he'd already gained entry. He still felt uneasy just letting himself into a big, old civic building like this, as if he owned the place.

'You coming or what?'

'Yes, yep.' Addison pulled the front door closed behind him, hoisted the tote bag back onto his shoulder, and followed Percy across the cleared town hall floor. With the wall-to-wall dividing curtain and all the chairs packed away after the Spooky Showcase, they could cut diagonally to a door flanking the stage on house right – or stage left, depending on your perspective.

'Mabel says you've been looking into Cilla Slay's death?'

'I have, yeah. There are still a lot of question marks.'

'I take it that's what we're doing here?' Percy said as he stepped through to the backstage area and up a short flight of steps before flicking a series of light switches. 'Hoping to clear up a few of those question marks?'

'I can't think of what else to do at this point.' Addison looked around himself, the bright lights illuminating everything – scaffolding, crates, racks, and the great black side curtains leading towards the stage itself – leaving nothing in shadow, unlike during the show. If he'd stood then where he stood now, he'd have been looking at the backs of the judging panel seated behind the sarcophagus.

'I've thought about what happened every which way,' Percy said. 'I've spoken to the backstage crew I was working with on the night and gone over the trapdoor and its mechanisms with a fine-tooth comb – I can't make head nor tails of any of it. And I can't help but feel responsible—'

'You mustn't, Percy,' Addison said, shaking his head. 'I said the same to Mabel. You cannot be responsible for the actions of others, not even partially. Nor should you take on any of the blame.'

'You are very kind and generous to say so, Addison. I'll be glad to know what happened and I'll admit I was pleased to hear you'd turned your mind to it.' Percy turned to face Addison as he reached a railing and nodded once. 'Anyway,' he said, injecting his voice with what Addison suspected was false cheer, 'you wanted to see below stage, is that right?'

'Yeah, I was hoping to see the trapdoor in action for myself.'

'We can certainly do that.'

Addison followed as Percy rounded the railing, revealing the top of a staircase previously obscured from view by a row of stacked crates. Percy descended into the darkness, the steps creaking faintly as he went.

After a moment's hesitation, Addison started making his way down too until Percy abruptly stopped. But then he reached to the side and flicked another switch, illuminating the space below stage.

Unlike upstairs, which had been flooded with light, down here there were only the occasional naked bulbs casting small pools of light at intervals across the width of the stage.

'Watch your head,' Percy said. 'Not the best clearance down here.'

Addison could see what the older man meant the moment he reached the bottom of the stairs. The thick timber beams holding up the stage forced Addison to hunch down and bend his knees before moving on. 'I doubt even Mabel could walk around down here upright.'

Less obvious but still noticeable was the drop in temperature below stage. Addison's skin prickled in response. He briefly rubbed some warmth into his arms, causing the tote bag of clothes from his great-uncle's wardrobe to swing awkwardly from his shoulder. He half wished he'd had a chance to stow it under his desk at the office before coming out again, but he wasn't about to miss this chance when it had been offered so swiftly and readily. He could also have left it upstairs, but he was here now and wasn't about to backtrack.

He followed Percy as he slowly made his way between the timber posts that held up the stage. The well-worn path ran in a direct line from the bottom of the stairs to the short ladder that led up to the trapdoor at centre stage. To either side of the path, Addison could make out cobwebs clinging to the beams overhead and random bits of detritus scattered across the floor, even in the low light.

He paused for a moment and toed the floor to the side, just beyond the direct path. His shoe left a smudge in what he could now see was a thick layer of dust coating the floor. From this, it was clear the path was not so much well-worn as just free of dust from the backstage crew coming to operate the trapdoor.

No sooner had he made this realisation than he felt the pressure behind his eyes ratcheting up and a sneeze bursting from him, his head bumping against the underside of the stage from the force.

'You all right back there?'

'Yep, I'm OK,' Addison said, lifting a hand to rub the back of his head. 'Just a bit of dust.' But then he was lowering his hand when his arm seemed to catch in midair. Surprised by the unexpected resistance, Addison jerked his arm down and away, resulting in a short, sharp tearing sound followed by the tote bag over his shoulder slumping open.

Looking down, Addison saw one strap had torn away from the tote bag on one end. He wrapped his arm around the bag and held it to his side, satisfied the contents weren't about to spill out, then turned his head to see what had caused the issue.

He spotted the culprit immediately.

On the timber post nearest him, about a third of the way down, was the head of a nail sticking out just a bit. And caught on it was a small, black scrap of fabric. The evidence suggested the nail had already snagged on a crew member's stage blacks and now Addison's tote bag had fallen victim too.

He must've said something aloud because Percy once again called out from further ahead. 'You *sure* you're all right? You're making a heck of a racket.'

Addison burst with unexpected laughter. 'Yeah, sorry. I was just caught up there for a sec,' he said before absently wondering if the health and safety investigator had noticed the nail too, if it might feature in their upcoming report. He made a mental note to mention the protruding nail to Gary Farnham so he could hammer it in on his next maintenance visit.

Careful to leave a buffer zone between the beams overhead and the posts to each side and himself, Addison caught up with Percy. He stood waiting at the edge of a large red square painted on the floor.

Beyond him were great stacks of collapsed trestle tables

which Addison knew could be pulled out from below the front of the stage into the hall itself for the Spring Craft Fair and the like. But Percy's attention was directed above them.

Positioned directly above the red square painted on the floor was another square. This one was formed by the bright lights on the level above illuminating the narrowest of gaps in the floorboards, the edges of the trapdoor obvious in the dimness below stage.

'See here,' Percy said, pointing off to the side of the ladder to a panel covered in bold yellow and black diagonal stripes – the universal pattern for 'warning' or 'danger'. If that wasn't clear enough, the words 'WARNING' and 'DANGER' also featured. Percy unlatched the panel, which swung down to reveal a large red lever handle which was connected to various cogs, metal arms, hinges, and hydraulic pistons – or at least that's what it looked like to Addison. He wasn't going to pretend to understand how it operated, only that it did.

'Make sure you're off the red square – yes, that's it.' Percy then demonstrated the trapdoor mechanism by gripping the lever handle in both hands, taking one deep breath and holding it before he pulled the lever down in one swift motion.

The trapdoor dropped open with a bang that echoed around the space below stage and a burst of light from the level above.

'Wow, that was loud,' Addison said once he'd recovered from the assault to his senses.

'Yes, sorry, I should've warned you. I've often thought I could do with wearing earmuffs when I'm down here—'

'But then you wouldn't be able to hear your cue?'

Percy nodded. 'That's right.'

'You timed the trapdoor openings well the other night,' Addison said. 'At the end of the first round when the losing contestants were banished and then when Little Red made Mabel "disappear".'

'Thank you. And yes, I was sure to discuss it with them beforehand. As you can see from down here, visual cues are no good – you can barely see the staircase that brought us down here, let alone anything else. So I was down here, ready and waiting, listening out for the right words so I could time my lever pull with a clap from our performers.'

Percy lifted the lever handle, reversing its previous motion, and the trapdoor swung back up with a *clunk*.

'Have you had any trouble with the trapdoor?' Addison said. 'Any signs of tampering?'

'Oh no, it works every time. Gary does a brilliant job keeping everything running as it should. And it looks and feels no different today than it did last Friday night. Here, you have a go.'

'What? Really?'

'Of course, it's straightforward. Don't worry, you're not going to break it. Here, come over here.'

Addison set his bag down as they swapped places and, following Percy's instructions, he threw open the trapdoor with a bang. 'You really do have to put your back into it, don't you?'

'Good thing I've been eating my spinach,' Percy said, lifting his arm for a bicep curl Popeye-style.

Addison smiled and then, just as Percy had done earlier, he reversed the manoeuvre until the trapdoor locked back into position with a satisfying *clunk*.

Not quite sure what else he hoped to find below stage, Addison activated his phone's torch light for a closer inspection of the trapdoor mechanism. It was as Percy said – as far as Addison could tell, nothing appeared amiss.

'All right,' he said. 'Thanks, Percy, for showing me around.'

'No worries at all. Unless you wanted another go on the trapdoor?'

'No, no. I think I've seen all I can see.'

'Very good. Latch that panel back up, will you?' Percy said. 'That's the one. And don't forget your bag.'

Addison collected his late great-uncle's clothes and followed Percy back the way they'd come.

On the return journey, Addison made a point of scanning each side of the path, noticing no shoeprints in the dust except for the smudge he'd left earlier.

They re-emerged into the bright lights above stage, which Percy flicked off again before they crossed the hall and stepped back outside. Meanwhile, Addison considered what he'd discovered.

He'd confirmed that below stage was accessed by a set of steps on stage left, in the wings behind where the judging panel had sat at the sarcophagus; that the trapdoor mechanism was below stage and out of sight of the rest of backstage; and that the operation of the trapdoor required conscious effort – that is, there's no way anyone could accidentally activate it.

All of that had been good to see for himself, even if he hadn't found anything to progress his thoughts on the situation. He had to hope it was too early to write off this exercise as a complete waste of time, that something he saw or heard might still prove useful as he picked up more pieces of this infuriating puzzle.

For now, all he'd earnt for his troubles was a torn tote

bag strap.

Still, grateful for Percy's time, Addison promised to buy him a coffee at Lynne's sometime soon as thanks, to which Percy said that would be unnecessary but very welcome indeed.

On the short walk back to the office, Addison conceded his amateur sleuthing was not making the cut, not this time. He was once again at a loss and knew the best course of action would be to put everything he'd heard and learnt to the actual professionals, specifically Sergeant Jake Murphy.

Chapter 32

Addison's afternoon dragged but at least he could look forward to seeing Jake that evening.

It sounded like most of the office would be coming out for the bonfire and fireworks display too – bringing family and joining friends. If his new workplace was at all representative of the town, then he anticipated much of Milverton would be in attendance.

The forecast, however, suggested the rain they'd been having on and off all week would *not* be in attendance, which was a relief.

Addison left the office a little late, deciding not to go home first but instead heading straight for the secondary school hosting the event.

Shadows were already lengthening as the sun lowered itself through the clear evening sky. It may have still been an hour or so until it dipped below the horizon, but it wasn't letting off any real heat anymore, leaving behind it a faint chill in the air.

It was a matter of minutes before Addison arrived at Milverton High School. There was a small visitors' car park to one side of the entrance and the administration block to the other, but it was the big white plastic arrow pointing skywards that told him what he needed to know. Cable-tied to a stake in the garden beside the path, the sign featured bold red letters oriented ninety degrees from horizontal that read 'EVENT'.

More arrows led Addison through a series of small, paved courtyards and covered walkways weaving his way past classrooms, all closed up and with the lights off. It may not have been the school he'd attended, but it still felt a little eerie to be there after hours – a place that would normally be so busy and loud. He also couldn't help feeling a bit naughty to be out like this on a school night.

The thought was interrupted by a twitch and a sudden elevation in pressure behind his eyes. Moments later the cause made itself known as he emerged from the built-up part of the school and stepped onto grass. And yes, his sinuses could confirm the lawns had recently been mowed, presumably earlier that day for this very occasion. Addison had to hope the hay fever tablets he'd taken that morning, as he did every morning, would see him through.

Staked into Addison's eternal nemesis was one final sign. This one was much larger than the rest, advertising the event as a fundraiser for the performing arts faculty, with students re-enacting scenes from Macbeth throughout the evening at quarter past and quarter to the hour. Further bullet points indicated the bonfire lighting would commence at seven o'clock; entries for the Guy-building competition were open until sunset; and the fireworks display was scheduled for nine o'clock, weather permitting.

Beyond the sign was a vast, open green space.

Addison rummaged through his very limited sporting knowledge to identify the two sets of goal posts at either end. They appeared to have a rugby field alongside a football field, with a cricket pitch between the two.

More importantly, they had food trucks, caravans, and stalls. There were, of course, staples like hot dogs, hot chips, burgers, ice creams, and candy floss, but Addison had also already spotted many other stallholders he recognised from the weekend before. And again, many a themed special, which was always fun.

New additions came in the form of entertainment, with a bouncy castle and similarly inflated obstacle course; go-karts puttering around a kidney bean-shaped course marked out with small, rectangular hay bales; and a makeshift stage set up on a truck's open-sided trailer, currently unoccupied.

Beyond the goal lines – still on the grass, but well clear of any buildings or trees – was a mountain of timber, branches, and logs.

The bonfire itself was only just now being lit, but lined up around it – at a distance, for now – were the scarecrow-like effigies. Made of straw and sacking materials, dressed in clothes that might very well have been rejected from Andy's vintage clothing store. Even from the far side of the field, Addison could make out a few in the classic form of Guy Fawkes; recreations of villainous cartoon characters; and a few with uncanny likenesses of current controversial politicians, awaiting their fiery fate.

Alongside all that were the fire engine, ambulance, and first aid tent – ready to go, just in case.

And finally, far away from anyone or anything else was a cordoned off area with a couple of figures in high-viz orange vests bustling about arranging an astonishing assortment of boxes and tubes – the fireworks.

Addison was about to start a slow circuit of the stalls when he spotted a familiar face making his way over. He felt his own face involuntarily exploding into a smile, but tried his best to dampen it down lest he look manic and scare the man away.

'Hey,' Jake said.

'Hey,' Addison said, his conversational abilities apparently limited to parroting the handsome man before him.

'Have you been here long?'

'No, I just arrived.'

'OK,' Jake said, sounding pleased. 'Did you want to have a look around?'

'Yes, let's,' Addison said, relieved to have something to do as he fell into step alongside Jake. The initial tension eased but Addison couldn't help wondering at the faint flutter of nervousness he seemed slow to shake off.

They wandered around the stalls together and, with plenty to point out and comment on, Addison soon fully relaxed into the situation.

Constables Sean McGiffert and Manaia Edwards had once again somehow been roped into being on duty. Addison's cheeks warmed when he received a wide grin and eyebrow waggle from Sean and a faint smirk from Manaia as they passed. It was likely because of them that their boss could have the evening off to spend with Addison. He made a mental note to get them each a pint as thanks next time he saw them off duty.

For now, however, Addison took the opportunity to bring Jake up to speed on his chat with Andy Leigh at the vintage clothing store and his nosing below stage at Milverton Town Hall with Percy Foster. Jake raised an eyebrow at that but didn't interrupt as Addison continued sharing his thoughts about the culprit either coming and going entirely unseen, or just not being noted because they were so often there. 'Who could move around like that? It didn't help that so many people have been getting dressed up all week—' Addison cut himself off, eyes wide with sudden regret. 'Oh, I am sorry, this is your night off and here I am rambling on.'

Jake smiled. 'That's all right. I understand.'

'What – uh – what else have you been up to this week?' Addison had meant the question in an open, general sense, but the moment the words were out of his mouth he couldn't help remembering the current state of Jake's living situation. He'd promised himself he would wait until they'd resolved Cilla Slay's untimely death, but he reasoned he couldn't keep pausing important things in his life every time someone unexpectedly died. If he did that he'd never get anything done.

Addison decided that no, he wanted to know. He wasn't going to have him and Jake awkwardly dancing around the topic, risking misunderstandings, miscommunications, missed opportunities...

Though, to be fair to them both, with everything going on, they hadn't seen much of each other in person and hadn't had the chance to discuss it.

Well, they had a chance now.

Feeling bold, and before he could second-guess himself, Addison raised the question of Jake's living situation himself. 'I heard you've been given notice on your place?' He kept his tone as light as he could manage.

Jake's step faltered briefly. He glanced in Addison's direction before recovering his composure and offering an unemotional, factual response that also got out ahead of any of Addison's immediate likely questions. 'Yes,' Jake said, 'the landlord hasn't renewed my lease. A family member of theirs is moving back to Milverton and my landlord intends to offer the place to them. So I have to find a new place. I haven't sorted out anything yet – haven't had the time, honestly. But Emily Smith is keeping an eye out for me. Not urgent, not yet.' He slowed in his response, turning to Addison as he did so. 'I have more important things to focus on, to spend my time on...'

Addison nodded. 'Cilla Slay's death.'

'Ah.' Jake paused, then said, 'Yeah, that too.'

There was a clear and obvious solution to Jake's living situation. They both knew what that solution would be but at the same time did not know what the other thought of that solution – *that* was an issue.

Addison feared he'd used up his day's quota of boldness in raising the topic of Jake's living situation and didn't know if he had any more up his sleeve to ask Jake to move in with him.

Addison knew that's what he wanted for himself, but he didn't know Jake's mind and there was so much tied up in the asking – a sense of obligation, either real or imagined; then there was the timing, so soon but what did that matter if it felt right?

He was going to go for it.

'You know, Jake...' Addison said slowly. 'If you wanted—'

'Boys!'

Addison and Jake simultaneously stopped in their tracks and whipped their heads towards the unexpected interruption.

Apparently their reaction had been more than their caller had anticipated, as she'd thrown her arms up, showing she wasn't a threat. It was Lynne Matthews of Lynne's Cafe, eyes wide a moment longer before she slowly lowered her arms, chuckling all the way down.

'Sorry, I didn't mean to alarm you, or sound so *condescending*, actually. "Boys"? You don't call out "Men!" though, do you? We're not in the army. Sergeant Murphy, Addison, good to see you both,' she said, sneaking a wink at Addison.

He couldn't very well say, 'Hi, sorry, can we swing by later? I was about to ask Jake to move in with me.' Instead, as he made his way over to Lynne's stand, Jake coming along with him, Addison rearranged his features into something he hoped presented pleasant interest and said, 'What do you have for us, Lynne?'

'Well! I went a little overboard. We have "Bonfire Brownies" with molten chocolate inside and crushed honeycomb sprinkled on top; "Explosive Slices" coated in popping candy and fizzing sherbet; and your classic s'mores, ready to be melted over one of the braziers they have scattered around.' Lynne's enthusiasm was infectious, and Addison found himself warming to it despite her unintentional, untimely interruption. 'But what I'm most excited about this year is my hot chocolate menu.'

With great fanfare, Lynne ran a hand down a small, hand-written blackboard. Before Addison had a chance to read it, she continued. 'I have milk chocolate *and* dark chocolate options, but also a range of adults-only alternatives.' Lynne quirked an eyebrow and couldn't help herself from chuckling. 'I've been trialling a few delicious liqueurs at home this week – a tough gig, let me tell you. So, tonight I am very pleased to offer boozy hazelnut cream, orange, and mint hot chocolates. Not all mixed together, mind – one liqueur per drink. And finally I have a salted caramel rum hot chocolate.'

Lynne stood back while her customers considered their options. She'd placed her hands on her hips while doing so, revealing yet another new apron. This one featured an illustration of Guy Fawkes holding a steaming mug above the words 'Remember, remember your fifth hot choc cuppa!'

Addison found himself absently counting with his fingers – turns out the rhyme had the right number of syllables. Even so, it didn't quite roll off the tongue like the original.

Addison didn't know whether it was their earlier tension, their general lack of contribution to the conversation, or their delayed decision making that Lynne had picked up on, but she looked between them both, frowning, and said, 'Is everything OK?'

'Yes, yes,' Addison said. 'Just…' What was he *just* doing? 'Just trying to figure out what I want.'

'Yes, of course.' Lynne was unconvinced. 'Big decision.'

'What do you want, Jake?' Addison said, slowly turning to face him as he asked the loaded question.

Jake returned the look, pursing his lips before breaking eye contact and addressing Lynne. 'Mint for me, please.'

Addison let out a shuddery breath before doing likewise. 'One of your boozy orange hot chocolates, thanks. And an Explosive Slice.'

Chapter 33

Their hot chocolates were everything Addison could've dreamed of – silky and rich and delicious and warming. With those to sip on and the various goings-on around them, Addison had to hope that – as far as Jake was concerned – their current silence was more comfortable and less strained than it felt to Addison.

He felt more than a little deflated having lost his momentum and now seemed unable to dredge up any of his former boldness. Perhaps a bite of his slice would give him the little boost he needed? At the very least, finishing it would free up a hand – to do he didn't know what, but at least it would be one thing he didn't have to worry about.

Addison took a bite and his mouth exploded.

With ears popping and jaw crackling, eyes wide and watering, his mouth gaped and a pained 'Ahhhhh' noise escaped him.

'Don't just hold it there.' Jake's voice somehow broke through Addison's sudden and overwhelming torment. 'Do something.'

'What?' That's what Addison meant to say, but with his mouth still open to the max it came out sounding more like

'Wahh'.

'Spit or swallow,' Jake said.

Addison was panicking too much to overthink what had just been said to him. He knew he wasn't about to spit, so took the other option, rapidly chewing through the explosions before swallowing the mouthful.

His eyes were still watering, and it took a while for the fizzing, crackling, and popping to fade until it felt like his jaw was only a little bit on fire, but also simultaneously ice-cold.

Eventually Addison wiped his eyes clear only to find Jake's eyes on him, somehow both concerned and amused, a combination with which Addison was becoming familiar.

He may have been wildly embarrassed, but at least the spectacle he'd made of himself had broken the tension, effectively resetting the atmosphere. Still, he couldn't hold Jake's gaze for more than a second before he laughed, shaking his head and looking away.

It was then that Addison got his second shock.

A strange sight to start, one he didn't initially recognise in the last of the sun's light; he'd only seen it later at night and lit from below with spotlights. It was a collection of ornate mirrors, scraps of paper, and caged self-portraits, all suspended from a skeletal gazebo frame. And standing alongside was the installation's creator in yet another black ensemble that was somehow even drapier than the last one Addison had seen.

Addison's first thought was that here Brodie Seatter-Dent was yet again, no doubt hustling for patronage. He could feel himself subconsciously warming up for a hearty eye roll when his second thought struck: arts funding. Quickly followed by a comment Andy had made back at the vintage clothing store – 'I would *kill* for that kind of funding.' He'd said it in a joking, offhand way, hadn't meant it literally.

What if someone else shared the sentiment but took it much more seriously?

Addison's earlier *aha* moment had turned out to be a dud, but this one he reckoned might be for real.

Starting with Brodie's tendency to dress all in black – which had much the same effect as the crew's stage blacks – allowing him to move about backstage unseen and undetected.

Even if he had been seen, his presence likely wouldn't have been noteworthy. By his own account, he'd been involved in helping with the show, at least early on.

There was another aspect of his preferred clothing choice that was relevant to the situation: the drapey layering of it all. With the addition of an accessory or two, he might look like he was attempting any number of Halloween costumes – the grim reaper, the Wicked Witch of the West, a malnourished vampire, the Babadook, the list went on. Just as the black fabric allowed him to blend in backstage, the semi-gothic aesthetic allowed him to blend in with the crowds enjoying Halloween festivities.

Brodie had been disguised in plain sight. He could easily have accessed the trapdoor mechanism below stage without being noticed—

Addison halted mid-thought as another struck him: the scrap of black fabric caught on a nail below stage.

He'd assumed it was one of the crew in their stage blacks, but Brodie was a very real possibility too.

Addison's thinking lurched again, eyes widening as he put his mind back to the vintage clothing store. Brodie's top, the one he'd worn on the night of the Spooky Showcase, had been on the 'New Arrivals' rack that very morning. The label even said something about it having a small tear. Could it be...

He couldn't be sure it was the same top, not without heading back to the store and asking Andy, but Addison liked his chances.

Backtracking a moment, Brodie may have been able to access the trapdoor mechanism below stage without being noticed, but surely his absence from where he was supposed to be – that is, in the audience in his seat – would be a different story?

No, Addison realised he'd already covered this. When asked about who he'd gone with to the Spooky Showcase, Brodie had dodged the question, instead spouting some existential, philosophical nonsense. Addison had to assume that meant Brodie had attended alone, or at least that nobody could vouch for his whereabouts at all times.

Then there was the twitchiness... Which was fine – people had their quirks and mannerisms – but on top of everything else, it really started to paint a picture.

Returning to the motive, it wasn't immediately obvious how killing Cilla Slay would solve Brodie's funding issue. Sabotaging a show which had been successful in getting arts funding didn't suddenly mean the funding would transfer to him and his staging of *Reflections of the Self*. The Spooky Showcase was done, the money was spent. Unless the attack on Cilla was some kind of attempt to clear out those Brodie deemed less deserving to make room for those practising what he considered *real* art?

Addison couldn't be absolutely sure Brodie was a cold-hearted killer, but he could be sure that Brodie believed in himself and his work. Was it enough to kill?

That aspect Addison was less sure of.

Everything else made sense. It all fit, even if he hadn't fully pinned down the proof – not yet, at least.

It just so happened Addison knew someone who might be able to use evidence – the potential proof – that was the scrap of black fabric and torn garment. If he took this to a certain Sergeant Jake Murphy, could the police wave their magic forensics wand, or whatever it was they did? Addison strongly suspected it wasn't that simple, but Jake would have the knowledge, experience, and resources to do what was required.

Or, Addison could collect the proof himself and *then* take it all to Jake, nicely wrapped with a bow on top?

No.

He dismissed that thought almost as soon as he'd had it – interfering with the evidence might very well invalidate it. And going rogue, not keeping Jake in the loop, had been what got him into trouble in the past. Jake had trusted Addison enough to ask him to keep an eye and an ear out on the night of the Spooky Showcase, so Addison had to trust Jake and take his thoughts to him.

'Brodie Seatter-Dent.'

'What?' Jake said, pausing with his minty hot chocolate part way to his mouth. 'The artist?'

'It was him. Brodie did it.'

'Did what?'

Addison lowered his voice, nodding to Brodie and his gazebo on the far side of the rugby field. 'I think he killed Cilla Slay. I don't know why, not exactly, not yet, but I will. Everything else fits.'

Jake gestured for Addison to join him off to the side, out

of the main thoroughfare running along the stalls. He took a breath, his expression dead serious, and said, 'Step me through it.'

Addison did just that, quickly summarising everything he'd heard and inferred, even making sure to voice his remaining quibbles – those being a definitive motive and verified evidence. Still, he was convinced of the strength of his case, that it was worth pursuing seriously.

Jake appeared receptive – genuinely, or just to humour him, Addison couldn't tell.

'Thank you for bringing this to me, Addison. I will take it seriously, I mean that.' Jake looked like he meant it too. 'We will investigate.'

Addison wasn't sure if it was what Jake had said or how he'd said it, or if Addison's frustration about Jake's unresolved living situation – which he recognised wasn't reasonable of him to feel – had come to a head, but he wanted to *do* something.

Something bold.

And he wanted to do it right now.

'I'm going to confront him,' Addison said.

'You are not.'

'Are you telling me what to do?'

'No. Well, yes, actually,' Jake said. 'I'm sorry, but yes, *please*?'

'Brodie did it. I can't fully explain *how* I know, not just now. I can't prove it either, not beyond a reasonable doubt – not yet, at least. But I know he did it.'

'And I believe you. I trust your instincts. But where would we be if the police went around arresting people based on *vibes*?'

'*Vibes*? I have a lot more than that.' Addison took a

breath in an attempt to calm himself. 'I'm not suggesting we go and arrest him. Just that we go and have a little chat with him? Brodie loves to talk, especially about himself. If we approach in the right way, ask the right questions, he's bound to slip up and incriminate himself. You can come with me, if you like, make sure I don't do or say anything you'd disapprove of. Actually, I would like you to come with me, please.'

Jake sighed. 'Just a little chat?'

'Yes.'

'OK.'

The moment the confirmation was out of Jake's mouth, Addison nodded and began striding across the rugby field, his expression determined.

Not to be left behind, Jake fell into step at his side.

Chapter 34

Addison and Jake must have made quite the picture as they strode across the field, because anyone in their path swiftly scuttled out of the way.

They'd already closed half the distance when Brodie Seatter-Dent – deep in what Addison could be certain was a heavily one-sided conversation – looked up and clocked their approach.

Even from this distance, Addison could make out Brodie's eyes flicking between them. Everyone in town knew who Jake was, even out of uniform, and Addison's expression must have betrayed their intentions, because the moment Brodie realised they were heading directly for him, his entire body stiffened.

He started backing away from the poor soul he'd been speaking at, stumbling in his haste and grabbing one of the gazebo's metal legs for support. Addison and Jake were closing fast when Brodie finally tore his gaze away from them, his hands scrabbling at the leg before pulling out a pin and shooting out the far side.

The gazebo's leg telescoped down, one corner of the structure dropping under the weight of the items hanging from it, unbalancing the entire installation further and sending the ornate mirrors and caged portraits crashing to the ground.

Addison and Jake drew up alongside Brodie's most recent conversational victim as they witnessed the whole thing collapsing into a tangle of bent poles and broken glass. It was over in a matter of seconds. And once past the initial shock, Addison was relieved to find nobody had been caught up in the installation's sudden destruction. All that remained were the wreckage and many stunned onlookers.

Jake must have reached the same conclusion, already moving off as he turned to Addison, flashed his eyes, and pointed his chin beyond what was now a large obstacle in their way. 'You coming?' Jake said. 'He's getting away.'

Addison didn't need any further encouragement, skirting around the destroyed installation after Jake in pursuit of the artist.

Brodie was surprisingly quick, with already half a field's head start on them, appearing as a mass of wildly flapping fabric that somehow didn't hinder his progress. However, the drapey black garments did not lend him the anonymity and effective invisibility upon which he'd previously relied. Here, in the middle of the Milverton High School grounds, surrounded by folk in their regular, everyday attire – that is, not in costume – and in the light of the setting sun, his outfit choice only made him stand out all the more.

As well as sticking out like a sore thumb, Brodie had to duck and dive around the meandering crowd, who weren't quite fast enough in scurrying out of his way, allowing Addison and Jake to gain ground.

As they closed in, Brodie's destination suddenly became clear: the bonfire. It was still early, but the flames were already crackling, snapping, hissing, and popping, and they were ramping up in size and heat with every minute that passed.

Brodie snatched the nearest effigy as he raced past, yanking it with surprising strength from where it had been driven into the ground. Addison couldn't help noticing this one looked remarkably like the Scarecrow from *The Wizard of Oz* as Brodie swung its sack-head with floppy felt hat towards the flames.

Eyes wild, sweat running down his face, and chest heaving with the exertion, Brodie swung the Scarecrow's flaming straw-filled head around to face Addison and Jake.

'Stay back!'

They did as instructed, halting well out of reach of Brodie and his oversized flaming torch. Even at that distance, they could feel the heat already pouring off the bonfire.

And Brodie was closer still.

'We just want to talk, Brodie,' Jake said, raising his voice to be heard over the crackling flames.

'No you don't!'

'Come on, Brodie, let's put that down and come away from the bonfire,' Jake said, motioning for Addison to join him in taking a few steps back, giving Brodie space to ease away from the fire. 'We just want to have a chat.'

'You're lying. You're trying to trick me. You will not make a fool out of me.'

Like the bonfire at his back, Brodie's torch only grew, the flames having fully engulfed the Scarecrow's head, now licking at his stuffed shoulders and chest.

'We just want to sit down with you, Brodie. Back there where it's a bit cooler.' Jake pointed behind them, away from the bonfire, taking another encouraging step back.

'I'm not stupid!' Brodie waved his oversized torch across his front and back again, lurching under the weight of it, his face glistening with sweat. 'I didn't do it, OK? I didn't.'

'We know,' Jake said, not taking his eyes off Brodie for even a moment. 'Everything is all right. It's getting a bit hot though, don't you think? Shall we come away from here, eh?'

Addison could see Brodie recognising he had no way out of this, that he was considering Jake's proposal.

After a long few seconds Brodie lifted his shoulder and upper arm in an attempt to wipe the sweat from his brow, all while maintaining a firm grip on his flaming Scarecrow.

The movement was enough to break what had formerly been total focus on his pursuers. Brodie caught sight of the gathering crowd, already a large semi-circle that had formed a few steps behind Addison and Jake, maintaining a safe distance, at least for now.

Addison chanced a glance out the corner of his eye, seeing a few spectators now had their arms in front of them, phones in hand, no doubt filming the unfolding situation.

Brodie spotted this too and the effect was instantaneous. His entire demeanour shifted – he straightened his posture, head held high, eyes slowly scanning the onlookers as he confidently wielded the flaming Scarecrow.

Where before he was a manic, sweating madman, he now appeared commanding, triumphant, and very much like he was in control.

'So, this is how it all ends,' Brodie said, speaking slowly and projecting his voice for all to hear. 'I, Brodie Seatter-Dent, always knew this day would come. I did not know it would be so soon, did not know it would be tonight – how could I? Not when the fire is blazing so hot and bright, not only at my back but also in my hands and in my very soul.'

The flames had moved on to the Scarecrow's arms and chest by this point. It was also at this point that Addison noted two uniformed officers – Constables Sean McGiffert and Manaia Edwards – had appeared behind Brodie, on either side of the bonfire, and they were slowly edging their way around, closing in on their target, ready to intercept if Brodie made a run for it.

'But why me? These hands which I have used to create, now stained with something I cannot wash off. Not blood, no. But intent, passion, conviction... I'll admit, to start, my intent was but a nascent flame. With these hands I did shunt aside the stage set piece while under construction, but it was Theo Robinson who faltered, cutting into his own finger.'

Brodie swished the flaming Scarecrow from one side to the other, as if underscoring his revelation.

'With these hands I did spill the water onto the stage during rehearsal, but it was Patrick Laurence – or "Lady Perry Less", I suppose – who slipped, breaking her leg.'

Again, this revelation was accompanied by a swish of the oversized torch. Addison couldn't quite believe what he was witnessing but, just like everyone else there, he watched on, utterly captivated.

'And with these hands I did trigger the trapdoor mechanism, but it was Cilla Slay who dove to her death.'

One more swish of the Scarecrow for the third and most egregious confession of all.

'But why, you ask?' Brodie said, apparently still not finished. 'Why did I do these things? For the sake of art – what else is there? We are sleepwalking into the complete dulling of the arts, catering only to the unforgivable stupidity of society. I refuse to allow it! What else could I do but clear the way for arts sector funding to go to art that truly matters? With the Spooky Showcase plagued by injury and death, such reckless productions could surely not attract future investment. I *killed* it, that so-called art, entirely unfit to label itself such. My efforts will make way for important, meaningful, worthy art to capture the funding it so rightfully deserves. Art such as *mine*.'

The artist briefly bared his teeth, eyes scanning the crowd as if in challenge before continuing.

'Even so, I did not mean for Cilla Slay to die. I meant to interfere, to disrupt – yes! But now she is gone, and I remain. The world goes on, so must we all.'

Brodie paused, appearing to reflect on his own profound words.

'Perhaps the meaning, the only truth in this contrived journey we call life, is that we get but moments – fast and fleeting – where we must choose who we are, who we want to be. And I chose. Some may argue about that choice, but none can deny that it was *honest*. That it was real.'

By now the flames had worked their way down to engulf the Scarecrow's midsection and beyond, getting ever closer to Brodie's hands.

'So, let them come and tear me away in the name of justice, of society, of whatever they think they represent. And I will go. Because I did it and I meant it and that – in the end – is all that matters.'

With that, Brodie raised his arms directly out in front of himself, both hands grasping the stake, holding up the now entirely engulfed Scarecrow, before hurling the whole thing up and back over his head, sending it soaring into the bonfire itself before he himself crumpled on the spot into a pile of lightly singed black fabric.

Gasps erupted all around, followed by a tentative smattering of applause which quickly faded.

Addison remained fixed to the spot, his jaw slack, wondering what on Earth he had just witnessed... An impromptu bout of unhinged improv? The slow and very public unravelling of a doomed narcissist's mind? A last-ditch attempt at relevance or notoriety? Or some kind of villain monologue?

Luckily, while Addison remained in a state of utter bafflement, the slowly stalking constables had taken Brodie's theatrical collapse as their cue to sweep in. Sean and Manaia got under an arm each and dragged Brodie away from the fire, across the grass, and directly to the first aid tent.

Addison caught Brodie sneaking an eye open, checking on the reception of his performance as he was pulled into the first aid tent and out of sight of his enraptured audience.

Diana and Scott – two paramedics Addison had met more times than he might have liked in his short time in Milverton – leapt into action the moment the constables deposited Brodie into their care, though the police remained close at hand, ready to take Brodie away once he'd been given the all-clear.

Sergeant Jake Murphy, meanwhile, took on crowd-control duties, but the onlookers took little convincing to return to the evening's other amusements now that Brodie's spontaneous and rather dramatic soliloquy was over.

Jake had a brief conversation with his constables at the first aid tent's entrance, which resulted in nods all round, a glance from Manaia and a grin from Sean, both in Addison's direction, before Jake returned to Addison's side.

'Hey,' Addison said. 'Don't worry about me. I'm just glad this is over. I'm sure you'll have plenty to do with—'

Jake placed a hand on Addison's shoulder, cutting him off mid-sentence. 'Edwards, McGiffert, and the team back at the station are more than capable of sorting this one out.' He shrugged, shaking his head. 'Brodie confessed to everything. Not much in the way of detective work to do now he's laid it all out for us. I'm not on duty, and I'm not needed on this tonight anyway. I have more important things to do.'

Jake paused, looking around them at the bonfire, the emergency services vehicles, the stalls, the bouncy castle, the cordoned-off fireworks area, and all the people back to enjoying their night out.

'Do you want to get out of here?' Jake said as he returned his gaze to the man at his side.

Addison smiled right back. 'I do.'

Chapter 35

Addison and Jake retreated to the safety and serenity of Harper House.

Though they did make a quick detour via the hotdog stand. After all the excitement and adrenaline, Addison realised he was starving. And he knew very well that he didn't have anything in the fridge for dinner, especially not anything he'd be willing to serve to anyone else, let alone Jake.

The hotdog was a calculated choice. Firstly, hotdogs were quick to prepare, so they could be on their way as soon as possible. Secondly, provided it wasn't over-sauced or overloaded with onions, it was portable and could be eaten on the move – again, a time saver. Thirdly, they were served in a bun which was itself edible – no waste, no mess, no fuss. Sure, there was the paper napkin, but he'd need that to wipe his mouth afterwards, just to be sure. Finally, hotdogs were just a little bit nostalgic – when else did you get a chance to have one but at a carnival-type event?

Not that Addison had shared any of this thinking with Jake, nor had Jake asked for it.

Hotdogs successfully demolished, they were soon clear

of the crowds and enjoying their twilight walk to Harper House.

At least, Addison wanted to enjoy it but was finding that easier said than done. The relative peace and quiet only created space for *thoughts*. He'd attempted to occupy his mind with an overly detailed analysis of the many merits of the humble hotdog, but apparently it wouldn't be so easily distracted.

It was over, finally over, and he looked forward to filling Mabel in on everything that had happened. She was bound to have already heard, knowing Milverton. Addison also knew his friend would be miffed to have missed all the action.

But no matter how relieved he was for it to be over, one thing stuck in his mind. One thing got in the way of his sense of complete, satisfying resolution.

'Brodie didn't kill Cilla Slay,' Addison finally said, unable to hold it in any longer, 'at least not directly.'

Jake hummed thoughtfully at this as they walked side by side. 'He was doing his best to make the whole production as dangerous as possible, though.'

'It was only a matter of time...' Addison trailed off, the impact of Brodie's misguided and spiteful actions really hitting home.

'Only a matter of time before the casualties became a fatality, yes,' Jake said. 'With a confession, attitude, and pattern of behaviour like his, I have to believe any jury would understand that the guilt lies entirely with him and the—'

'Punishment will fit the crime.'

'Right,' Jake said with a nod as they turned up the dark, tree-lined driveway to Harper House. 'But that's not for us to decide – the courts will work out the details. I think it's safe to say the only art Brodie creates for a very long time will be from behind bars, his only audience his fellow inmates.'

Addison groaned. 'I feel for them. Such a cruel and unusual punishment.'

They both laughed darkly at the thought.

It had been a busy week. In just the past seven days Addison had attended a whole bunch of events, investigated the sudden death of Cilla Slay, and started a brand-new job. But now, walking and laughing with Jake, it felt to Addison like at least some of the pressure was beginning to lift.

It would be nice to have a night in, Addison thought as he opened the front door, and having Jake there too would be extra nice. Alone together, just him and Jake—

'Meow.'

Addison, Jake, *and* Keith – how could he have forgotten?

The cat's opening protest was short and sharp, but the subsequent *meows* were each a slight variation on what came before, as if articulating a new outrage each time – 'Where have you been?' and 'What time do you call this?' and 'What is he doing here again?'

'Sorry,' Addison said to Jake with a wince. 'I'd better feed the little terror. Come through, if you like.'

With Keith's wet food, dry food, and water bowl replenished, Addison returned his attention to Jake, who was highly amused but doing his best not to show it.

Addison needed to unwind properly, perhaps a drink… He thought on it for a moment, then, pretty sure he had everything he needed, he said, 'How about a sidecar?'

Jake's amusement shifted to confusion. 'What? The – uh – motorbike attachment?'

'Oh, can you imagine? Like Gromit's little capsule thing on the side of Wallace's bike?' Addison laughed. 'No, but I think that might be where it got its name. The cocktail, I mean. It became popular in the twenties – the 1920s, not the 2020s – like a hundred years ago. It's delicious.'

'I trust you.'

Addison didn't know what to say to that, so focused on assembling their cocktails. 'It's two parts cognac, one part orange-flavoured liqueur – think Cointreau or triple sec – and one part fresh lemon juice.'

Addison shook the ingredients with ice, strained the chilled mixture into two cocktail glasses and, feeling a little fancy, even garnished each with a lemon twist. He slid one glass along the kitchen bench to Jake and picked up the other.

Jake accepted his glass. 'What should we toast to?'

'Oh, right.' Addison set his drink back down, reached into his pocket and pulled out his wallet. 'Look what I got yesterday,' he said, pulling out a crisp piece of paper, unfolding it, and presenting it to Jake.

He looked down at the official-looking slip with the testing station attendant's signature, then up at Addison.

'My proper card with a photo and everything on it should arrive in the post shortly.'

'Well done.' Jake beamed. 'Very well done.'

'Thank you,' Addison said, his cheeks warming at the praise. He inclined his head to obscure the undoubted rosiness before folding up his temporary licence and putting it away.

Jake raised his glass. 'To our newest learner driver.'

'Finally catching up with the teenagers.'

'Hey.' Jake raised an eyebrow. 'Just because you're

allowed to sit the test at sixteen doesn't mean you have to, or that you should.'

Addison shrugged but smiled.

Jake tried again. 'To life-long learning.'

This drew a laugh from Addison, but he raised his glass nonetheless and they both sipped.

'Oh, yeah. That is delicious.'

'I may not know how to drive a car or keep my nose out of other people's business,' Addison said, 'but I can definitely bake a cake and mix a drink.'

'That you can,' Jake said, taking another sip before nodding down at Addison's wallet. 'Anyway, you kept that quiet.'

'I didn't want to say anything until it was done.'

Jake huffed out a breath. 'I can understand that.'

'Speaking of keeping things quiet,' Addison said, setting his glass down, leaning his hip against the bench, and looking directly at Jake. 'Your tenancy coming to an end? Your imminent homelessness?'

'I'm not about to be—'

'Jake.' Addison cut him off as he turned to face him front on. 'I think you should move in with me,' he said, coming straight out with it, before taking a breath, glancing down with a little less certainty. 'Only if you want to, of course.'

Jake was silent and stayed that way until Addison looked back up and met his gaze. He opened his mouth a few times, as if going to say something before thinking better of it. Eventually, he simply asked, 'Are you sure?'

'Yes,' Addison said, not missing a beat. 'I am.'

A small smile tugged at the corner of Jake's mouth. 'Is Keith sure?'

Addison laughed. 'That I am less sure of…'

'Well, in that—'

'Keith doesn't get a say in the matter,' Addison said with conviction. 'Oh, I'm sure he won't be impressed to start, but he'll come around, I know it.'

'Yes,' Jake said.

'Yes, what?'

'Yes, I want to move in with you.'

'And Keith?' Addison said with a smirk.

Jake laughed. 'And Keith.'

Addison's smile threatened to take over his entire face, but before it could, he reined it back in and put his lips to work on Jake's. In response, Jake wrapped his arms around Addison and kissed him right back, yet somehow still managed to laugh through their locked lips.

They pulled back after a moment, eyes glistening, smiling at each other.

And then there was a *bang*.

Eyes wide, Addison said, 'What was that?'

Jake checked the time: nine o'clock. 'That'll be the fireworks display starting.'

'You know,' Addison said as more pops and bangs erupted in the distance. 'You know, I reckon we might get a better view from the bedroom window upstairs?'

Jake's response to that was a deep, full laugh. 'Addison Harper, you don't have to play games to get me upstairs.' He smiled and landed another quick kiss on Addison's lips. 'All you have to do is ask.'

'All right, then,' Addison said before flying out the door. 'Race you to the top.'

Bonus material

Do you want a peek backstage? Maybe sample a few spooky cocktails?

One particular scene was a lot of fun to write but didn't quite fit into the book for pacing reasons. 'Mabel's Magic Moment' is the extended version of Chapter 11 which is over 50% longer than the version published in this book. It features a bit of fun and flirtation, some extra Mabel, and a sneaky peek at a magician's secrets!

I've also brought together Paul's Killer Cocktails in case you wanted to try a spooky tipple for yourself. Cheers!

Already on my author mailing list?
You're amazing! You can access the bonus material from the exclusive content page that I've linked in my emails to you.

New reader / not already on my author mailing list?
You're amazing too! You can join my author mailing list – it's free! – to access the bonus material by visiting my website: www.gbralph.com

You'll also see more from Milverton in the next book in the series. Turn the page to investigate…

Addison will return...

Killer on the Kelvin Explorer
The Milverton Mysteries #5

Addison Harper and Sergeant Jake Murphy are off to a shaky start with their new living situation. So, when Addison has the chance to get out of town and clear his head, he's quick to climb aboard.

The day's scenic railway journey features a powerful steam engine pulling lovingly restored heritage carriages. On the train, passengers enjoy dramatic landscapes and endless cups of tea. When it comes to driving Milverton's tourism, Addison can see they're already on the right track. Unfortunately, a death en route threatens to derail not only the day's excursion but any future marketing efforts.

Passengers have been promised an unforgettable day out – and they're going to get it.

Killer on the Kelvin Explorer traverses New Zealand's picturesque lower North Island and is the latest in a wonderful cosy mystery series. Investigate *The Milverton Mysteries* for a chaotic cast of local busybodies, delicious baked treats, a demanding and disdainful ginger cat, a very slow-burn romance with a rather appealing policeman, and of course… murder!

Scheduled for release in September 2026.
Pre-order today, or buy now if it's already out:
www.gbralph.com/killer-on-the-kelvin-explorer

Thank you for reading

I had the best time writing *Fright on Stage Right* and I hope you enjoyed reading it!

If you did, please tell your friends – personal recommendations are the best. Also please consider leaving a review wherever you bought this book, on book review sites, and/or on social media. This is important in making my work more visible to other readers as each review gives the books a little boost and means others are more likely to stumble across them.

For my latest updates, free short stories, and to accompany me on my journey to bring out the next mystery in Milverton, you can join my mailing list via my website: www.gbralph.com. You can also find my other stories there, and links to my social media if you'd like to drop me a message – I'd love to hear from you!

Acknowledgements

Can you believe we've reached the end of Addison's *fourth* misadventure in Milverton?

Halloween gave us a spooky start and Guy Fawkes brought us to an explosive end. I think these two annual events were ideal for giving this book the nighttime feel I wanted. Add to that my love of live theatre – no matter whether we're going to a play, musical, opera, ballet, concert, stand-up comedy, improv, drag, dance, burlesque, magic, acrobatics, whatever – a night at the theatre, or a bar with a stage, is always a great time!

I wanted to capture at least a little of that fun and drama in this book. I wasn't shy about leaning into the nineties nostalgia either, removing any doubt that this story was written by a millennial. But we're not here for a debrief, we're here to say thanks to all the wonderful people who helped support me, my writing, and my books!

To the improv comedy and drag performers of Palmerston North who provide endless laughs and much inspiration.

To the good people behind the Off the Page writers series – a partnership between Palmerston North City Library and Massey University – who consistently bring such intelligent and articulate writers and speakers to share their thoughts and expertise with us.

To the librarians of the Palmerston North City Library

for shining a spotlight on my books, for letting me check out so many titles, and for having me take up space while I'm writing the next book.

To Louisa, Corey, Serena, and the team at Bruce McKenzie Booksellers for enthusiastically putting my books into the hands of local readers.

To Gareth and Louise Ward, AKA The Bookshop Detectives, and the team at Wardini Books for hosting me and my fellow local mystery authors for a cracking evening of clues, crime and craft in Napier.

To Craig Sisterson and the Ngaio Marsh Awards for inviting me back to join their 'Mystery in the Library' author panels in both Palmerston North and Whanganui this year.

To the team at Tantor Audio and Philip Battley for bringing the wonderful audiobook editions to readers.

To the book bloggers and online content creators who help to share the excitement and raise the profile of my books.

To the readers of early drafts of this book who gave me brilliant feedback: Julian Barr, Angela C. Nurse, Paul Austin Ardoin, Greg Low, A.J. Lancaster, Mel Harding-Shaw, Derryk Butcher, Bing Turkby, Rosie Stirling, and Hollie Fisher.

To Chris Zable for doing a fantastic job of copyediting this book into shape. Of course, any remaining errors are entirely my own.

To the Word Racers who are up at all hours offering encouragement and/or a kick in the pants, whichever may be required at the time.

To the Speculative Collective for being such a lively and engaged community of authors, sharing all the ups and downs of both the creative and the business sides of writing, editing, publishing, and promoting books.

To my very talented bunch of local author friends who are always up for coffees and brunches, walks and talks.

To my partner, my family, and my friends – your support means everything.

And finally, thanks to you, my amazing readers. Whether you're enjoying the audiobooks while out for a walk, sharing your Milverton-inspired crafts online, getting in contact to ask for my preferred scone recipe, tagging me on social media when you're out sipping a cocktail, or just quietly devouring the books at home, you make my many, many hours of tapping away at the keyboard so worth it!